The
Salt House

~~~ *a novel* ~~~

Lisa Duffy

TOUCHSTONE

New York   London   Toronto   Sydney   New Delhi

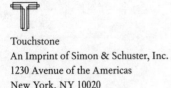

Touchstone
An Imprint of Simon & Schuster, Inc.
1230 Avenue of the Americas
New York, NY 10020

First Touchstone paperback edition June 2017

TOUCHSTONE and colophon are registered trademarks of Simon & Schuster, Inc.

For information about special discounts for bulk purchases, please contact Simon & Schuster Special Sales at 1-866-506-1949 or business@simonandschuster.com.

The Simon & Schuster Speakers Bureau can bring authors to your live event. For more information, or to book an event, contact the Simon & Schuster Speakers Bureau at 1-866-248-3049 or visit our website at www.simonspeakers.com.

Interior design by Jill Putorti

Manufactured in the United States of America

10 9 8 7 6 5 4 3 2 1

Library of Congress Cataloging-in-Publication Data
Names: Duffy, Lisa, 1970- author.
Title: The salt house / Lisa Duffy.
Description: First Touchstone paperback edition. | New York : Touchstone, 2017.
Identifiers: LCCN 2016030718 | ISBN 9781501156557 (trade paper) | ISBN 9781501156571 (ebook)
Subjects: LCSH: Families—Maine—Fiction. | GSAFD: Domestic fiction.
Classification: LCC PS3604.U3784 S25 2017 | DDC 813/.6—dc23
LC record available at https://lccn.loc.gov/2016030718

ISBN 978-1-5011-5655-7
ISBN 978-1-5011-5657-1 (ebook)

For Thomas Wotton Wheble

Tell her this
And more,—
That the king of the seas
Weeps too, old, helpless man.
The bustling fates
Heap his hands with corpses
Until he stands like a child
With surplus of toys.

—STEPHEN CRANE,
THE BLACK RIDERS AND OTHER LINES, XXXVIII

The
Salt House

Kat

The night Mom threw Dad out we had a dinner party at our house. We lived on the first floor of a tan two-story on the bay side of town. Mom grew up there, but on the top floor, where Grandma lived.

Mom loved to cook and play games, and Dad loved Mom, so they entertained often, or they used to at least, before Maddie. Jess and I were always included. Mom said it was because she liked having her favorite people around. "Am I one of your favorites, Hope?" Dad sometimes asked, his dark eyes drilling a hole into the back of Mom's head. You got the sense he was holding his breath when he asked the question. It would get him a laugh and a hug, but over her shoulder, Dad wasn't laughing. In those moments, if need had a face, it would've looked like Dad.

I was in charge of coats at the party. I'd sulked about that all afternoon and told Mom that carrying coats to the bedroom didn't seem like an important job, since it was summer and who wore a coat in June?

Mom was on her knees on the kitchen floor, looking for the Crock-Pot, half her body missing inside the cabinet, the sound of pans bumping against one another ringing through the room. I heard her say something about June nights in Maine and how they sometimes had a chill to them, but when she sat back on her heels, her eyes were a little wild, and there was a dark smudge on her forehead, and still no Crock-Pot.

She looked at me and must have seen how serious I was, because she sighed and told me to go set the kids' table then, with whatever plates I wanted, which seemed like a much better job.

That's how Jess and I got to drink Shirley Temples in old mismatched fancy glasses, set with our best china and cloth napkins just like the adult table. It was perfect, even though Jess told me to stop calling it the kids' table, since it was just me and her sitting there and she was almost seventeen and only home on a Saturday night because *everyone* except for her was on vacation somewhere else.

I kept quiet because once Jess got in one of her moods, forget it. It wasn't worth pointing out that by *everyone* she meant Carly and Betsy, her two best friends, and they only visited family for a couple of weeks each summer. Betsy down to Kittery, and Carly up to Boothbay. Each one less than an hour away, which, in my opinion, didn't count as a vacation. But Jess *always* had to be right, so I didn't argue with her.

The Alfonsos arrived first. They came with their sheepdog, a hulking black-and-white thing with patches of skin peeking from where his fur should've been. He crept close to the floor when he walked and lowered his sad eyes like he knew he was overstepping. He'd had some sort of breakdown after Mrs. Alfonso went back to work full-time, leaving him alone in an empty house.

They got another dog so he wouldn't be lonely, a long-haired retriever named Molly. Mrs. Alfonso said she'd never seen him so happy. Then Molly got hit by a car six months later and died. He started losing hair after that. *Separation anxiety,* Mrs. Alfonso told Mom, wringing her hands and sighing as she watched him hunker down under our table, his large body hitting the floor like a sack of potatoes.

So sorry for the inconvenience, Mrs. Alfonso repeated over and over. Mom shushed her and rubbed Mrs. Alfonso's shoulder and said she understood. Sometimes, Mom said, love isn't convenient. Mom had a big heart like that. Dad rolled his eyes but stared at Mom like he could devour her alive. I didn't think it was whatever anxiety the doctor called it. Looked like a broken heart to me. I'd seen that before.

The Donovans and the Martins came next. The last ones in were Mom's friend, Peggy, and a man who held out his hand to Mom and said his name was Ryland Finn, but she should call him Ry, and Mom said, "Oh, what a great name," and waited like he might have a story about it.

But he just shrugged and glanced over her shoulder into the room behind her, as if he were searching for something he'd lost. Then nobody said anything until finally Mom said, "Well, let's get you two introduced, shall we?"

We started with mussels in marinara sauce, one of Mom's specialties and easy to make, since Dad brought them home from the shop whenever Jess and I asked. Dad was a lobsterman and did some shellfishing on the side, which we loved. We could never get enough steamers, mussels, and clams on the half shell. Dad said we were spoiled, ate like queens. But he winked at Mom while we dug in.

They played charades after dinner. Dad put up a fuss about playing, but Mom talked him into one round. He got *To Kill a Mockingbird*, and Mom thought he was acting out a horror movie. She guessed bird when he flapped his arms but finally got it when he pretended to play a harp. Dad said he should've done the harp bit first, since Mom was a writer and always remembered authors. Mr. Finn said he didn't get the harp bit, and Peggy looked at him with tired eyes and said Harper Lee wrote it. Mom got up to put coffee on, and everyone looked at the couple whose turn it was next, except for Mr. Finn, who was sitting behind the group, watching Mom as she left the room. I watched Dad, watching Mr. Finn, watching Mom.

Later, in my bed, long after I should've been asleep, I listened to Mom and Dad clean up after everyone left. The kitchen and my bedroom shared a wall, and my dresser sat on the opposite wall from my bed, across from the kitchen doorway, its tall mirror reflecting the round table, giving me a clear view of the room. In our small house there wasn't much I couldn't hear.

Sometimes I loved it. Hushed voices carrying me to sleep or the noise from the television drifting in and out. Sometimes I hated it. Especially when Mom and Dad fought, their voices low and angry. Mom usually stomped off and went to bed upset. Dad never knew when he pushed his luck too far. Grandma said when it came to Mom, Dad lived with his heart on his sleeve and his head up his ass.

I heard Dad turn off the music and settle into the kitchen chair as Mom did the dishes in front of him. He was wearing what he called his dress clothes, which meant just a clean pair of jeans and a T-shirt that wasn't stained or ripped. Dad always said he was a mess, hopeless when it came to fashion, a disaster next to Mom. She'd overheard him once and rolled her eyes at him and said, "Give me a break, James Dean. What you mean is you don't have to do anything to look good. Unlike some of us."

I had no idea what she was talking about until I searched *James Dean* on Jess's computer, and besides the fact that Dad had dark hair and kept it short, they did sort of look alike. Except instead of a cigarette, Dad smoked cigars, and that was just once in a while and only ever outside because Mom said the smoke got stuck in the rugs and pillows and curtains, and it was bad enough that she already had to deal with the smell of fish.

Which wasn't true, because Dad always left his boots and coat outside in the hallway and showered first thing when he got home, and I'd never smelled anything on him besides soap and the aftershave he sometimes wore.

But some days Mom acted like that. Like everything Dad did bothered her. And then she'd complain when he stayed out of her way, out on the boat for hours and hours.

Like that made any sense.

Now Dad leaned forward in his seat, and suddenly Mom was there, his arm on her waist, his forearm huge around her middle. He pulled her into his lap.

She gave a halfhearted laugh and tried to stand, but he hugged her tighter, moved her legs across his lap, and leaned back in the chair with her.

"Shh, just sit with me," he said.

His fingertips ran the length of her thigh, and his other hand played with the black hair that hung down her back. I wanted to look away. I knew I shouldn't be watching, but I couldn't pull my eyes away from the mirror. Jess and I used to make silly faces when Mom and Dad kissed and hugged. I didn't remember the last time we got the chance to do that.

"Jack, stop. Let me just finish." Mom patted his leg and gave him a quick peck on the cheek, but her voice was high and tight, and her body looked stiff and uncomfortable on his lap.

"Leave it. I'll finish them. I just want to sit here for a minute with my wife."

Mom's wrap dress had come loose, and he traced the opening with his finger. I saw her stiffen and move his hand away. She held it in her lap, where it was no longer covering her chest, and pulled her dress closed with her free hand.

"Let me finish," she said. "Then we can go to bed together."

I wasn't sure if it was what she said or the way she said it, but everything changed right then. I saw it in Dad's reflection in the mirror, the way his face went hard, the way it was most of the time.

Abby, my camp counselor who got sent home at least once a week by the recreation director with instructions to put on shorts that were not *so* short, told me once that she didn't know how I could live with someone as *hot* as my father. But why didn't he smile more? she'd asked me. I didn't know what to say because he was *my father*, and who was I supposed to live with? I lied and said that he smiled all the time, just not at her.

Truth was, he never really smiled at anyone unless it was me or Jess or Mom. It was just the way he was.

But now he wasn't smiling at all.

"What?" Mom asked.

"Nothing," he muttered.

She hugged her arms across her body as if a cold wind had come through.

"I'm asking you to wait until I'm ready, and you're upset."

"You're not asking me to wait," he said. I didn't so much hear it as read his lips. That's how soft it came out.

Mom stared at the floor, and I heard the clock in the kitchen ticking away time.

"What does that mean?" Mom's voice cut through the silence like a dull knife. "What do you think I'm asking?"

He shut his eyes and sighed, a long one that seemed to empty him out, the way he sank deeper into the chair. "You know what, Hope? I don't know what I'm saying. Let's drop it."

"You work a hundred hours a week. You disappear out there." She waved at the water behind our house. "But when you're ready for me, well, sound the alarm."

He looked at the ceiling for a minute, then back at her. He didn't speak.

"Say something," she said.

"You don't want to hear it."

"Try me, Jack. At least you're talking instead of disappearing on that boat."

"Disappearing? And what do you call this? This right here."

"What right here?"

Dad shook his head, his eyes on the floor.

"What?"

He looked up, studied her. "You haven't been ready in a year," he said in a flat voice.

Mom stood up, and the air seemed to leave the room. "That's not true," she said.

"No? When was the last time we were together and you didn't do this . . . vanishing act that you do?" His hands made a large circle in the space between them.

"Stop it," she said, and her arms went around her body again.

Dad picked up his beer, took a swig of it, and slammed the bottle down so hard, the table shook. The noise made Mom jump. My first thought was he was going to be sorry tomorrow.

"Stop what? Trying to make love to my wife, or trying to figure out why she hates it when I touch her?"

His voice was thick and gravelly. I pulled the blanket up higher on my face. I hated that his eyes reminded me of the sheepdog's.

Mom went to the sink, gone from my view. I heard a drawer open and the clinking of silverware.

Dad put his head in his hands. When he looked up, I saw his

eyes and yanked the covers up so only a tiny sliver of space was left to see through. I knew that look.

"You had an admirer tonight," he said calmly, as if giving her the weather. But he was watching Mom, staring at her so hard, I thought it must hurt to be on the other end of it.

"Oh, please," she said, and muttered something under her breath I couldn't hear.

"What's that?" he asked.

"I said I don't need this crap."

"What's crap is you pretending to not notice him noticing you."

Mom walked over to my doorway to where the light switch sat on the wall and flicked it on, as though she hadn't been able to hear Dad without the light on.

"Him who?" she asked.

"Your new buddy Finn, that's who."

"Ry?"

"Ry?" he asked, pronouncing the word with force. "I didn't realize we were using nicknames."

"It was how he introduced himself."

"Well, Finn, oh I'm sorry, *Ry*, couldn't take his eyes off you."

"Don't pick a fight with me, Jack," she warned.

But he already had. Even I knew that.

"Why did you invite him?" he asked, as if it were the craziest idea she'd ever dreamed up.

"What do you mean why did I invite him? He's Peggy's *husband*. The reason for the party was to introduce them to some of our friends."

"I don't want him here again," he told her. He leaned back in the chair and crossed his legs out in front of him. He might have looked calm, but I saw his jaw pulse. "Did you hear me? They're not allowed to come over here again."

She was leaning against the doorframe now. I could see her face in the light. I watched as she raised her eyebrows at him and held them there, the way she did sometimes at the dinner table when Jess and I fooled around too much. Just a glance up from her plate, barely a movement at all, really, a flick of her brows, a tilt of her head. It stopped us every time.

"Allowed?" she asked. There was no sound coming from the kitchen, and then I heard her say in a voice that was high and wobbly, "*Allowed?*"

I leaned in closer to the mirror at the same time she moved off the wall and took two steps toward him. There was a force to her step that scared me. Dad seemed scared too and sat up quickly, pulling his legs in as if he might need them to fend her off.

"Get out," she whispered.

Dad's eyes closed, and I wished in that moment that by some miracle he'd suddenly fallen asleep. Mom was patient, but Dad had pushed too far. I knew this was what Grandma meant when she said Dad sometimes put his head up his ass.

The sound of a chair scraping against the tile sliced through my bedroom, and I peered out through the spaces between my spread fingers. He patted his pocket for his keys, and I rolled my eyes, embarrassed for him that he didn't see them sitting only two feet in front of him on the kitchen table. Mom saw them, though, and snatched them up and held them in her hand under her folded arms.

"Give me the keys, Hope."

"So you can leave here in a fit and wrap yourself around a tree?" She tightened the belt on her dress and said in a low mutter, "If I wanted you dead, I'd do it myself."

It was a line I'd heard them use on each other all my life, always in a joking way: Mom watching Dad fillet fish with his thick bear-paw hands—*Give me that knife. If I wanted you to lose a finger, I'd wait until you ticked me off and do it myself.* Or Dad catching her wrestling the full barrels down to the sidewalk for the garbage pickup—*Let me do that, baby. If I wanted you flat on your back, I'd put you there myself.* And so on and so on and so on.

But tonight, it wasn't a joke.

Dad stared at Mom, and then leaned in until his face was inches from her, and his voice was a growl.

"If you want me dead, keep it up. You're doing a hell of a job."

Mom sucked in her breath, loud and sharp, like she'd just bumped her hip bone on the edge of the table. There was a frenzy of movement, and I heard the front door open, and what sounded like Dad's coat hit the front hall with a thwack. Mom stomped into the kitchen, and something hard hit the wall again. I looked out from under the covers just in time to see Mom launch his shoe from the kitchen, through the living room, clear through the front door, where it landed with a loud thump.

"Jesus, Hope. Calm down." Dad snapped out of it, but it was too late.

Mom took two big strides in his direction, and there was not another sound as the door slammed shut. The house went silent.

I sat up in bed, hugged the blanket to my chest, and strained my neck to see around the corner. Mom rounded the opening and caught my eye. She let out a small noise, walked into my room, and sat on my bed. I put my head against her, pressed my cheekbone against the sharp edge of her collarbone, felt her heart pulsing on the flat part of my cheek.

She smelled like baby cream, and I wondered if she was still using the tub of Johnson's on her arms and hands like she did after Maddie died. She'd sit on the edge of her bed and massage the thick white cream on the insides of her forearms, where the skin's so soft, and then drop her head in her arms and rock that way until I got her for dinner. I thought it was weird. It was the same cream she used to rub on Maddie's bottom after she changed her diaper. But a lot of things got weird after Maddie died, so I stopped thinking about it.

Mom nudged me over and sank back. I looked at Mom curled up in my bed, and I pictured Dad standing in the hallway in his socks with his coat and shoes strewn all about, and then I remembered what Mom said earlier to Mrs. Alfonso about love not being convenient.

2

Hope

An hour passed before Kat's face softened and her breathing changed to the familiar timbre of deep sleep. I lay next to her in bed and wondered whether Jack was sleeping in the truck. Or more likely, he had a spare key stashed somewhere, and he'd gone to the boat. Or maybe to the Salt House across town.

I closed my eyes, but sleep was impossible. The argument with Jack had me twisting and turning in Kat's bed, restless from a current running through my body. Difficult now, with all the words hurled at each other, to pinpoint what we'd fought about. But something Jack said turned over in my mind.

When was the last time we were together and you didn't do this vanishing act that you do?

Men like Jack didn't say such things. Not out loud, at least. It seemed the point of no return. For both of us.

For Jack, it would have been saying it out loud—admitting I was letting him down in some way—that he had expectations. Needs.

For me, hearing him say it, even now, made my body jolt. My hands clench.

It was a year last week. The anniversary of her death. The beginning of the longest year of my life. Of our life. Our marriage.

We need to not let this thing destroy us, Jack said last week. When he said *this thing*, he meant my grief. But he never used that word.

In bed, when he wanted to make love and all I could muster was to kick off my pajama bottoms and press my lips against the side of his neck where I knew he liked, Jack had questions. Are we ever going to make love like we used to? Are we going to move on from being sad all the time?

He didn't use the word *grief*. Grief was too serious. Being sad was temporary, fixable. Grief was deeper, unchangeable, forever.

He didn't say this, but I knew.

I didn't tell him that my grief was as familiar to me as a worn sweater covered with loose threads and filled with the smells and sounds of a thousand cold nights and frosty mornings.

Grief and me, we had a history.

On most days something benign brought my grief calling. The smell of apple juice in the morning. A lost diaper in the bottom of a handbag found buried under shoes at the bottom of my closet. A forgotten pacifier I stumbled upon when I pulled the bed out to vacuum.

This grief had separated into various faces, each with its own smell and feel.

Holidays and birthdays were sure to bring one, if not all of them, piling in like crazed partygoers trampling over one another in their haste and excitement. On those days, I didn't get a word in edgewise; they were overwhelming.

Pity was my favorite. Pity had a calm, soothing voice. She made me rest in bed, and she never stopped talking about how un-fair this all was. She patted my back and rubbed my arm, and she smelled like the kind of cinnamon toast my mother used to make for me when I was small and tired and out of sorts. The kind that's crispy on the edge, soft and gooey in the middle with swirls of butter, sugar, and cinnamon seeped deep into the belly. Pity knew I didn't deserve this fate. She repeated again and again how unfair it was that this happened to me, when mothers all over the world gave up their children willingly. Some neglected or abused them. Pity was compassionate; pity understood; pity knew I could not just get on with life.

Anger was the opposite. He was needy and smelled like air the hour before a hurricane struck, and I was left cold and empty after his visits. He didn't speak to me; he screamed in my ear that I was robbed. He was enormous with piercing eyes and a viselike grip that grabbed hold of my arms and shook me when I didn't respond. He wasn't happy with simple tears; he wanted action, repayment, retribution. Somebody was to blame for this, he said. Don't give me that healing crap. Anger wasn't satisfied until I was angry. He giggled when I lashed out at Jack, chortled when I threw my pocketbook with the diaper across the room and followed to stomp and tear at it.

This grief had softened in the last month or so. A better word surely applied, yet this was how it felt. A dulling of the sharp edges. An imperceptible shift inside of me. Simple things—a morning two weeks ago when the clock struck noon before I thought of her—a night when Jack and the girls were at the table, and he made them laugh. He looked at me and winked. I smiled and left the table to wash the dishes. But my hands trembled as I washed the silverware. I saw the hollow space at the base of his throat. I imagined the skin against my lips.

But later in the evening, Jack fell asleep in front of the television, and when I woke up, there was crying throughout the house.

I'd been dreaming about Maddie, and now there was crying and maybe it was all a bad dream. The bedroom was dark. The sheets tangled around my legs. I kicked them off, stumbled to the door, and yanked it open.

Then I was racing around the corner to the sound, to Maddie, and there was Jack, sitting up slowly on the couch, dazed, his eyes trying to focus through the haze of sleep.

And there was Tom Selleck on the television screen, holding a howling baby.

Jack said, "Babe?" and my open palm slammed down on the remote so hard, the battery cover popped off, and I yelled, "Goddammit, Jack!"

And then there was silence. Jack was wide-eyed. When he came over and put his arms around me, I leaned into him and found the hollow space at the base of his throat and pressed my lips against it.

But all I felt was the pounding of my own heart, and all I heard was a crying baby that did not belong to me.

This was the thing not just threatening to destroy us—it was destroying us.

I climbed out of bed, careful not to wake Kat, and tiptoed into Jessica's room.

She was normally a deep sleeper, and I was thankful when I found her snoring lightly. One less casualty of tonight's war.

I sat on her bed and stared into the darkness of the doorway across the room, empty of her things now: the changing table replaced with a file cabinet; the crib packed away in the basement; a desk with a calendar hanging above it in its place. As if to say, *Look, see? Time goes on.*

I drove Kat to school the other day, and as I pulled out of the drop-off area, I saw a class of preschoolers gathered around a teacher. I circled around and parked in the visitor space and studied each one of the girls, wondering if Maddie's hair would have been long like the girl with the polka-dot raincoat. What sneakers would she have liked? Would her eyes have stayed the same deep blue? Would the birthmark on her tummy have faded? I sat in the car, paralyzed. Not able to move. Sometime later, I drove away. This was my life now. Time unaccounted for. Days lost.

I used to write. It was what I was doing when she died. We'd gone to the grocery store. By the time we got home, she was cranky and hungry. I settled her in the high chair and she pushed macaroni around on the tray, every third one making its way to her mouth, while I put the groceries away. Jack called at lunchtime, and I put the phone to her ear and watched a gummy smile spread across her face at the sound of Daddy's voice.

We cleaned up, and after I changed her diaper, I gave her a kiss and hugged her tight. I remember thinking I could just sleep with her in the rocking chair, but my column was due and her nap was my only writing time. I put her in the crib, under the small soft blankets. There were more than usual, but she started to fuss when I tried to take some of them out, so I let her be. Kat had climbed in the crib that morning and let Maddie cover her with stuffed animals and blankets. I didn't see the harm in letting her nap among the extra baby blankets.

I remember making a cup of tea and settling at the kitchen table. I'd joined *Parent Talk* magazine more than a decade ago as a staff writer after doing freelance work for years. Jess had just started full-day kindergarten, and the local office in Portsmouth was full of women, mostly my age, balancing work with raising children— just what I was looking for after the solitude of freelance work.

But even after ten years, my bad habit of finishing my column at the deadline hadn't changed.

After fifteen or so minutes of writing, I went to her doorway and looked around the corner. She was busy pushing blankets around the crib, babbling to herself. She was making a racket when her chubby hands hit the crib bars, but she was content, so I moved out of her line of sight. If she saw me, the crying would start for certain.

My memory blurred from there on. I don't know how much time passed before I went to wake her. I wouldn't have wanted her to sleep past two o'clock, so maybe another half hour, but I don't recall the exact time.

I also don't know if it was the color of her face or the lack of movement when I picked her up that made me scream. I've gone over it in my head more times than I can count, and all I remember is the metallic taste in my mouth and the sound of a train thundering in my head. I don't remember the ambulance ride or the room where we waited or the hospital chaplain who held my hand.

They found a quarter-size heart locket lodged in her throat. Jack and I had given the necklace to Kat for her birthday two weeks before. She hadn't taken it off since.

They'd jumped and played in the crib that morning. Kat's necklace fell off and slipped in the folds of the blankets. It was Maddie who found it. I imagined the delight on her face when she found it. I pictured her sitting on her small bottom, her plump legs crossed in front of her and the necklace draped over her chubby hands, her fingers settling on the locket, a shiny heart of sparkling silver. She knew it was Kat's.

Had she brought the locket to her nose to smell it and give it a taste and it slipped down her throat by accident or did she get right to it, slamming the necklace in her mouth with both fists? Was she scared? How long had she struggled before she lost consciousness? What went through her mind in her last moments? These were only some of the questions I would never be able to answer.

The only thing I knew was that as I sat writing on a clear nondescript day, my daughter died twenty-two feet away from me without calling my name or making a noise. I knew that in the middle of the afternoon, without any warning and within an hour, it was possible to lose your life.

Those first months after she died were a blur. My mother flew up from Florida the day after we lost her. She stayed for two weeks, and then went back to Florida, to her own life. It was a process she repeated nearly every month. And somehow, the year passed and here we were.

It seemed we were through the worst of it—I could breathe again, at least. I could open my eyes in the morning and take a breath without feeling like a slab of granite rested on my chest. I lost track of the number of days this past year, I simply closed my eyes again, let that crushing weight sink my body deeper into the mattress.

Jack was the opposite. He got up every single morning—sun or rain or snow—and went to the boat. As if his sanity depended on it. And maybe it did. Perhaps in his own mind, putting one foot in front of the other suggested forward motion. Perhaps his inability to talk about any of it, to *cry* even, was the very thing that allowed him to get up and get moving.

Not that his grief wasn't as far-reaching as my own—it was. I saw it in the weary lines tugging at the corners of his eyes, and in the pounds melting off his already lean frame. But movement seemed to heal Jack, or at the very least, keep his mind occupied.

There was a part of me that knew I deserted him, left him to his own grief, his own way of dealing with it. He didn't dwell on the moment like I did. He didn't obsess over how things might have gone differently. How she'd still be here if I hadn't been writing, if I hadn't given Kat the necklace. Stop, he'd say to me, with his hand up, not wanting to listen. Not willing to live in a moment that was gone. Irretrievable. But I was still there, on that day, and we were moving farther and farther away from each other.

I'd put life on hold for a year.

I hadn't been back to work since she died. My editor, Josie, kept the column filled with ads—she was giving me time, encouraging me to come back, insisting our readers missed the column. But when I sat down to write, I was back on that day. Had she called out for me, and I hadn't heard her because I was occupied? Why hadn't I checked her crib, knowing that Kat had played in there? There must have been some noise . . . some indication of her struggling. Why didn't I have a video monitor?

These weren't just random thoughts. They were comments posted online after the local news ran a short article about her death. The article wasn't specific—just the facts—her name, age, a short blurb about how choking was the cause of death. One sentence revealing she had been put down for a nap in her crib and was found unresponsive by her mother. At the end of the article was a *Comments* link. I'd clicked on it. I can't say why. Perhaps only because the link was there. I'd stumbled across the article as it was, only online for the first time in weeks to send my coworkers at *Parent Talk* an email thanking them for the dinners that showed up on our doorstep every night.

Jack had walked in the room and found me wide-eyed at the computer. He leaned over my shoulder, glanced at the screen. *Internet scum,* he growled, and yanked the power cord from the wall so hard, the pins on the plug bent at odd angles.

I waited until the following day, when Jack was at work, to turn on the computer again and search for the article. I scrolled down to the *Comments* section.

Most were condolences, well wishes, an occasional OMG! or Devastating!

Then there were the others. Not many. Enough, though. Enough to confirm every fear, every voice in my head.

Where was the mom? Ever hear of a monitor??? Video monitor maybe?! Morons!

Sh*tty parents! NOTHING should EVER be in crib to choke on! WTF-they desrve everything they got! Poor baby!!!!! Wouldn't happen in my house!

Nice parenting-NOT. RIP sweet baby!!!!!!!

I hadn't written since that day.

When I got on Jack for working so many hours, he'd look at me like I was living in some imaginary world where mortgages didn't exist.

We'd taken out a second mortgage last year to renovate the Salt House, a dilapidated farmhouse across town passed down to us from Jack's grandfather. Nothing to look at except for the view. Water as far as the eye could see. The view at our house now wasn't anything to shrug off, but the street was busy, full of triple-decker homes built almost on top of one another.

We were supposed to be living in the Salt House now. The plan had been to rent out this house and move across town once renovations were complete.

But I hadn't been back since she died.

There wasn't an inch of the house that didn't remind me of her. The screen porch where Jack and I had made love. The bathroom upstairs where I'd peed on a stick and watched the plus sign appear while Kat and Jess played on the lawn below. The sunflower garden in the backyard, where she'd crawled while I weeded and pruned.

Jack had been patient, given me time. But our savings were gone. The money we'd taken out to renovate the Salt House was gone—we were close to finishing the renovation before she died—and we were paying two mortgages now. I'd mentioned putting the Salt House on the market months ago. Letting someone else finish the renovation. He'd looked at me, and the look on his face made my cheeks burn, my insides twist.

But we were out of time, and money.

Over the years, I'd built up a handful of women's magazines I contributed to on a regular basis—articles for *Ladies' Home Journal, Family Circle, Glamour,* and *SELF.* Tips on how to lose the baby weight, or the best places to vacation with toddlers in tow. But I hadn't taken a freelance job since she died.

And even though my work at *Parent Talk* clocked in at typically less than twenty-five hours a week, it was twenty-five hours' worth of income that had disappeared from our weekly budget. For more than a year.

Josie had called last week and asked, in a gentle tone, if I was thinking about ideas for the column. I told her I'd have something for the September issue, and apologized again. She'd shushed me, telling me the column wasn't going anywhere. I'd felt my face flame anyway, feeling as though I'd been taking advantage of our relationship.

Josie and I had grown close over the years we worked together. She had four boys and often said, with her formidable stature—she'd been captain of the volleyball team in college—and penchant for chaos that a house full of boys suited her just fine. But after too much wine one night, she'd admitted she and Cal had tried for a fifth, and she'd miscarried. And now they were done trying. Four children, all healthy, was more luck than she could ask for, she'd said, with a wistfulness in her voice. When she'd excused herself to the bathroom, her eyes were wet as she left the table.

I knew they'd been trying for a girl. I saw the way she ran her fingers absentmindedly through Kat's hair when she stood near her. She brought the girls gifts when she visited the house: hair-brushes with their names written on them, tiny barrettes Kat would let Josie put in her hair (forget it if I tried). She'd taken pleasure in buying clothes for Maddie, and I knew when we lost her, Josie felt as if she'd lost one of her own. And I knew our friendship blurred the lines when it came to my job.

I said this to her on the phone, admitted I felt guilty, and told her I would understand if she wanted to ask someone else to write the column. But she'd refused. Our readers don't want someone else, she'd said. Our readers want *you*.

I didn't argue with her. I wanted to write the column. I hadn't wanted to *stop* writing the column. But the words wouldn't come. I'd sit at my desk, the screen blank and the cursor blinking at me. Sometimes, I'd sit for ten minutes before I gave up. Other days, hours. In the back of my mind all those voices rising up. *Who are you to write a parenting column?*

What sort of mother doesn't notice a necklace in her daughter's crib? What kind of mother doesn't know her child is choking twenty-two feet away from her?

I'd written the first column years ago after Josie and I went to lunch and I told her how, the night before, Jess had lost her tooth. Kat had been up teething all night. I'd spent the night rocking her in the chair, and when I woke up, morning had come but the tooth fairy hadn't. I had only stray change in my purse, and when I tiptoed into Jess's room to leave the money under her pillow, the coins clanged as they slid from my hand to her mattress. Jess opened her eyes, and even though my hand was already out from the pillow, I saw she heard them fall from my hand. I saw she knew what it meant too.

I told Josie, in that moment, I felt like a failure. How there was an awful sinking *I'm the worst mother in the world* feeling.

I told Josie I wanted a do-over. Josie laughed, and said, *Honey, don't we all.* Then she said maybe our readers would connect to something like that. So I went back to my desk and wrote my first column.

I wrote about how you can love your child with something that surpasses logic and reason and words, and you can still screw up. Even with the best intentions and loftiest goals, sometimes, as a parent, you fail. I wrote how so many of these moments stare back at you and say, *See, you were told being a parent would be harder than you imagined, the hardest job in the world, and you didn't believe it.*

Did you?

3

Jack

The spare key to the truck had wedged itself between the pages of the Ford manual. I emptied the glove box onto the front seat, swearing at the hair bands that were tangled with the bungee cords coiled in a tight circle. Now that Jess had her license, I let her take the truck once in a while. Between the clothes on the backseat and the flip-flops strewn on the floor, it looked like she'd moved into the old truck.

I thought about stretching out on the backseat and letting Hope calm down before I went back in the house. But after twenty years together, I knew to keep away from her until she cooled off. The boat wasn't great for sleeping, but it'd do for the night.

The drive to the dock was less than a mile if you stuck to Main Street, but I took the road by the water. The one I drove six mornings a week, before the sun came up, to *Hope Ann,* my lobster boat—and home away from home.

Hope used to call it that, with a smile. Now she called our house my other home. She'd call me on my cell to ask if I'd be home for dinner. *You know, your other home,* she'd say, and I'd hear her frown through the phone.

The light in the center of town blinked yellow. I slowed, turned into the lot, and parked in front of the shop in the space marked

Down East Lobster—the only space open even at this time of night because of the Wharf Rat, the local bar on the harbor. Boon had put up the sign last summer one morning after he'd circled the waterfront for more than an hour and ended up in a parking spot in the *goddamn next fucking town*. Quinton Boonalis was sweet and good-natured, Hope liked to say, until he wasn't. I thought the sign was foolish, with the town dead for almost nine months out of the year. But Boon had never gotten used to the changes in our hometown. As kids growing up in Alden, the town seemed to have sprouted up from the water. Evergreen-dotted cliffs shot straight up out of the Atlantic, and the low-lying roads near the mouth of the bay sat underwater in the highest of tides, as if the surrounding water was intent on reclaiming what had been rightfully hers.

Now, some thirty-odd years later, the influx of visitors and summer people had changed the geography of Alden, with new bridges connecting the once-submerged roads to make access possible to houses perched high on pilings.

As much as Boon complained about the changes in Alden, we both knew the summer folk were good for business. And business was what mattered to Boon.

When we started Down East Lobster Supply, I'd fish and Boon would sell. Now I still fished, but we had a handful of guys from Alden who sold their catch to us. We sold some of our lobster out of the shop, or to local restaurants. But it was our shipping business that allowed us to keep our price per pound competitive. *The Freshest Lobster in Maine Delivered Straight to Your Kitchen* was how we grew from some kids just out of high school hauling traps to lobster dealers.

Not that we were rolling in it. But it was a living. A tough one at times, with long hours and hard work.

And some years were not worth thinking about. When the recession plowed in the summer of 2008, lobster prices dropped below the price of ground beef. Record harvests glutted the market. Too many lobsters, not enough buyers.

That was two years ago, and some of the guys were still having a tough time of it. Hank Bitts had fired his stern man and brought his wife aboard in his place. One less man to pay.

They were loyal, our guys. Mostly because of Boon. Last I'd looked in the books, we had five hundred out to Tom Clover, whose engine had shit the bed at the beginning of the season, two-fifty out to Hank Bitts for a root canal for his wife, and almost a thousand out to Stan Grady, who was waist deep in legal bills after his wife caught him almost as deep into Dawn Milney, the busty hygienist from Village Dental.

The guys had a field day with that one over the radio. Stuff like, "Hey, Grady, I thought the nurse was supposed to do the drilling," and, "Stan the Man, you go to the dentist to have a cavity filled, not the other way around." And so on and so forth. So much of it I'd finally yelled over the radio to shut up or get off the channel. They were good guys, but enough was enough.

The back deck of the Wharf Rat was full of people, even though it was almost closing time. I blocked out the noise, the music. All I wanted was quiet. And sleep. I climbed over the rail of *Hope Ann,* the deck still slick from when I hosed it off earlier.

Below deck, the cabin was crammed with foul-weather gear piled in heaps, crates of WD-40, liters of oil, and coils of line stacked three high. I pushed the mess over and spread out on one side of the cushioned V-berth.

I hadn't wanted the dinner party from the beginning.

Hope had suggested it one night when I got home from the boat. I'd started to say I could do without it—but fine if that's what she wanted—when she'd scowled and said I'd always hated parties. Why should this one be an exception?

She said it in the way she spoke to me lately, light and airy but cold. Like fake snow blown from a can. She looked over at me after she said it, and her face softened when she realized my mouth was still open, my unfinished sentence lost in the air.

"It's the decent thing to do," she said. "Peggy's new to town and it's what we would have done before." Her eyes filled when she said this, and I knew "before" meant *before* Maddie died, *before* we became who we were now.

Part of me wanted to see Hope do something . . . anything . . . that she would have done before we lost Maddie. I didn't question the party because of it. I didn't know anything about Peggy except that she'd moved to Alden last year, and somehow she and Hope had met and hit it off.

And then, before I knew what was what, the party had come, and Finn was standing in my kitchen. I was stunned, speechless when he appeared in the doorway across the crowded room. He said, "Hey, man," and Hope introduced him as Peggy's husband, and then she frowned at me when I didn't cross the room to shake his hand, only nodded my head.

I didn't mean to bring Finn into the fight with Hope; she didn't know anything about that time in my life. But I wasn't any good at fighting about one thing when it was really about another, and before I could stop it, Finn's name came out of my mouth, and then Hope said his name: *Ry.* The way she said it, so easy, rolling off her lips stained red from the wine—I snapped.

Not from anger, though. Not at her. Even though it came out that way. Even now, thinking about that time, my body felt heavy, weighed down. If Finn felt the same about his role in the mess, he hadn't shown it.

I'd heard him ask Hope at dinner what someone had to do to get a boat named after them. She was at the other end of the table, and people were talking in various conversations. But I tuned out everything but them, nodding now and then to show I was listening to the Martins discussing the proposed budget for the town's new fire station. But I was listening to Finn, watching his every move.

His voice was playful when he said it. *So what does someone need to do to get a boat named after them?* He put the emphasis on *do* and leaned toward her when he said it. If he meant to startle her, it didn't work. He didn't know Hope. She laughed, as if it were a ridiculous question, and pointed at me.

"Marry him," she said.

When Hope excused herself to the kitchen, Finn looked over at me and saw that I was watching him. *It's quite a boat you got there,* he said, his words slurred.

I ignored the comment, pretended the noise between us at the table had drowned out his voice. The last thing I wanted was to ruin the night for Hope.

But he found me on the back deck smoking a cigar later that night, the rest of the party inside.

"Got another one of those?" he asked, gesturing to the cigar in my hand.

"No," I said, even though there were a dozen of them in the drawer inside.

He leaned against the railing in front of me. When he crossed his arms, his shirt strained against the movement. His biceps were small boulders.

He hadn't changed much in the twenty years since I'd seen him. Deeper lines cut his too-tanned face, and a blond crew cut spiked with gel showed more scalp than hair, but he had the same girth from high school.

He'd been a juicer back then, a linebacker who broke the opposing quarterback's leg in the last game of the season, even though our team had been up by three touchdowns. His buddies had high-fived him after the game, saying, *You* told *him,* like a team wasn't really beat until an ambulance showed up.

I heard he'd gone into the army or navy after high school, or maybe it was the coast guard. Probably whoever would take him after the DUI. After he smashed his truck into the stone wall at the edge of Jeremiah Road and the cops found him with a broken nose and his hands covered in blood.

The cops had assumed the broken nose was from the impact. Only Finn and his buddies who'd jumped me knew it wasn't. They also assumed the blood all over his hands was his, but they were wrong about that too. Most of that blood had belonged to me.

I flicked my cigar in his direction, and he sidestepped to avoid the ash. It was a slow, wobbly step. He leaned back against the railing to steady himself.

"I guess I'm a little drunk," he said when he caught my eye. "Tell your wife I'm sorry to be the drunk asshole at the party."

"I guess times don't change." I leaned down, ground the tip of the cigar into the metal sand bucket on the step.

"Got me there, good buddy." He shook his head in an aw-shucks kind of way, as though we were old friends just shooting the shit. "Cut me some slack. It's a party after all. Who would've guessed our wives would end up friends?"

"Go find your wife and go home," I told him. "Party's over."

He blinked, his grin wobbling. "Well, so much for small talk," he said.

I got up out of the chair and stood in front of him, the stench of booze hitting me. Whiskey, maybe, or scotch. Stuff I never went near. His eyes were glossy, red rimmed, and his wide, flat face was damp with sweat, even though the night was cool. If he wasn't drunk now, he had been at some point in the night.

Finn cleared his throat, stood up straighter. "We're grown men now, Kelly. What happened between us was a long time ago. I was hoping we could put it behind us."

He'd been a shadow standing over me. I'd been passed out on Pop's boat, sleeping off the twelve-pack Boon and I had split after work. There was a flash in my mind of the steel tip of a leather boot. The thud as it slammed into my head.

Without thinking, my hand went to the scar above my eye. I felt the thick line that sliced through my eyebrow. Boon always said I was color-blind. I never told him my right eye had taken the brunt of that blow. That the doctor told me my vision in that eye would never be the same. That it would be hazy, unfocused. Permanently.

"Is that what you came to tell me?" I asked.

"You say that like I just showed up here. You forgetting that I came here because I was invited?" His voice was upbeat, a nervous twitch on his lips that he forced into a smile.

"Not by me you weren't," I said.

He nodded, as though he'd known this all along. "Fair enough. I figured you hadn't connected the dots with Peggy and me. But hey, no worries in case you're wondering—man-to-man—I kept my mouth shut. Figured with the wives and all. I don't need Peggy yammering at me about the past. And Hope seems like a fire-cracker, like if you set her off, well—"

"Don't talk to me about my wife," I interrupted, and he stopped talking, the smile slowly leaving his face.

In the distance, the foghorn at Breakwater Light let out a warning.

I didn't speak. I knew if I did, I'd tell him Hope didn't know anything about that time in my life. And he'd also hear that I didn't want her to hear it *now*. Not after the year we'd had. Not after everything she'd been through.

Finn held my eyes before he gave a small shrug. "I was hoping we could do this on friendlier terms. Let bygones be bygones." He paused. "You know, you've got quite a business going on, you and Boon. Fishing pretty much all the harbors from what I hear. No water left for folks not selling to you."

"No water left? It's the Atlantic."

"You get what I'm saying."

"Actually, I don't. So spit it out."

His face colored. "Now I remember why I kicked the shit out of you. Here's the deal. I want to fish my waters again. The waters you moved in on after I left."

I waited. Not sure I heard him right.

He'd worked as the stern man on his father's boat for a couple of summers in high school, just like every other kid in these parts who was related to someone in the fishing business. I'd fished with Pop, my grandfather, ever since I'd turned ten.

But I'd kept fishing. I'd fished ever since.

"I've got a forty footer with twin diesels and a pot hauler. I've got a buddy who's got a license. What he doesn't have is territory that's pulling anything but crabs. But you do. And you've also got strings where I used to haul." He cleared his throat, bolder now.

It didn't surprise me that he had a twin diesel boat, even though every working lobsterman around here fished with a single engine. Two engines were twice the worry, twice the maintenance, twice the cost.

Pop's inshore territory had always been the western edge of Turner Point. Finn and his father had fished near us. But that was more than twenty years ago, before the older Finn died, and Ryland had disappeared off the face of the earth. And the territory had become mine.

There were no lines in the water. Nothing you could see. But there might as well have been. It was water, fluid and moving, but territories were made out of concrete. Mess with them and you might get your gear cut, your driveway full of nails, your tires slashed. And that was if whoever you messed with was in a good mood.

"You've got traps where I used to haul," he said again. "I can see taking over since I was gone. Now that I'm back, I should have rights to fish it." He said it in an offhand way. Like we weren't talking about how I put food on my table.

"It's my territory. Go near it and we're going to have a problem."

"It was my territory. Ask anyone who fished with us back then, and they'll tell you it belongs to me. Your partner there. Boon. He knows."

"Well, go ask him. Last time you guys saw each other, I heard he was pretty reasonable."

His hands balled into fists when he heard this. "I don't have a problem with Boon. He kicked my ass. I'll give him that. But he was just looking out for you. Like I said, water under the bridge."

"I had nothing to do with that. He went looking for you all on his own. I guess he figured you wouldn't be so tough one-on-one. And he was right. Wasn't he? Rumor was, you were a rag doll when he got done with you."

Finn's lips twitched. He looked like he might come at me, but he took a deep breath and stayed at the railing.

"Look. We can go back and forth about this forever. I have no interest in what happened back then. And I didn't come here to be your buddy. I don't like you. You don't like me. That's fine. But fair's fair. You've got traps all over the place. Your buoys. All *over* the place.

You've got your trawls out there, the shop, guys selling to you." He ticked these off on his fingers. "We're talking about your scraps here. All I'm asking for are your goddamn scraps while I get my business going. A strip of water. A strip of water that used to be mine."

"Used to be. It used to be your water," I said. "And it's staying that way. You want to work these waters? Do what I do. And every other fisherman around here does. Find some open water and fish it. And when you come home with nothing, go out the next day and do it again. And that strip of water isn't just a scrap. It's how I make my living. That water feeds my kids, pays my mortgage. And it belongs to me."

He watched me, his face blank. "Don't lecture me about fishing. I've been doing it as long as you, just in different waters. And I've got kids to feed and a mortgage to pay as well. That water doesn't belong to you. It was mine and you took it. And I think it's time you stop taking things that don't belong to you."

From somewhere inside the house came the sound of glasses clinking together. I looked over and saw Hope standing in a small circle with two other women. Their silhouettes were dark shadows through the sliding glass door. They lifted their glasses and drank a toast to something. Hope turned, and the light across her face lit her smile.

The slider opened, and Jessie stepped through the opening. She didn't pause when she saw the two of us. She walked right over, crossing the porch quickly until she stood next to me, so close that her chin brushed the side of my shoulder.

"Mom needs you," she said.

"Go back inside. I'll be there in a minute," I said, and turned back to Finn.

But she slipped her fingers around my wrist, pulling me toward the door.

"Dad. It can't wait. She said now."

I looked over at her, and her eyes were wide. She said it in a strong voice. But I heard the shake in it. I took her hand off my wrist and gestured for her to walk.

I heard Finn say to the back of my head, "Thanks for the hospitality."

"What's going on?" I asked Jess when we were in the house.

I saw Hope in the living room, her back to me. I started to walk toward her when Jess grabbed my arm.

"Dad. Wait."

"Jessica," I said, exasperated.

She looked out the door at Finn. I looked past him to the window behind where he was standing. The window in Jess's room.

"She doesn't need you. Don't be mad," she said, watching me. "I heard voices and looked out my window, and you looked like you were going to hit him. What were you talking about?"

"Just business, Jess."

She eyed me, not convinced.

"Plus, I don't hit things that big." I tugged her ponytail, trying to lighten the moment.

She gave me a weak smile, and I put my arm around her shoulders and led her into the living room, away from Finn on the deck. She'd stayed glued to my side the rest of the night, and the party had ended soon after.

Instead of hitting something as big as Finn, I'd picked a fight with Hope, the one person I was trying to bring back to me.

I was failing, though. Nothing I said or did made any of it better. She kept telling me it wasn't anything I could fix. That she needed time. That me pushing her to feel better, to make love, to spread Maddie's ashes, all of it was too much. So I went to work. Out on the water, where every movement mattered.

I reached into my back pocket and pulled out my wallet. The light was dim, but I didn't need it to study the pictures anymore like I used to right after she died. I knew them by heart, every last detail, as if by studying them I could breathe life into them.

There were two, taken on a rare warm October day when we decided on a last-minute picnic at the Salt House. Hope was lucky and snapped a picture of the girls without them noticing. Kat is six and slight in build. She is holding Maddie, who is in her diaper, her legs ringed with baby fat and wrapped around Kat's waist. Her head is resting on Kat's shoulder and she is sleeping. Both arms are around Kat's neck. She is under a year in the picture but Kat has thrust a hip out to support her weight, and her gaze lands directly on Maddie's face.

In the other picture, we are lounging on the blanket, and Hope is laughing at something outside of the picture. She is sitting between my legs with her arms wrapped around my thighs. My face is nuzzled in her long black hair. I'm looking straight at whatever caught Hope's attention. Jess's legs are draped over Hope's feet, and Kat's fingertip is clearly in the side of the picture. I don't remember what it was that we were laughing at. But it must have been Maddie. Because we are happy.

And she is the only one missing.

4

Jess

"Dad's gone," a voice said in the dark. I opened one eye. Kat was in front of me. I blinked, sleep blurring my vision.

She was sitting with her legs folded under her on the edge of my bed, her face invisible under the brown curls tangled around her face.

"Go back to sleep," I muttered, and pulled her sideways until she toppled over in a heap next to me.

The bed dipped and she popped upright like a coiled spring. She swiped at her hair, pushing it off her forehead. Her eyes were two blue circles staring at me.

"Did you hear what I said? Dad. Is. Gone." She pulled the pillow from under my head, and the side of my face bounced off the mattress.

"Jesus, Kat! Knock it off—"

"Shh! Listen! Mom's in there." She pointed at her door. "They had a fight last night, and Mom threw Dad's shoes out the front door and now he's gone."

She stood in front of me. Fists clenched, the vein on her forehead a bulging dark line. She was a bomb. A four-foot bomb waiting to explode. Or implode.

We did an experiment in Physics last year with a can of soda

and a hot plate to learn the difference between explosion and implosion. How an object that implodes reacts from the inside out,
collapsing into itself.

I looked at the clock. 5:58. On a Sunday morning. This was my
family now: an implosion experiment in action.

I swung my legs over the side of the bed and sat up.

"Slow down. And calm down. Mom and Dad have fought before. They always make up. Big deal."

Even as the words left my mouth, I heard the lie in them. I
couldn't remember a night my father hadn't slept in our house.

But this was the new us. The post-Maddie us.

"You didn't hear this one. Plus, Smelliot on the bus said Mom
was over his house and he heard they were getting a deforest."

"A what?"

"A *de-for-est*," she said, pronouncing the word so hard, the vein
on her forehead pulsed.

"That's not a word. And what is a Smelliot?"

"It's not a what. It's a who." She disappeared into her bedroom.
A second later, she returned with a stack of lined white paper, a
row of staples running crooked down the side. She flipped through
them, paused on one, and thrust it at me.

I took it, my eyes following her finger to where her handwriting was dark and precise on the thin lines.

"Read," she said.

*On bus, minding my own self like mrs. whitley says to do when
Elliot jumps to the seat next to me. Hey Ding-dong he says and
he pinches my arm so hard my eyes water. Are you gonna cry
now, Kat Poop, he asks and his stupid friend in the seat in front
of us is laughing. I tell him my eyes are watering from the way
he stinks. And then I call him Smelliot. His friend laughs and*

*points his finger like I got him good. Smelliot's face gets all red
and he comes even closer to me and says your mom was over my
house talking to my mom about how your dad is never home.
Your mom and dad are getting a deforest, Ding-dong. The Big
D he says over and over until I put my hood up and he shoves me
and goes to the back of the bus.*

I flipped through the pages. There were drawings on some,
scribbles on others, but most were filled with her small handwriting. She snatched it away, the edge of the paper slicing my finger
as it whizzed out of my hand.

"Cut it out. I only let you read it so you could see that word. It
is a *diary*, you know," she hissed.

I sucked on my finger where a thin line of blood had formed.
"It's a bunch of paper stapled together. Why don't you get a diary
that actually says *diary* on it so someone doesn't lose a finger?"

She reached for my hand, looking sorry now. I waved her away,
and her shoulders slumped.

"I had one Grandma bought for me, and I hid it to keep it safe,
but then I couldn't find it. And when I told her, she bought me another one with a lock on it. Then I put the key in a safe place, and
now I can't find that. And if I tell her, she'll buy me another one,
and then I'll feel bad when something happens to that."

"You're a mess," I told her.

"Don't say anything to her," she pleaded.

I rolled my eyes. Like I didn't have better things to do than
tell on my eight-year-old sister to my seventy-year-old grandmother.

"Anyway. I told you I didn't hear him wrong," she said, holding up the papers.

"It's called a divorce. Who is this kid, anyway?"

She ran over to my desk and grabbed a pencil.

"Peggy's son. Spell it."

"What?"

"Spell that word."

"Kat. Stop. You're overreacting. Maybe Dad just went for a walk."

"All night? I checked their room. Mom is in my bed, and their bed is still made."

I sighed. "That doesn't mean they're getting divorced."

"And Smelliot? Why would he say that?"

She was gripping the sides of the chair, and her eyes were wide. A bead of sweat rolled down her forehead.

Kat never mentioned that she was being picked on by this kid, but that didn't mean anything. She was like my father that way. They pushed away the things that bothered them and filled the space with movement. Always busy, always doing something, no time for sitting around mulling things over.

"How old is this kid?" I asked.

"I don't know. He stayed back a grade when he moved here. Wait, that's it," she said. "Next time he picks on me I'll say they kept him back because he was too smelly to go to middle school."

"Maybe he picks on you because you say things like that."

She twisted her face at me. "I say things like that because he calls me Kat Poop."

"Have you tried ignoring him?"

"Ignoring him? He's this wide and this tall." She spread her arms out and up. She looked up at me, and I saw my father's face. All angles and slopes with the way their cheekbones stuck out. The same deep-set eyes. Full of worry now.

"Does he pick on you a lot?" I asked.

She shrugged, as if to say, *That's not the point.*

"Why don't you tell Mom? She'll say something to Peggy."

"No way. Then he'll think it bothers me."

I eyed her. "It does bother you."

"What he *said* about Mom and Dad bothers me. He only picks on me because I beat him in every race in gym. Then he blubbers to Mr. Scott that I stay behind him on purpose and cut in front at the finish line."

"Well, do you? You know how you get."

"What's that mean?"

"It means you're little competitive, Kat. And by a little, I mean a lot."

She scowled. "I hate when you say that. Mom too. Besides, even Mr. Scott told him to stop whining about it, so it's not my fault."

"Well, don't worry about it, then. He probably just said it to get under your skin."

She looked doubtful. "You didn't hear them last night. They said mean things. Like Dad told Mom she was killing him."

I narrowed my eyes at her, and she nodded.

"*Killing* him," she said again. We didn't say anything for a minute, and I knew Kat was picturing my father saying those words. Picturing my mother hearing them.

Kat had her head down, and she was playing with the necklace around her neck, running the locket up and down the chain. The locket was so small, I couldn't see it underneath her fingertip.

She'd been determined to put a picture of my parents in it, but by the time she cut the photograph to fit, all that was left was my father's eye, a sliver of nose, one side of my mother's face.

My mother had replaced the locket with one half its size. So little, it would slip down even the tiniest throat.

Not that I wanted to know this. I didn't have a choice in it. Kat thought my sister just stopped breathing. But I'd come home from school too early to not know the truth. There'd been an ambulance outside. In her room, paramedics kneeling over her. An arm peeking out, a necklace wrapped around her hand.

Kat looked up at me now, her eyes on me, looking for some kind of answer, and suddenly my heart was hammering in my chest. I didn't have any answers. This was new territory for me and Kat—I was eight years older—I'd always had the answers to anything she needed. But it was typical big-sister stuff—how to braid hair, how to do a back flip off the dock without whacking your head, how to change out of a wet bathing suit under an oversize T-shirt or the best way to cook a s'more without scorching the marshmallow.

This past year her questions were out of my league. Question after question, and not a single one had an answer. Why wasn't Maddie in a graveyard like Grandpa? Are we ever going back to the Salt House? Do I still say I have two sisters now that she's dead?

I'd been angry at first. Angry with my parents for giving Kat the necklace. Angry at Kat for wearing it in the crib. Then all that anger faded away, and there was just the feeling of missing her.

And then months passed, and little by little, even that faded. I forgot what she smelled like. I had to look at pictures of her to remember the shade of her eyes, the color of her hair, the shape of the birthmark on her tummy.

My mother was the one I worried about the most right after Maddie died. The way she cried all the time. Seemed like every day, at some point, her face would crumple, and she'd go in her bedroom and lie on the bed.

My father was the opposite. I'd never seen him cry. Not even once. And now, it seemed like all that not crying had built up and spilled out his pores, changing him on the outside. You couldn't look at him without flinching.

It seemed like the only thing that had lived in my mind the past year was worry. And sadness. And more worry. My family was falling apart, and I'd spent the whole year worrying about it, thinking about it, and now it just seemed too much. Where were my parents? What were they thinking, fighting like that in front of Kat?

I took a deep breath, made my face stay expressionless so Kat wouldn't see that I was upset. I leaned over and turned on my computer. I never let her play with it, and her eyes lit up.

"Stay here, and I'll see what's going on, okay?" I asked calmly.

She sat down and took the mouse, her eyes focusing on the screen. I left her looking through my photos and hurried through Kat's room. My mother was spread out on her back, her long hair fanned out on the pillow.

In the kitchen, the stench from the mussel shells in the trash turned my stomach. On a regular night, Dad wouldn't have let them sit inside.

But we weren't exactly regular anymore.

I took the trash bag of shells down the stairs to the backyard. The lawn was still wet from the dew, and by the time I reached the water, small pieces of grass were wedged in the spaces between my toes. Seagulls circled above as the last of the shells tumbled out of the bag into the bay. I put the bag in the outside barrel and headed to the kitchen to start on the piles of dishes.

I'd just turned on the kitchen faucet when I heard the front door open and Kat's feet pounding on the floor. I shut off the water and turned to see my father standing in the doorway with Kat's face buried in his neck. He hugged her, then peeled her arms off his neck and hung her upside down, her legs still wrapped around his waist. He tickled her stomach, and a giggle filled the room.

"How about a ride on the boat today? It's a beauty out there,"

Dad asked in a voice that sounded like fluff, sweet and thick and sugary.

I wanted to tell him that Mom was spread out on Kat's bed like a dead person, but the look on his face stopped me. He looked scared, like the kind of scared when your smile is bigger than it should be and it doesn't match your face. Like the way I used to make Kat's Mr. Potato Head. I'd snap in the angry eyebrows with the serious eyes but finish him off with the big, red, shiny smile for a mouth. Kat hated it, said he looked all wrong. Crazy, she'd say.

He looks like he went crazy.

"I'm babysitting," I said quickly. Too quick.

Kat, who was standing now, looked suspiciously at me.

Dad said that was too bad, but clapped his hands together and said to Kat, "Come on, Kiddo. I get you all to myself today. Let's hit it and grab some breakfast."

He told Kat to go brush her teeth, and I followed her into the bathroom and closed the door.

"Where does that kid live? The one that's picking on you," I asked. I wet a tissue and wiped a glob of toothpaste from the lip of the sink. Some of it was on her sleeve, and I held her wrist and tried to clean it.

"I can do it." She wrestled away from me and stuck her arm under the water.

"You mean Smelliot?" she asked, and I nodded.

"I dunno. He gets on before me and doesn't take the bus home. Why?"

"I thought you said he was Peggy's son."

"Yeah, so?"

"Peggy left a dish here last night. I'm going to drop it off."

"No she didn't."

"What?"

"Mom gave me the job of taking pocketbooks and coats to the bedroom. She had a big, floppy bag, but that was it. If she had a dish in her hands, I'd have seen it."

Who knew if this was true? Maybe it was; Kat's memory was incredible. She was known for it in our family. Forget what Dad gave Mom last Christmas? Or where we went to dinner after the beach that day last summer? The answer was always the same. Ask Kat; she'll remember. And she would.

I grabbed her by the arm and pushed her down until she was sitting on the closed toilet seat.

"Do you trust me, KK?" I asked. It was Grandma's nickname for her, and she let her jaw relax.

"I want to find out what that kid said to you about the divorce. I lied to you because I knew you'd want to come, and you can't."

She started to argue, but I shushed her.

"Just go with Dad, please," I said in a hushed voice.

"Only if you tell me what he says." She held up her pinkie. "Swear it."

I sighed but stuck out my little finger. She wrapped her little finger around mine, and we pinkie swore. She made me hold it longer so she could double-check that my fingers weren't crossed behind my back.

After she left the bathroom, I went back to the dishes in the kitchen. I was halfway through the pile in the sink when I felt my father's hand on my shoulder, his breath on the side of my cheek.

"Stop, Jess," he said in a whisper. "That's not your mess."

He shut off the water. "I meant to do them last night. Leave them." He rolled up his sleeves, took the sponge from my hand.

"Mom's in there," I said, pointing to Kat's room. He followed my finger with his eyes.

I waited, but he didn't speak.

"Kat thinks you didn't come home last night," I said.

"I'll talk to her," he replied, avoiding my eyes, and I nodded, even though I knew he wouldn't.

"What happened?" I pressed.

"We had a little . . . disagreement." He fumbled over the word, his voice trailing off.

"About what?"

"Nothing important, honey," he said wearily, and rubbed the back of his neck.

"I'm not a kid, Dad. You don't have to pretend like nothing happened."

"You are a kid, Jess," he said, his voice thickening. "You're my kid. And nothing happened other than your father being a jerk. I was a jerk. That's all."

"You always say that."

"Say what?" he asked, tilting his head at me, his eyebrows squished together.

"That it's your fault. You always take the blame. Like Mom is always right." I crossed my arms in front of me.

"Well, statistically, she is," he joked, trying to making light of it. He saw the scowl on my face and walked over to me, put his arm around my shoulders. He smelled like cigar smoke, and I wrinkled my nose at him and stepped away.

"See," he said, "another thing your mother's right about. The smoke does stink."

In my whole life, I'd never heard my father say one bad thing about my mother, not even when he was joking around. He gave me a lopsided grin until I gave in, my scowl fading away. He went back to the dishes, and I left him there, knowing that was the end of that conversation.

I was walking through Kat's room when I heard my name. I

turned, and my mother was propped on her elbow, looking at me from Kat's bed.

She squinted at the clock. "You're up early," she said, her voice hoarse with sleep.

"Kat woke me up," I muttered.

Kat came in the room and skipped over to my mother, talking a mile a minute about going on the boat with my father. I went in my room and shut the door, not caring that it slammed behind me.

Several minutes later, there was a knock on my door. My mother's head appeared in the doorway, a forced smile on her face.

It was on the tip of my tongue to tell her that I knew about the fight. About her throwing my father's shoes out the front door. About him telling her she was killing him. About him sleeping on the boat last night.

But I waited, wondering if she would tell me the truth.

"Sorry that Kat woke you," she said. "She asked me to sleep with her last night, and I didn't hear her get up. Are you going on the boat with Kat and Dad?"

I felt my insides flip, a trembling in my arms and legs.

She was standing in front of me pretending everything was fine.

And my father was in the kitchen, with his angry eyebrows and serious eyes, and a crazy, too-large smile plastered on his lips.

"I'm babysitting all day," I told my mother, lying straight to her face, a sense of satisfaction running through me.

Not even the slightest waver in my voice.

~ 5 ~

Jack

Kat was quiet on the boat. She put on the life jacket I handed her without her usual grumbling and scooted on her hands and knees over the cushioned seat at the bow, a half-eaten doughnut hanging from her mouth. Sprinkles dotted the corners of her mouth like misplaced freckles, and they fell from her face when she pitched the last of her doughnut over the rail to the seagulls hovering in the sky above.

The drone of the engine filled the air as we left the dock and turned east to where the bay opened into the mouth of the Atlantic. Kat was on her knees, her hands on the rail and her body pitched forward. A spray washed over her when we hit a small wave, and she looked back at me and laughed. I winked at her and stretched my arms up to the sky, my lungs on fire, the tightness in my back not giving an inch.

Morning had come before I felt like I'd slept at all, and by the time I got home, Kat was worked up about my not being there. She didn't say it, but she climbed up me, wrapped her legs around my waist and her arms around my neck, tight as could be, just like she used to when she was a toddler. When I mentioned going out on the boat, a light came back to her eyes, and I'd let my breath out. It had been stuck somewhere in my chest since I'd walked in the door.

Hope was in Kat's bed, her eyes closed. I'd pulled the shade down and covered her with the blanket. When I leaned down, pressed my lips to her forehead, and whispered that I was sorry, I felt her head move, a nod, and then her eyes were on me, asking me questions, even though she didn't say a word. When I didn't say anything, she turned away from me.

And then Kat was in the room, whispering, *Bye, Mommy,* and pulling me by the hand to hurry up and get moving.

Kat had asked if we could haul traps. She loved to throw the females back in, but it was the middle of June, and Maine law didn't allow for hauling traps on Sundays between June and September. I told her this as I fastened her life vest before we left shore, and a scowl had settled on her face. She'd brightened when I said we could stop at the shop.

She asked if Uncle Boon would be there. I shrugged, not wanting to disappoint her again. Boon wasn't her uncle, but we'd been buddies for as long as I could remember, so when he'd given himself the title, it stuck. I doubted we'd see him at the shop, though. Sunday was Boon's fishing day.

I kept the skiff as shallow as I could to avoid the choppier swells with Kat sitting like she was. The shoreline of Alden followed along in a blur of balsam firs and rocky cliffs. The land curved inward farther up, and we followed the bend into Calm Cove, a large horseshoe-shaped inlet full of long piers and docks. White mooring balls bobbed on the surface, and I slowed the engine to a crawl as we passed the No Wake buoy.

Rows of wooden pilings held up the long wharf at the water's edge. I slipped the skiff into the small space next to *Hope Ann.* Kat climbed out onto the pier and took the rope I threw her to tie us off. She'd mastered the figure eights but still needed help with making the last loop and securing it to the cleat.

The sun lit the aluminum ramp as we walked up the incline to the landing. A handful of people sat in white plastic chairs above us, drinking coffee from to-go cups. It wouldn't be long before the Wharf Rat filled with the afternoon crowd and music blared from speakers disguised as rocks in the corners of the roped-off deck.

Kat skipped down the deck and stopped when she reached the splintered back door of the shop. She stuck her hand out for the keys, and I handed them over to her. She took the key ring, a jumble of silver and gold keys of various shapes and sizes, and flipped through them methodically before she lined one up with the keyhole and stuck it in. I leaned against the shingled wall, settling in while she searched for the right one.

The door opened on the first try, though. Boon stood before us with a smile on his face, as if he lived there and just happened to hear us at the door. His thick frame filled the doorway, his black hair slicked back. He was dressed in his usual gear: pressed khakis, boat shoes, a shirt with our logo on it. Boon got on my case for working too much, but he wasn't fooling anyone. There was no off button when it came to Boon and work. He just did it in different clothes than I did. Behind a desk instead of inside a wheelhouse.

"Aw, come on Uncle Boon. Dad was letting me open it with the keys," Kat said, her voice full of blame.

"Come on yourself, fancy pants," he said, turning her by the shoulders. "Go back out, and I'll shut the door. You can open and close it until the cows come home." Kat scooted out while I called after her to knock if she got stuck.

There was a pot of coffee on in the kitchen. I poured a cup, took a sip, and felt the hot liquid light up my lungs.

The shop was closed on Sundays, and I wondered why Boon was here. I'd only stopped in because Kat wanted to sit on the edge of the thigh-high lobster tank and stick her hand in the shallow water to lift them out one by one.

I threw the half-filled cup in the trash and walked down the hall. Boon was still at the door, throwing the deadbolt each time Kat unlocked it. She shouted at him from the other side of the door through her laughing to stop. I leaned against the wall and watched until the noise from the two of them made my head throb.

"Boon. Let her in. You're cranking her up."

"That what uncles are for," he said, without stopping, the *click clack* of the lock bouncing around in my head. A game of Ping-Pong in my temples.

"You're not her uncle, and I've got a hell of a headache." I reached around him and yanked the door open. He looked at me sideways while Kat fell in a heap at his feet.

After she settled down, I left her by the lobster tank and found Boon in the freezer checking the thermometer.

"What's up?" I asked.

"Got a call from the alarm company that the temperature in here had dropped, but I don't see an issue. We might need to replace the sensor." He glanced at me. "You look like shit. I heard it was a long night."

I shrugged, ignored him.

"Hope sounds as tired as you look."

"What'd she call you? Christ."

The freezer door was open a crack, letting in the warmer air, but the chill wrapped around me. I'd been on the water by four in the morning all week and stayed out later too. Lately it seemed like it took me twice as long to get the job done. There was a pain in my back that came and went, and with it so did my breath. Now, with my head pounding, and my body aching, the frigid air made me feel weak.

Boon watched me with a blank look. "When you didn't answer your cell this morning, I called the house. Hope answered."

"So you know the whole story, then. We had a fight. I'm an asshole. Let's drop it."

He walked past me, leaned out the door, and yelled to Kat, asking if she was okay. When she yelled back that she was fine, he closed the freezer door until only a small sliver of light came through.

"You are an asshole," he said, "but I didn't need Hope to tell me that." He said it lightheartedly, but it fell flat in the air between us. I'd heard his lines my whole life. Normally I'd throw him a chuckle, but today I had nothing left in my tank.

"You look like shit," he said again. "When is the last time you ate? You haven't been this size since high school."

I was down to the last hole on my belt, cinched as tight as it would go to keep my pants from falling off.

"Yeah, well, you've got a beer gut big enough for both of us."

"You know it's all muscle," he joked. I didn't answer because I did know. Boon hit six feet in middle school and started shaving soon after. I caught up to him in height but not in size or strength. He may have looked bulky and slow, but under all that bulk was a guy who could still kick my ass with one hand tied behind his back.

"Why the hell are we in here?" I asked, and moved to push past him, but he put his hand on my chest to stop me.

"Wait." He looked back at the door. "I don't want her to hear me," he added, like we weren't in a steel icebox a room away with the door shut.

"The bank called last week looking for you. . . . I took the number down." He reached into his pocket, held out a piece of paper.

I took it, shoved it in my back pocket, and mumbled thanks, avoiding his eyes as I walked around him to the door.

"Wait a minute," he said, stepping back, blocking my exit.

I looked at him, let my face do the talking. He put up his hands.

"Just hear me out," he said.

"It's freezing in here, so it better be important."

"You never get cold," he said accusingly.

"I look like shit, and I'm cold when I never get cold. Is that it?"

"Look. What I've been thinking is that . . . it makes sense . . ."

"No," I told him, knowing where this was going.

His eyes snapped up. "At least give me the goddamn respect of hearing me out."

"I've been hearing you out for the last year," I said. "You don't need my help in here, and I don't need your help out there. We cut fifty-fifty. You sell and I catch. The way it's always been. What you're talking about is charity. Give *me* the goddamn respect of calling it what it is."

He threw up his hands. "What I'm talking about is a friend help-ing out a friend who's down on his luck. We wouldn't be standing in this fucking building if it wasn't for you. And I'm in here cash-ing my paycheck sitting in a warm room while you're out there killing yourself."

"I'm out there because I want to be. How many times do we have to go around about this? I'd slit my throat if I did what you do all day."

I pushed past him, opened the freezer door, and walked to where Kat was standing above the lobster bin, holding one in each hand.

"Look, Dad," she said, "they're twins."

"Let's go, Kat."

"Ten more minutes. Please?" she asked.

"Five," I warned. "Meet me outside."

On the deck, the sun wrapped around me like a blanket. I leaned against the building and breathed, squinting against the pressure in my chest.

Boon came out of the shop and stood in front of me, his shadow blocking the sun. I felt a shiver run through me, even though the thermometer mounted on the wall read almost eighty-five degrees.

"You're an accident waiting to happen right now," Boon said calmly. "You don't have an ounce of fat on you, and you're hauling traps like we're just starting up. You pulled in the same catch last week as the Frazier brothers, and there's two of them and a stern man. The same stern man that you fired, by the way. Still haven't explained that one to me."

"Nothing to explain. My boat. My stern man. I wanted him off. You're the one that hired him."

"I hired him because I wanted to give you some help after . . . what happened. Not to mention, he's the hardest-working guy around."

"And he never shuts up. Talked all day about nonsense."

"You fired him for talking? Was he allowed to take a piss, or did you dock his pay for that too?"

"Look, Boon. Let me do my job and you do yours. It's worked that way for years."

"What's worked for years isn't just hard work; it's smart work. This . . . here . . . is not smart work."

He was getting worked up. Boon style. Face red, eyes blazing. Ready to blow. I stayed calm. We'd done this enough times to know what happened when we both let go.

"Let me worry about it. It's not your problem," I said.

He leaned forward. "Now, I'm going to talk and you're going to shut up and listen. The guy I own a business with—a business that a lot of people depend on to make a living—is either going to hurt himself or hurt somebody else out there. You think that's not my *problem*? I hired that stern man because somebody should be out there with you. You're stressed, you're tired, and you're weak. Do you know what I'd call that? You know what any betting man would call that? A trifecta for disaster." He glared at me. "And that's not a race you want to win, Kelly. That's not a race you even want to run."

He was in my face, trying to keep his voice down. From the side-glances of the people on the deck, he wasn't succeeding.

"That was me talking to you as a friend," he said, looking around, lowering his voice when he noticed the eyes on us. "Now I'm talking to you as your business partner. Cut back your time out there, or I'll do it for you. We're running a business here. You're not a one-man show calling the shots. You fuck up out there, you're taking more than just yourself down. You hear me?"

The veins on the side of his neck bulged. He was meddling, as usual.

But he was right. Everything on the water was earned. Mostly your reputation. If I was careless and somebody got hurt, it was not only bad for business. It was the end of our business.

I gave him a nod. He stepped back and shook his head at me. A look on his face said he wasn't sure how much more of this he could do.

I couldn't explain any of it to him. How being out there, hauling trap after trap, hour after hour, made the day go by. And the next one. And the next one. Until the days made weeks, and the weeks made months.

I couldn't explain that's how my life made sense now.

"Answer me one question, and then I'll let it go," he said, calmer now.

I met his eyes, waited.

"Is it the Salt House?" he asked. "This business with the bank?"

I nodded, swallowing a gulp of shame. I hadn't been late on a payment in my life. Sure, maybe when I was younger and we were just getting the business off the ground, I'd been overdue on an electric bill or a phone bill. But that was because I spent most of my time on the water and was barely on land to take care of things.

Not because I didn't have the money.

Hope and I had always done okay. More than okay, in my eyes. We didn't take fancy vacations or drive new cars—mine was an old Ford, Hope's a 2008 SUV, safe enough to get the kids here and there, but no car payment. Neither of us were big spenders—although the number of shoes in Hope's closet baffled me—we always had enough extra money after the necessities for the good stuff: lessons, instruments and summer camps for the girls, a membership to the boat-club pool, one weekend each season that Hope and I snuck away by ourselves, and a couple of trips every year for Hope and the girls to visit her mother in Florida.

And then came the past year.

The extra mortgage, just enough to update the Salt House, coupled with Hope not working was enough to deplete our savings, leave us living paycheck to paycheck. Now we were coming up short. I'd covered the June payment, put the check in the mail yesterday, but it was already two weeks late, and I didn't even want to think about July.

I shut my eyes, opened them, and heard Boon's voice. When I focused, he was talking animatedly, his hands punctuating the air. I tuned in midsentence.

". . . let me help finish it. We can bang it out in a couple of weeks. Have you in there in no time."

"No sense in finishing it if I can't get my wife to step foot in the front door," I said, and Boon's expression changed, his eyes telling me he had no idea.

"She wants to sell it," I confessed. "Keeps talking about starting over somewhere new. You know, without all the . . . stuff attached to it. Memories or whatever." I cleared my throat, suddenly exhausted.

The door opened and Kat walked out. Her eyes darted back and forth between the two of us, her smile fading. But Boon grabbed her and swung her around. She giggled and wobbled when he placed her on her feet.

"You know who's been asking for you?" he asked Kat.

He whistled, and seconds later, a tiny, hairless dog bolted from around the corner, and Kat ran to meet it.

"Kitty!" Kat squealed, bending to pick up the miniature dog, who jumped in her arms and crawled up her front, resting her head on Kat's shoulder.

"Can you take her in and get her some water?" Boon asked.

Kat nodded and carried the dog inside.

"That's a dog?" I asked.

"I take her for rides in the truck, and I'm in Karen's good graces for the week."

Karen was his girlfriend, a tiny woman who wore colorful scarves and had a paint-your-own-pottery business in town. They'd been dating for more than a year, a record for Boon.

"Kitty?"

"It's named after her favorite country singer."

I let it drop, unable to muster the energy to needle him.

"Why'd you call anyway?"

"To see if you wanted to go fishing."

"I fish for a living, Boon."

"Well, sit in the chair and drink beer, and I'll fish."

"So I can watch you fuck up the line and not catch anything? I'll spend my whole day untangling your mess."

He didn't argue with me. He knew it was true.

"Come over to the house instead. Kat can play in the pool, and I'll flip you a burger."

"I've got to patch things up with Hope," I said. "Clean up the mess from last night. And when the mess is clean, I've got a stack of traps in the back of the truck that need fixing."

He squinted at me. "This is what I'm talking about. Let me hire some high school kid to fix them for ten bucks an hour."

"They're my traps. I fix them."

He sighed. "Do me one favor. Okay? I know you, and I know you like to handle your own shit. But promise me you'll come to me before things get out of hand with the house. Banks aren't fooling around now. The recession and all. They're snatching up homes like it's a game of monopoly. I can help, you know. . . . I want to help—"

"You've helped enough, Boon," I said, remembering pulling out my checkbook to pay for Maddie's funeral services only to find they'd been paid in full; the envelope of cash Boon claimed had been left on his desk for me from an "anonymous donor"; the new engine for the boat he'd said he won in a poker game.

Boon started to argue with me, and I put my hand up; we both knew I wouldn't borrow money from him to dig me out of this hole. That was a rock bottom I wasn't willing to hit. If I did, I wasn't sure I'd be able to get back up.

Pigheaded. Stubborn. That's what Boon called it. Maybe it was. Or maybe it was just Pop, his words in my head from all those years ago, remembering when I'd brought home a slingshot from school when I was a boy, the wood sanded smooth, glossy from a fresh coat of varnish. I'd gone down to Pop's boat to show it off.

"Where'd you get that?" Pop had asked.

"I borrowed it from a friend," I said, anxious to dig one of the rocks out of my pocket and give it a try.

"Give it here," Pop said, and held out his hand.

"It's not dangerous," I argued. "I'm only going to shoot them into the water."

"Listen to me," he said, taking it from me and putting it gently on the sorting table. "Give this back first thing in the morning."

"Why?" I whined.

"Because first you borrow, and then you beg," he told me. "There's some wood down below. Go sort through it and find a piece without knots." Two days later, after a long night in Pop's workshop, my fingertips raw from all the sanding, I owned a slingshot.

Now, Boon stepped back and threw up his hands. "You know where to find me if you need anything." He stuck his hand out for me to shake, and when I took it, he pulled me into his shoulder, held me there in a grip.

"Hang in there, brother," he said. I tipped my head and he slapped me on the back and stepped through the door.

Kat came out a minute later, the dog on her heels. She reached down and held the tiny animal with one hand and closed the wood-trimmed screen door with the other. The dog stood on her hind legs, clawed at the screen, and let out a flood of high-pitched barks that ended in a low, humanlike whine.

"Don't cry, Kitty. I'll see you soon," Kat crooned.

We walked down the dock, Kat's footsteps matching my own. She reached out and grabbed my arm and swung from it like Tarzan, the braids in her dark hair twisting like vines with the motion. When her feet hit the gangplank, she looked up at me and smiled at the loud noise it made.

Her eyes stayed on me too long, though, and I knew she was

watching me, like she had been all year. Watching, waiting, I guessed, for me to make everything better. There were no words to fix it, though. At least none that I owned.

In the weeks after Maddie died, with Hope holed up in our bedroom, and my mother-in-law in the kitchen, baking, mixing, and icing, as if our sanity could be salvaged by a cupcake, or a homemade crumb cake, or a slice of carrot cake, if I could have, I would've slept on the boat.

I didn't know what to say to the girls back then. Especially Kat's questions about Maddie. Why did she just stop breathing? Where was she now?

Of course we didn't mention the necklace.

How do you tell a seven-year-old that her baby sister died choking on the necklace she got for her seventh birthday? You don't. You lie. You say she just stopped breathing. You tell her sometimes that happens to babies. You say she's safe in heaven now. You say too much. You say too little.

And still she asks and then you stop saying anything because no matter what you say, there's that same broken look on her face. So you work twelve-hour days on the water. Hours when there are no questions.

On the boat with Kat, I pushed all of it out of my mind. All that mattered now was putting this past year behind us. I focused on that thought, untied the line, and shoved us off the dock into the black water.

Above us, back at the shop, the dog named Kitty carried on, her cries following us, her high-pitched whine calling over and over for my daughter to come back.

The sun had burned through the morning fog, and the sky was cloudless now. Kat sat on the seat and raised her face to the sun. The skiff moved smoothly over the water, and when I looked over at Kat again, she was curled up on the seat, her sweatshirt under her head as a makeshift pillow, her eyes closed.

I turned the skiff away from home, heading in the other direction, out to the Salt House.

It was named after a rocky spit of land on the easternmost point of Alden, connected to the mainland by a long wooden bridge. Great Salt Bay stretched out in front of the house, and Olde Salt River snaked past it, visible only from the bathroom window.

The dirt road leading to the front door was marked by a wooden sign that read only *SALT* after time and weather erased the remainder of the words.

Pop said the sign had always been that way. From the first day he'd moved there, when he was just a boy.

When I was little, I'd imagined his family had moved to Alden for the beauty of it, for the water.

But Pop had a different story.

His father, Seamus, married with three kids by the time he was twenty-five, hated the water. He couldn't swim and hadn't held a fishing rod in his life. But his wife, Lydia, inherited the house from someone on her side of the family, and since Lydia was pregnant again, and not at all happy about bringing another baby into their already cramped duplex in South Philly, they sold whatever they couldn't fit in their station wagon and drove straight through the ten-hour ride to the house on Great Salt Point.

Pop would tell the story of that drive over and over through the years. Some details would change; the places they stopped to eat or the things they took with them, but his memory of seeing the house for the first time never faltered. The way he'd make his eyes open as wide as he could, let his jaw hang open like it had a loose hinge. *It was paradise,* he'd say, *effin' paradise,* with a whistle through his teeth.

It was a poorly constructed barn made into a ramshackle farmhouse by Lydia's self-proclaimed carpenter uncle. Rooms added to rooms with no logic; a hallway, long and narrow that ended at a wall, as if the uncle decided at the last minute that he'd grown tired of all that work and the room was no longer necessary. The walls were empty inside, not a speck of insulation. Cedar closets in the bedrooms, almost as large as the rooms themselves. *Guy had those moths tapped down,* Pop would say, shaking his head, *no matter if the people inside were frozen solid.*

But that morning when Pop pulled up in front of the house, the sun was shining on a slope of grass that wandered down to the dark blue water. For a city boy who'd never seen the ocean, it was paradise.

To please Pop even more, the house came with a boat, just a dinghy, but it had a motor and wasn't in bad shape. Seamus wanted to sell it, and Lydia didn't care much for it either. She was a young mother of three with one on the way. She had little use for a boat unless it was bringing food to the table or helping her with the mounds of laundry. But Pop wanted that boat, and he knew getting through to his mother was his only hope of keeping it.

He made it his mission. When he wasn't pestering her, he was working: painting the buoys that had sat unused on the boat for years: a bright green ringed with blue, the same color as the family coat of arms his mother hung next to the cross in the kitchen. He took out library books on lobstering and taught himself how to restring the old wooden traps that were piled in a heap against the back of the house. And he kept at his mother. And at her, and at her, and at her. After three months, she relented with one condition. He wasn't to go out on the boat unless his father went with him.

Pop would chuckle when he got to this part of the story. His mild-mannered father had whipped around to his wife when he heard this bit of news and said, "Have you gone feckin' nuts, now, Lydia?"

But Lydia had gone nuts, she told them both. Absolutely out of her mind from that boy on her all the time about that damn boat. She had her hands full enough with the other kids, and besides, a lobster or two a week, maybe some fish here and there, wasn't the worst thing that could happen.

So two mornings a week at the crack of dawn, Seamus and Pop motored out and set two traps, all that Pop managed to salvage from the old heap. The boat had fared better than the gear, and the blue dinghy, with its tinny buzzing motor, became my grandfather's home away from home.

Seamus clung to the sides of the boat, white-knuckled and pale, for the near dozen trips they took. Finally he put his foot down and told Lydia that his son was more than capable of going out alone, and for the love of Pete, what was he going to do if something happened anyway? Pop would always act out this part of the story, mimicking his father. "It's not that I can't swim, honey," he'd say, a wild look in his eye. "I sink, Lydia. *Sink*."

By the time I was born, Pop had built up steadily from those two traps to more than five hundred. When he died, Hope and I had inherited the house, and even though Pop had put in a wood-stove and done some updates, it was still rustic living, and with the girls so young, we'd only used it as a summerhouse every year.

Now it was another ten minutes before the house was in front of me, set back from the water. The lawn overgrown, a layer of green mold covering the back stairs, as thick as two-day stubble.

Hope had been the one to suggest renovating the house, moving into it for good. *Can you imagine, baby,* she'd said, *waking up to this? What a gift.*

We'd jumped in with both feet finally. Never in my life did I think I'd have two mortgages. But it was only supposed to be for a few months while we did renovations. We had a crew come in, and Boon was usually good for a day's work as long as I had a cooler full of cold beer.

We'd planned to move in at the end of summer last year and have the girls settled before school started.

Then she died. We hadn't been to the house as a family since. I knew Hope hadn't been back at all.

But I couldn't stay away. Sometimes I drove over and mowed the lawn. Checked the house to make sure there were no problems. I didn't feel the same way Hope did. She was afraid to go back. Afraid of all the memories piling up on her. I felt the opposite. But the more I pushed at her, the more she shut down.

Hope had suggested we sell it. She'd said it once. And once only. I stayed silent. Because if I spoke, the words would have been that we wouldn't come back from selling it. Our marriage. We wouldn't make it back. Not just from her forcing me to do it. But from her giving up on it. Giving up on us.

Looking at the house now, with the water shimmering in front of it, and the yellow clapboards so bright, it seemed hopeless. I had no idea how to get Hope to change her mind. How to make her feel how she did once about the house. *What a gift.*

6

Jess

I crossed the street on my bike and headed to the wide paved road that divided the town like a lazy river.

It took me ten minutes to reach the town dump, and I turned left down the pebble-strewn street that led to the housing development where this kid lived. Peggy's address had been in the book on my mother's desk, and now I hopped off my bike and pushed it slowly, trying to read the numbers on the doors. The Finns' house was number 25.

I'd lied to Kat. I wasn't there because of what this Elliot kid said to her about the divorce. I was there to tell him to stop picking on her.

I couldn't make Kat stop worrying about my parents, but I could tell this little bully that if he called my sister Kat Poop one more time, the varsity wrestling team was going to show up at his house and twist him into a human pretzel. It was an empty threat— I didn't know anyone on the wrestling team—but he wouldn't know that.

Of course, if he wasn't outside playing, my plan was useless. But Kat had told me he carried a basketball with him everywhere he went. It was a hot Sunday in June. Worth a bike ride over to see if this kid was outside shooting hoops in his driveway.

I was lost in this thought when I heard a train whistle, right on top of me, it seemed. My heart flipped and I flinched, catching something out of the corner of my eye. On the steep incline across the street, a train rumbled by, chugging past the houses sitting below it. When it was out of view, the air had a dead silence to it.

Then came the sound of a ball bouncing. The *thump, thump, thump* of it coming from a house down the street. I pushed the bike in front of me until I stood a house away from two boys playing basketball in a driveway. A large tree stood on the strip of grass between the sidewalk and the street, and I leaned my bike against it, shielding my body behind the wide trunk.

Number 25 was a small box of a house, sandwiched between two others. Chipped-gold-plated numbers sat above each plum-colored door. A black metal mailbox was mounted next to the door with the word *Finn* stuck on it in individual stickers, each letter sitting lower than the last, with the last *n* hanging off the bottom edge of the mailbox, as though even the name wanted to run away from the house.

Train tracks sat high on a steep slope behind the row of houses, and a massive chain-link fence ran as far as I could see to the left and right. From where I stood on the street, the rooflines of the three houses seemed to be holding the tracks up. I studied number 25 and imagined there were times in that house that it felt like the train was rumbling right through it. A hundred tons of smoking black metal steaming around the bend into your pancakes, all warm and syrupy on a cold winter morning.

No wonder why this kid was hassling Kat. I'd be angry if I lived here too.

I was leaning against the tree, staring at the house when I felt a puff of air on the back of my neck, thick and earthy, like the smell in the back of my father's pickup truck after he hauled the wet leaves from the lawn to the dump.

I turned quickly, the sharp teeth of the bike pedal digging into my ankle. I hopped to get away from the bike, my foot slipping off the street curb, twisting as I fell. I landed on my butt on the street, my hands slapping the pavement underneath me.

I looked up. Standing in front of me with a half-burned cigarette in one hand and a plastic cup in the other was Mr. Finn.

"Boo," he said quietly.

He wore a shirt that said *Plumbers Lay Good Pipe.* The sleeves were cut, the fabric torn and stretched, giving the impression that his huge muscles had ripped through the material.

I heard something over my shoulder and turned to see the two boys pointing at me and snickering. My ankle was throbbing, my hands pulsing from smacking against the street. I bit the inside of my cheek, forced the tears back into my eyes, and stood up.

Mr. Finn sucked on his cigarette, blew the smoke out of the side of his mouth, and said in a short bark to the boys, "Get over here."

They stopped laughing when they heard him, and the smaller boy lagged behind the tall one as they walked over to us.

"You think that's funny?" Mr. Finn asked, gesturing at me with his elbow.

The tall boy looked at me, and I could tell by his eyes that he thought it was funny, and when he looked at Mr. Finn and shrugged, the smaller boy took a step back, away from all of us.

"Go home, you little pissant," Mr. Finn said, and the smaller boy took off down the street like he knew what would happen if he had to be told twice.

"Here," Mr. Finn said, holding the cup out to me, his cigarette in the other hand.

I took it, and he reached out with his free hand and slapped the back of the boy's head. It was a sharp clap in the air, and I dropped the cup. It hit the ground and splashed onto Mr. Finn's pants.

The liquid was clear, small drops on my hand that felt sticky and thick.

"Ah, shit," he said, swiping at his pants. "So much for a little hair of the dog."

I reached down and picked up the cup. My hand shook when I held it out to him.

"I'm sorry," I said.

He took the cup, waved off the apology, and flicked the boy's chin up with his index finger. "Who raised you? Don't embarrass me. Apologize to this young lady for laughing at her when she was in pain."

"Sorry," the boy mumbled, looking at his feet.

"Hey, ding-dong. Look her in the eye. Like you mean it."

I saw the words in Kat's handwriting. *Ding-dong.*

So this was Smelliot.

Damp strands of dark brown hair were plastered to his forehead, and a bead of sweat rolled down his round cheek. He looked about Kat's age, but she was right about his size. He was big for his age, chubby, though, the baby fat on his still growing body more noticeable next to his father's sculpted frame.

He'd dropped the basketball when his father whacked the back of his head, and now it rolled down the street, wobbling to a stop on the iron grate over the street sewer.

Mr. Finn had his son's neck pinched between his thumb and his forefinger. Before I could tell him I didn't want an apology, Smelliot said he was sorry again, this time looking straight at me, and Mr. Finn let go of his grip on him.

We both watched him walk away and disappear into the house marked 25.

When Mr. Finn looked back at me, he narrowed his eyes.

"You're that girl from last night, the older one." He crossed his arms, studied me. "You look like your mother," he said, his eyes moving down the front of me.

I took a step back from him, and his eyebrows went up. His eyes were glossy, the alcohol on his breath turning my stomach.

"Did I scare you with my boy just then?" he asked, taking a step closer to me.

I froze, stopped breathing, a lump in my throat. I shook my head.

"I sure hope not. I was just teaching him his p's and q's. Nobody likes a boy to grow into a man with no manners. Know what I mean?"

He ducked his head so he was looking up at my face.

"I bet your Daddy taught you all about that, huh? Right from wrong."

I heard the sneer in his voice. I met his eyes and promised myself I wouldn't look away. I'd come for a bully. A harmless one, I thought. And instead, I got Mr. Finn.

His body was huge. Every part of him thick and solid and filling up space in front of me. But his eyes were empty. Gray and flat, colorless against the red of his face.

There wasn't a part of me that wanted to be standing there, inches away from him. But I couldn't move. I didn't know what my father and Mr. Finn had been arguing about, but I knew the tone of my father's voice well enough to know he'd been angry. And it was obvious that Mr. Finn was either drunk or a jerk. Maybe both.

Now all the emotion from this morning flooded my mind. The pain in my ankle was a white heat spreading up my leg. The word *ding-dong* swirled around in my head. Kat's face flashing in front of me. My father's scared eyes and crazy grin.

My head spun, a small hurricane building inside of me, and before I could stop it, words spilled out of my mouth.

"My father taught me a lot of things," I blurted, standing on one foot as tall as I could. "One of them was not to hit people."

Mr. Finn's eyes lit up. Flashing from dull gray to slivers of ice.

"Well, see, you're a girl, so I wouldn't expect you to know the difference. But that was a tap. Not a hit. See, a tap says, 'hey, listen up, kid,' but a hit. A hit's something different. A hit puts somebody on the ground." He watched me, waiting for my response.

When he didn't get one, he leaned closer. "Ask your father. Ask him if he thinks someone who gets hit by me would still be standing."

I heard a rattling noise and turned to see a rusted silver pickup truck behind us on the street. We shuffled to the side so it could pass, and it parked directly across from us. The door opened, and a boy stepped out of the driver's seat and glanced over at us. Mr. Finn tipped his chin up as a hello, but the boy didn't return the greeting. Mr. Finn turned to me again, and I felt my body stiffen, but he stepped away, talking as he backed up.

"Tell your mother I said it was a great party. And don't forget," he warned, pointing his finger at me. He walked backward until he reached his truck. A loud rumble filled the air as he drove away, disappearing around the bend.

I leaned down, looking to see how bad my ankle was, when suddenly there was a shadow over me. Dark and large. I sucked in my breath and stood up quickly. The boy from the truck put up his hands and stepped back.

"Whoa. Sorry. Didn't mean to scare you. Here to help."

"Did I ask for your help?" I snapped. "What is this? The sneak-up-on-people street?"

I turned away from him, hopping on one leg over to my bike.

"Wait a second," I heard him say, and I looked over my shoulder at him.

"You're bleeding," he said. "Look." He pointed to the line of blood running down my ankle, dripping over the side of my flip-flop.

I wanted to get on my bike and ride away as fast as I could, but the pain in my ankle was making me nauseous. I hopped over to the curb and sat down.

The boy walked over to his truck and leaned in through the open window. When he came back, he handed me an old beach towel.

"It's clean," he said, gesturing to my foot. "Use it."

I reached out slowly and took it, mumbling a thank-you and pressing it to my ankle. After a minute, I lifted the towel and saw the cut was just a deep scrape, but the side of my foot was swollen.

"It looks like it's sprained," he said, and I glanced up, trying to get a look at him out of the corner of my eye.

He had a baseball hat pulled low on his forehead. He wore a baggy T-shirt with tan cargo shorts so worn that strings of fabric from the frayed edges dangled around his knees.

I reached down and pressed gently against the side of my foot, a bruise already spreading over the swollen area.

"Do you need a lift somewhere?" he asked. "You can't ride that." He pointed to the bike.

The only thing I wanted was to leave this street. I stood and put my weight on my good ankle.

"I don't live far. I can hobble."

"You don't live far as in next door? Because that's about how far you'll get."

"I'll be fine," I said.

He looked at my ankle and shrugged. "Okay. Hold on."

He walked over to the bike and wheeled it over to me. I took a step, and a sharp pain shot up my leg. I winced, and he grabbed my elbow, taking the bike from me with his other hand. I had no choice but to lean my weight on his forearm for support.

He was only inches from my face now. The brim of the baseball hat had shielded his eyes until he looked at me. His face was sharp and angled, a shadow of brown stubble on his chin. He smelled like my skin after a day at the beach. But it was his eyes that made me suddenly aware of how close he was to me. They were green. The color of the inside of a kiwi, with specks of tan and black in the center.

Besides an awkward kiss with Robbie Messina in back of the gym at the eighth-grade dance and the two times I'd slow-danced with Josh Brown at the semiformal, this was the closest I'd been to a boy.

But even the word *boy* seemed wrong.

He wasn't a man, but man*nish*—more man*nish* than Josh Brown would ever be.

"Hello?" he said, craning his neck at me.

He'd been talking to me, and I'd been thinking about how man*nish* he was. I dropped his arm and hopped back a step. He stood with his arm extended, as if he wanted me to know I could still grab hold if I needed to.

"Look. Are you sure you don't want a ride? We can throw your bike in the back of the truck."

I shook my head, hopped back to the curb, and sat down, thinking about what to do next.

"Okay. Well," he said, taking his hat off and running his hand through his hair. It was brown, and curled up at the ends from where his hat had pressed down. "You can't walk. You won't let me drive you anywhere." He paused. "I have a phone inside. You can call your mom . . . or dad . . ."

"No!" I said, remembering the lie I told about babysitting. "Nobody's home. . . . My parents are out on our boat for the day."

"How about a friend, then? Look, I know I scared you earlier, and I'm a stranger, but I can't just leave you here on the street . . . hurt and bleeding . . ."

"I didn't say you scared me." I blushed.

"I didn't mean it like that," he said. "I just meant I sort of snuck up on you over there. And you're smart about the ride. I mean, I wouldn't want my daughter getting in a car with someone she didn't know."

"You have a daughter?"

"What?"

"Oh, nothing. I thought you meant you had a daughter."

He smirked, raised his eyebrows. "It was sort of hypothetical."

I blushed again. I didn't know if it was the pain in my ankle or his kiwi-colored eyes, but suddenly I was nervous, frazzled.

"Wait a second," he said, a look crossing his face. "How old do you think I am?"

"I—I don't know," I stammered, not wanting to study his face with him staring at me the way that he was. "I've never seen you at school, and it's a small town, so I just figured you were older."

"How old?" he pressed.

"I don't know." Thinking, *Does it matter?*

He tilted his head to the side and waited. Apparently, it did.

I shrugged. "Nineteen. Twenty?"

His lips formed a smile. It was clear this was good news to him.

"Stay here," he said then, and disappeared down the sidewalk.

I leaned back to see where he went, but his truck blocked my view.

I thought about getting up and making a run for it on my bike.

The last thing I wanted was for Mr. Finn to come back. Not to mention how embarrassing this was.

Suddenly I felt almost hysterical, as if either tears or laughter might come pouring out of me. I put my head between my knees and told myself to breathe.

This was ridiculous. It had been a stupid idea to come here. Who did I think I was? Some sort of Wonder Girl riding my ten-speed across town to save the day? I wished I could call Carly or Betsy to come get me. But both of them were on vacation.

I talked to Carly last week, and she couldn't stop talking about the bonfires at the beach every night, how much fun they were.

And Betsy had gone tubing with her older sister and a bunch of their friends. I'd listened to her talk for what seemed like forever about the bridge they'd jumped off and the boys she'd flirted with.

"What are you up to?" she'd asked, and I'd mumbled, "Not much," and changed the subject.

What was there to say?

That the big event of my summer so far was sitting at the kids' table with my sister at a dinner party at my house? That my mom had thrown my dad out of the house, his shoes as well, and now my little sister was convinced my parents were getting divorced, and the only thing I'd come up with was this brilliant idea of threatening some kid, and I hadn't even managed to do that.

I felt silly sitting there. Like a small child instead of someone about to turn *seventeen*.

I pictured my father tugging my ponytail like I was a toddler last night when I asked him what happened with Finn, and telling me I was a *kid* when I asked about his fight with my mother. Refusing to allow me to date, even though all of my friends had been allowed to date since middle school.

My father and I had argued about it months ago, but he refused to budge, said that when I went to college, I could make my own decisions but as long as I was under his roof, it was his rules. I told him his rules were ridiculous. My mother had chimed in that she thought I was old enough, *responsible*. But he'd stormed out of the room, my mother frowning after him.

I closed my eyes and tried to breathe. A minute later I felt a cool pressure against my ankle and looked up to see the man*nish* boy crouched in front of me, pressing an ice pack against the swollen part of my foot. He was holding a rolled-up Ace bandage in his other hand.

"Okay if I wrap it?" he asked, and I nodded, the cold immediately dulling the pain.

He held the ice pack in place, winding the bandage around it and over my foot in loops, until my foot looked like it was covered in a tan cast.

I lifted my foot, turned it from side to side. "Not bad."

"That's what premed at Stanford gets you," he said, blowing on his fingernails and polishing them on his shirt.

"Really?" I asked, impressed.

"No." He shrugged. "I did a lot of skateboarding when I was younger. My mother was always wrapping one injury or another. I paid attention."

"Is that offer for a ride still good?" I blurted before I lost my nerve. My father's face flashed in my mind, and I pushed it away.

There was a fluttery sensation in my stomach, and my heart was knocking in my chest.

It wasn't beach bonfires and tubing, but at least it was *something*.

He looked surprised, but he held his hand out and pulled me up when I took it. I hopped over to his truck, the door creaking when

I pulled it open. I buckled my seat belt while he put my bike in the bed of his truck.

There was a tall metal pail on the floor at my feet, and when he opened his door to get in, he reached over and grabbed it quickly.

"Let's give you some room for your foot," he said, lifting it away from me and placing it on the seat between us.

Inside the pail was a coil of rope, the handle of a saw jutting out from the top, a pair of pliers tangled in the rope.

I swallowed, feeling my heart speed up.

The door shut, and he put the key in the ignition, the truck sputtering a few times before it started. He pulled away from the curb and did a U-turn.

"We won't break down, I promise," he said, looking over at me. "That's all you need, I bet. To be stranded on the side of the road with some guy you don't even know."

I gave him a weak smile, eyeing the contents of the pail, thinking maybe this wasn't the smartest idea. But it was too late now. We were turning off the street, onto the main road. He turned left, and I gulped, felt for the handle on the door.

"Where are you going?" I asked.

He looked over, startled.

"How do you know I don't live that way?" I pointed in the other direction. I glanced at the sharp teeth of the saw, then back at him.

"Because unless you're a mermaid, you live this way," he replied. "That way ends at the ocean."

"Oh, right," I said, turning my head to look out my window so he wouldn't see the red on my cheeks.

"By the way, what was that all about when I pulled up back there?" He gestured with his head in the direction of where we'd come from.

I didn't know how to explain it to him, or even how to explain why I was there. I said the only thing that popped into my mind.

"It's a long story. But that guy, the one you saw me talking to, is a total jerk."

He looked over at me, his expression blank.

"I don't even know your name," he said.

"It's Jess. Well, Jessica, but everyone calls me Jess."

"I'm Alex," he said. "Well, Alexander, but everyone calls me Alex."

"Well, nice to meet you," I said, smiling at him.

"Nice to meet you too, Jess," he said, not smiling. "I'm the total jerk's son."

7

Hope

The weeks passed quickly. Jack and I moved around each other carefully. My mother was visiting again, and she was a buffer between us, another body filling the space.

Last night over dinner, she'd mentioned that she was going back to Florida soon. She wouldn't be back for a while. Maybe not until after the New Year.

Jack had looked at me, raised his eyebrows.

Later, in the bedroom, he came in and stood in the doorway, a look on his face that I knew well. I felt my body tense.

"You heard your mother. She's leaving," he said.

I didn't answer him. I knew what was coming next.

"She's been in your closet for a year," he said quietly, looking over my shoulder into the darkness of the closet.

He was looking at Maddie's ashes, nestled on the top shelf of my closet between my heaviest sweaters and covered with her worn baby blanket. I'd put them there to keep her safe and warm. I may have told Jack this at some point, but I'd never repeat it now.

Now the ashes were just another fight.

Jack wanted to spread them. I wasn't ready.

He waited for me to speak. When I didn't, just sat on the end of the bed looking at the floor, he cleared his throat.

"She's been in there for over a year," he said again, and this time I heard the blame in his voice. I felt a surge of anger roll through me. Before I could stop myself, I scowled at him.

"I know she's in there, Jack. Do you think I just forgot?"

We'd argued, and gone to bed without speaking, and when my alarm went off, Jack's side of the bed was cold and empty. He hadn't said good-bye before he left for work.

Now, I was in my mother's kitchen, having a cup of tea while Kat got ready for camp. The sugar wasn't fully dissolved in my mug, and I was listening to my mother tell me how Roger had sent her the kindest letter, and she'd cried when she read it.

"You should go home to him," I said. "He misses you."

She spooned a dollop of honey out of the jar and held it out to me. I waved it away, and she put the spoon in her tea instead.

"He understands that I want to help up here. He's no stranger to this kind of stuff, you know." Roger was my mother's boyfriend, a widower who'd lost his wife after a long battle with Alzheimer's.

"When are we going to meet him?" I asked, blowing on my tea.

My father died of a heart attack in his sleep when I was sixteen. If my mother dated after my father died, I didn't know it. When I went to Emerson College in Boston, she moved to Florida. She'd started dating Roger right before Maddie died, and now, a year later, we still hadn't met him.

"Let's not worry about that. I'm here to help you, and Jack, and the girls. To do what I can to make an unbearable time more bearable." She patted my hand.

I thought back to the days I couldn't manage to get out of bed. My mother had dropped everything and basically moved in, taking over the daily care of the girls—cooking, shopping, cleaning. Had I thanked her? Was there even a way to say thank you for that? I reached over and squeezed her fingers.

"I don't know what I would've have done without you," I said. And it was the truth.

"Well, like I said. I'll be here for a few more weeks. And then I do have to get back."

I thought of the argument the night before with Jack. The weight of it sat heavy on my chest.

I took a deep breath. "I need to figure out some stuff before you leave."

My mother looked up from her tea.

"Just things. You know. That I want to do. Before you leave."

We were quiet then. I knew if I said the word *ashes*, if the word even stayed too long in my mind, I would start crying.

And I didn't want to start crying on another random morning out of the blue.

My eyes filled, though, and I swallowed hard to keep the tears from spilling over.

My mother reached out and put her hand over mine. "I know," she said.

"I know you do," I said, grateful for her support.

She sighed. "No. I mean I really know. I wasn't going to mention it, but I'm no good at that. I took a bath last night, which I never do . . . but I have all these bath salts Roger keeps sending me piling up in the bathroom. Anyway, apparently there's a heat vent in the bathroom that connects to your bedroom."

"So you heard us arguing about—" I waved my hand for her to finish so I wouldn't have to say it.

"About spreading her ashes. Yes. I heard a little before I managed to get a towel on and get out of the bathroom to give you privacy. I'm not trying to interfere. I'm not. It's just . . . if I can help, is all."

I nodded, a knot in my throat. "I know Jack's ready. And he has every right to be. It's been a year. I get that. It's just . . . hard."

"I know it is," my mother acknowledged. She started to say something, then paused and brushed a crumb off the table.

"What?" I asked.

"Have you talked about the Salt House?"

"Talk? No. It's another thing we fight about."

"Well, you'll be ready when you're ready."

"I wish it were that easy, Mom. I wish I could name one single thing between me and Jack that was easy right now."

"Well, you know what they say. Falling in love is the easy part. It's staying in love that requires work."

She stood up, squeezed my shoulder, and went to the sink to take the rollers out of her hair, leaving me to ponder this nugget of wisdom.

There seemed to be nothing that couldn't be solved by one of her quotes. Half the time, it was simply annoying. The other half, she was right.

I watched her at the sink now, letting my mind wander back to a time when it had been easier between me and Jack.

I'd met him more than twenty years ago on the same dock he fished out of now.

I'd taken a job as a reporter for the *Sun Herald* after college. One of the first pieces I was assigned was to write a profile on a Maine fisherman. My editor suggested I head east as far as Lubec, to get someone *authentic*. I assured him Alden had plenty of those.

My research was limited to a trip to the Wharf Rat. I knew that some of the lobstermen who worked out of Calm Cove had a drink before heading home.

Sure enough, Big Jim and Little Jim, a father-and-son duo, were sitting at the bar. After three rounds, and my repeated assurances that I was a local, they invited me to tag along.

I met them at dawn the next morning, and they looked as though they hadn't gone home from the bar the night before. Smoke swirled around the cigarettes hanging from their lips; the round button top of a stainless flask peeked out of Big Jim's flannel chest pocket.

"Here's your Lois Lane," Big Jim said to his son, pointing to me standing above them on the wharf.

Big Jim hadn't seemed too keen on my coming out with them. He'd barely looked my way the entire time we'd sat at the bar. Little Jim had been the one to invite me. He was a scrawny guy with small eyes that darted to and from my face when I talked. Now, he looked a little too pleased to see me.

I noticed a guy on a lobster boat on the other side of the wharf. He wore a flannel shirt under orange bib pants. His dark hair was damp and combed. He was drinking a cup of coffee, and his boat was immaculate, the hull gleaming and bright even from where I stood thirty yards away.

"Who's that?" I asked.

Little Jim looked over his shoulder. "Who? Kelly?"

I looked at him, and he scowled. "Ah, you don't want him."

"Is he a lobsterman?" I asked.

Big Jim came up behind us and spit a large ball of phlegm into the water, where it floated away like a giant oyster.

Little Jim put his arm around my shoulder, the stench of fish making my breath catch. "Come with us. We're more fun."

"My grandmother's more fun," Big Jim sneered, a half grin forming on his lips, only the second time I'd heard him speak.

"And she's fuckin' dead!" Little Jim added, punching my arm like we were old buddies.

"You know what? I'm not feeling so good," I lied. "Go on without me. I'll catch you tomorrow."

Little Jim looked disappointed, but Big Jim shrugged and went back to loading traps on to the stern.

I walked back toward the gangplank and waited until the Jims had their engine running before I took a quick turn and walked over to the coffee guy. He was coiling a rope, the muscles on either side of his neck straining when he made the last loop, tightening the circle.

"Morning," I said.

He looked over at me, returned the greeting, and bent down, storing the rope in a crate that was neatly packed.

The deck was wet, freshly hosed. Nothing looked out of place. His boat was cleaner than my kitchen.

I waited until he stood to introduce myself and explain that I wanted to do a special-interest piece on the life of a lobsterman. He said something about an oxymoron, and I laughed—a silly, almost hysterical noise—because he was standing a foot away from me, his dark eyes staring at me so directly that I thought of retreating, tracing my steps back to the darting side-glances of Little Jim.

But he was looking at me, waiting for me to continue.

"I was going to go with them." I pointed to the boat motoring out. "But they're kind of, um . . ."

He followed my finger with his eyes and held up a hand when Big Jim waved to him. "Kind of what?" he asked.

"Oh, I don't know. Rough, I guess."

"They're good guys." I heard something in his voice, as though I'd overstepped.

"They said you weren't any fun."

"That so," he said.

"Well, no. That's not exactly true. What they said is that their grandmother who is dead is more fun."

"Is?"

"Present tense. She *is* dead and *is* still more fun."

"Ah."

"Why is that?" I asked.

He took a sip of his coffee. "Maybe they're necrophiliacs," he offered.

"Good word," I said, impressed.

"You know us rough lobstermen. When our knuckles aren't dragging on the ground, occasionally, we read a book." His tone was light, but he didn't smile when he said it. My face colored.

"So can I interview you?" I asked.

"Today's not good," he said, turning away from me, placing his coffee in the cup holder by the steering wheel.

"Okay. How about tomorrow, then?"

"Not good either."

"Look, you can just say no if you don't want to do the interview."

"Okay, then no. Your best bet was those two." He pointed at Big Jim and Little Jim, their filthy boat now a speck on the horizon.

"Can you throw me that line?" He pointed to the cleat on the dock and started the engine. I knelt down, unwound the rope, and held it out.

"Throw it." He gestured to the back of the boat, and I tossed the line where it landed with a thud. He put a hand in the air as a good-bye, the same wave he'd given the Jims. I watched as he motored away.

Up on the wharf, a guy holding a clipboard waited while I walked up the gangplank.

"That went well, huh?" He looked amused, a light in his eyes.

"What?"

"I'm Boon," he said, offering his hand, "his friend." He nodded to the boat growing smaller in the distance.

"Oh," I said, shaking his hand. "I asked if I could interview him."

"I know." He flicked his head at the bar next to him. "Our buddy owns the place. We were there."

"Where?"

"At the Rat. Yesterday. Kelly and I were there."

"No you weren't. I was the only one in there besides the two guys I was sitting with at the bar."

"We were in the kitchen, through the server window at the bar. You couldn't see us, but we could see you."

I felt my face grow hot, and then something occurred to me. "Could you hear me too?"

He grinned. "We weren't eavesdropping. I promise. I only noticed you because Kel couldn't get his jaw off the floor. I don't think he blinked once."

I looked at him sideways. "Well, why didn't he come out and say hello."

"I told him to. He said you were out of his league."

"Funny way of showing it," I said.

"It's not personal. Besides those two characters, you're not going to find anyone willing to talk about fishing. Not from around here, at least."

"I didn't know there was a code of silence. Why the secrecy?"

"Territory, trap placement, fishing routes . . . it's what makes some guys haul a big catch, and some guys come home empty-handed. Anyone making a living at it isn't going to want that printed in the local paper."

"And the Jims? What's with them?"

"A pretty girl is what's with them," he said, and my face went red. "Hell, I saw Kelly considering it. And that says a lot."

I felt foolish now, remembering how sure of myself I'd been coming to the dock.

"Come back tonight," Boon said. He had one of those faces that seemed to be perpetually smiling, his mouth pulling up at the corners, as if life was one big joke and he was the only one who knew the punch line. "I'll make sure he's there," he promised. "He may not answer any questions, but at least you can say you spent time with a local lobsterman."

"No way," I said. "I'm not going to chase him for an interview." Even though I knew that I would, that my interest in him had surpassed an interview.

"Okay, then. Where can he find you?"

"Why do you care so much?"

"Because he's my buddy," he offered.

I gave him a doubtful look.

"And he's a good guy," he continued, "who sometimes gets in his own way."

The bag on my shoulder was getting heavy. I nodded in a dismissive way.

"And he rarely looks at anyone the way he looked at you."

I tilted my head sideways. "That's a line."

He held up his hands. "Swear to God."

"Rarely?"

"As in never," he said, then squinted one eye. "Well, not never. He looked that way when we were in sixth grade and Gina Marie, my brother's girlfriend, got drunk and taught us how to shotgun a beer without using her hands. Come on. Just tell me a place tonight. Give him one chance. If you don't like him, at least you'll get a free dinner."

I considered it. What did I have to lose?

"Fine. Orphelia's. Seven o'clock."

"Orphelia's?"

Orphelia's was not only one of the best restaurants in town. It was also the most expensive.

"I don't know if he owns a tie."

"Well," I said, "if buying a tie is a deal breaker, then tell him not to show up anyway."

But Jack had shown up. I was sitting at the bar when he walked in wearing a blue blazer, a white shirt open at the neck, and no tie.

There were two women sitting next to me drinking martinis. I saw them glance at the hostess stand, and when they saw him, one woman quietly growled to the other.

He saw me, walked over, and sat next to me. I felt the women behind me staring at him over my shoulder.

"Boon said if you showed up, I should ask you to marry me on the spot."

"You don't even know my name," I said.

"It's Hope."

"I meant my last name."

"I know what I want it to be," he said.

"What's that?"

"Kelly."

I wrinkled my nose at him. "Do you always use lines like that?"

He grinned. "No. But Boon said by all means, don't be you. Be charming. So I'm taking his advice."

"So this is you charming."

"This is me charming."

"Where's your tie?" I asked. "Your friend said you'd have to buy one."

"Boon says a lot of things that aren't true. I own ties. I just don't like wearing them."

"So Boon says things that aren't true?"

"All the time."

"So when he said you couldn't stop looking at me the other night . . . that was a lie?"

"It was a lie."

"Oh," I said, feeling my face flush.

"I wasn't looking at you. I was ogling you."

"Is this the real you or the charming you?"

"Come out with me tomorrow and find out," he said.

We'd made it through the afternoon before our first kiss. We stayed below deck until the sun went down. He never hauled one trap, and I never asked him one question about being a lobsterman.

A year later, I became Hope Kelly.

"Earth to Hope," my mother said, waving her hands at me from the sink. "Did you hear what I said?"

"Oh, sorry, Mom. I was just . . . daydreaming. Start again."

"I was saying that I was thinking about something the other day. Something I don't think I ever told you."

"What's that?" I asked, blinking, not wanting to come out of the memory of me and Jack on the boat.

"I used to stutter when I was younger. Not a bad stutter, but enough to make me not want to talk. Mostly only with the *Y* words, but still, you'd be surprised at how many words start with the letter *Y. You,* for instance."

"I didn't know that," I said. "When did it stop?" I'd never heard my mother stutter. Not even once.

"*Yesterday,*" she said, her eyes roaming the ceiling. "*Yellow, year, yes.* That was a doozy, the *yes.* I'm lucky my head's not wobbly on my neck after all the nodding I did. Anything to keep from saying *yes.* The way I'd go on forever, ya, ya, ya, ya, ya. Like that *S* was just running away from my tongue, torturing me."

"Mom."

Her gaze came down from the ceiling, and she squinted, bringing me into focus. "Oh. Sorry. Anyway, this went on for some time . . . they didn't do the stuff they do now to help kids, and my mother used to interrupt me, finish my sentences. She was trying to help, but you know, that doesn't help."

"I imagine not," I said, glancing at the clock on the wall. I was going to be late getting Kat to camp. "So you stuttered . . ."

"So the year I turned ten, the school decided to put on a play. *The Wizard of Oz*. Which was exciting as it was, but then the PTO got involved, and someone's husband was on the board of selectmen, and somehow it was decided that the play would be held on the enormous stage at the town hall, the biggest one in three counties, and tickets would be sold to the public. Well, I wanted to be Dorothy, of course, but I was terrified of auditioning for the part because of my stutter. So your grandfather spent hours with me going over the script. Hours and hours we practiced. I still stuttered on some words, but he convinced me that I'd always regret it if I didn't at least try. Hardest thing I ever did, but I went to that audition."

"That was brave."

"Yes, it was. Wasn't it?"

"Did you get the part?"

"No." She shook her head. "Jennifer Ann Maloney got it. I didn't even audition because Ms. Waters pulled me aside the minute I got there and said she'd heard me in chorus and didn't I have the prettiest voice! That's what she said. I'll never forget her saying that. She asked me if I wanted a singing part in the lullaby league. I almost fell over with shock. Of course, I said yes, because you don't say no to a compliment like that. And the lullaby league . . . turns out they had the most beautiful costumes in the play. And we got to dance, well, it was just hopping from foot to foot, but in that costume, it seemed like ballet."

"Did you stutter onstage?" I asked.

"I never stuttered when I sang," she said blankly.

I cleared my throat. "And the stutter stopped when?"

"I don't know. It just sort of went away. Strange."

I waited for her to continue, but she reached up to her head, felt one of the rollers, and looked at the clock.

"I'm going to look like an ancient Shirley Temple if I don't get the rest of these rollers out." She bent over the sink, pulled a roller from her head, and placed it on the dish towel.

"Okay. Tell me. What's the connection between you stuttering when you were younger and spreading the ashes?"

"It's not a direct one," she said. "But I know you think spreading her ashes is going to be hard. And, I thought I'd tell you about something that I did that was difficult as well."

She glanced up, a curl flopping over one eye. "I guess my point is that sometimes in life what you think is going to happen is nothing like what actually happens."

"It was a lovely story, Mom. Thank you for sharing."

"I did love that play," she told me from inside the sink.

Ten minutes later, I was on the floor of my bedroom, one flip-flop in hand while reaching for the other under the bed, when I heard singing coming from the heat vent that was level with my head. I heard a toilet flush, and then my mother's voice singing over and over: *We represent the Lullaby League, the Lullaby League, the Lullaby League. And in the name of the Lullaby League, we wish to welcome you to Munchkinland.*

I sat on the floor and looked at the closet, and suddenly there was no air in the room. I closed my eyes and tried to envision the moment the wind lifted her ashes. I tried to fight against the suffocating feeling, tried not to think about how she was gone and all that was left were memories and ashes and I didn't know how to live with either of them.

A minute passed. I opened my eyes and listened to the sound of my mother's singing trickling through the vent. I pictured a ten-year-old girl with an awful stutter in a beautiful costume hopping from foot to foot, singing her heart out on one of the largest stages in three counties. And note by note, my breath returned to my body.

Kat

My sister's ashes were in a box in Mom's bedroom closet, hidden behind boots she used to wear out to dinner with Dad.

The boots were leather with high heels, and when she wore them, Dad always said something like *Holy Smokes*, or *Shazaam!*, and looked at her in a way that made me giggle, with his eyes crossed and tongue hanging out.

Last night I'd heard Dad say to Mom that now that Grandma was leaving, they should spread Maddie's ashes. I was brushing my teeth in the bathroom outside their room, and I heard him say it in a careful way.

"She's been in your closet for over a year," he said, and then my Mom said she wasn't ready. And I'd made a face at myself in the mirror because how can you not be ready for something after a whole year?

I never knew why sometimes I'd find Mom standing in the doorway of the closet, staring into the dark inside with her face tilted up and eyes closed like she was praying to the shoes. She looked like she wanted to step right in and disappear. She'd catch me watching her from the hallway, and say, "Go play, Kat," in a whispery voice that made me want to do anything but play.

I hadn't slept at all last night, waiting to sneak into the closet and see what Dad was talking about. But now with the closet full of wild things, I wasn't so sure.

From where I was standing down below, the boots sat under a cover of dust, just the round toes poking out from the lip of the shelf, like two ugly mushrooms growing there in the dark.

Mom had gone upstairs to visit with Grandma, and from the alarm clock next to the bed, she'd been gone three minutes. I figured I had another fifteen before she came looking for me. Twenty if Grandma started telling stories about the ladies at her old-age place and what she called their ninny pattering. They'd go on forever about that.

The two open windows on the far side of the room were full of light when I'd dragged the chair over and climbed on the wooden seat. But now, in the shadow of the open closet, a dead smell came out at me, and those two mushrooms got bigger each second. Reaching down for me, it seemed. A breeze came through, and the belt hanging on a hook next to me twisted, like a snake hanging off a limb, sending me hurrying back to the doorway.

This was stupid, wasting time like this. Mom had left me with strict instructions to get dressed.

I heard footsteps upstairs and froze. The chairs scraping against the floor above me sounding like they were sitting down for breakfast in the bedroom with me.

I didn't know why Grandma visited so much from her other house in Florida. It had a pool and shuffleboard outside her front door. Upstairs there was hardly any room. Just a bedroom with an old bed covered in a white blanket with all these little round pompoms hanging off the edges of it, and a kitchen that reminded me of the one on Dad's boat.

In the living room, there was the most uncomfortable couch there ever was, with awful clear plastic covering it. It made me sweat just thinking about sitting on that couch on a hot day, the way the skin on the back of my legs would peel off the plastic inch by inch, just like a caterpillar's legs pulling off the tree down back, long strips of skin clinging to the bark until they finally popped off.

I took a deep breath, two giant steps, and climbed back on the chair. I stood on my tiptoes to reach the box and shut my eyes tight when the back of my wrist touched the mushroom boot, expecting it to be slimy and wet, but it was fuzzy and warm. There was a blanket covering the box, and I unwrapped it, and put the blanket back on the shelf, fluffing it to make it look like there was something inside of it. The box was light, and I was careful not to drop it when I jumped off the chair. I put the room back the way it was just in case Mom came down—the chair back in its place between the windows and the closet door shut tight.

In the bathroom, I locked the door and set the box with my sister in it on the bathroom counter. Now that I had her here, I wasn't sure what to do with her.

Nobody ever said anything to me about why she wasn't buried in a graveyard, like the one in the next town over where Grandpa was buried. Grandma just sat me and Jess down once, a few days after Maddie died, on the awful couch upstairs, and used some big word that meant that Maddie would go to heaven and her body would go back to dust. She said we could sprinkle this dust in Maddie's favorite place.

I told Grandma that was weird because Maddie's favorite place was our cat, Orange Kitty's, water bowl. She loved to crawl over and slap at the water until it went all over the kitchen floor. Mom finally got fed up and put the water bowl on the counter, but that was only until Orange Kitty's fur got in Dad's coffee.

Grandma had taken off her glasses after I told her all of this and squeezed the little dents on the side of her nose. Jess had swiped at me with her hand and told me to hush up and just *listen*. But Grandma didn't say anything more. She just asked if we had any other questions, and even though I did, I didn't want Jess any madder at me than she already was. So I just shrugged, and then Grandma took us to the kitchen for ice cream.

We never talked about Maddie's dust again. Not because I didn't ask. Even Jess, who used to tell me everything, clammed up tight every time I brought it up. And Dad wasn't much of a talker to start with. Whenever I asked him to explain anything, he'd just tell me to ask Mom; she could explain these things better than him.

But that wasn't true either, because Mom just got tears in her eyes, and very quiet, and then Jess would yank me aside and whisper at me to stop it. *You're* upsetting *her,* is what she'd hiss at me.

The last time I'd asked Mom where Maddie was, she pulled me tight against her, my face pressed into her side, and said she was right there, and always would be, her finger pointing to somewhere around the area of my chest. I'd looked down at my shirt when she said this, as much as I could with her holding me as tight as she was.

"Here?" I asked her, to double-check, because the only thing I saw was a chocolate ice cream stain, and that didn't look anything like Maddie.

But she just said, "Of course. Can't you feel her, Kat? Because I can. I feel her."

And then she started to cry with my face still smashed against her.

I looked at the box sitting on the counter in front of me. I turned it around and upside down before I saw the small sticker on the bottom. It said: *Unlock: Turn box upside down, listen for sound of*

metal peg dropping (shake if necessary). Keeping the box upside down,
slide bottom panel toward side with sticker.

I turned it over and over. No sound. I shook it. Nothing. I
turned it and shook it at the same time. Still nothing. I was running
out of time before Mom came looking for me, and I still had to get
the box back in the closet.

I turned it upside down and ran my fingers along the edges,
settling on the two creases on one edge where it looked like the
bottom panel might slide out. They were narrow slots, too small
for even a fingernail. The dental floss container sat on the counter
next to my toothbrush, and I pulled a length out long enough for
me to slide it between the two cracks. I gathered the two ends in
one hand and held the box with the other, and gave a sharp tug.
The panel pulled loose, and a strip of white plastic sat inside. The
rest of the panel slid off easily, and I saw the back was just like my
sea life jigsaw puzzle, set in tracks that I couldn't see until it was a
little bit open.

I took the package out. It was just a big Ziploc bag, like the bags
Mom used for my sandwich in my lunchbox. I put it on the counter
and stared at it. I could see a straight line the color of a shadow
where the ashes ended and air filled the rest of the bag.

I wanted to feel something looking at it. But there was nothing
about it that reminded me of Maddie. It looked like fireplace ashes.
Not like the ones that sat in the bottom of our woodstove, all black
with chunks of wood mixed in. But the light gray kind. The kind
of ash that came from the hottest fire there ever was.

Maybe if I touched it, something would happen. Maybe my
finger would tingle, or a shock would pass through me. I wanted
something to happen. Anything. It opened easily, and some ash
blew at me. I closed my eyes, lifted my head like Mom did when
she prayed to Maddie in the closet, and pushed my finger deep into

the pile, all the way up to the knuckle. I waited, swirled my finger around and waited some more.

My stomach growled, and the drip from the faucet made me want to pee, and my arm burned from being in the air the way it was. And that was it. Maddie wasn't here at all. It was just a pile of ashes.

This is what my parents were fighting about? Spreading these? I took my hand out, and stared at the ash on my finger. I looked at the toilet, the water at the bottom of the bowl. If mom couldn't do it, I could. It'd be one less thing for them to argue about.

I picked up the bag and stepped over to the toilet.

Then I thought about what Grandma said about Maddie's favorite place.

From somewhere in the house, I heard a door shut.

I froze, waited, in the back of my mind Mom's voice telling me I better be ready when she came down.

I went back to the counter, wiped my finger on my pajamas and closed the bag, rolled it tight like it had been and put the box back together. I couldn't hear anyone walking in the house, even with my ear pressed to the door.

The house was still empty. I went to my room and put the box in my bottom drawer, way in back, rolled up in my long underwear and tucked under my snow pants, where Mom wouldn't look. At least not before I got them out of the house.

I was standing in front of my bureau when Mom walked in.

"You're moving slow today, Kat," she said. "I told you to get dressed twenty minutes ago. Let's get going. You have camp."

Her eyes passed over my shirt, and then she motioned to the bureau. "Come on, no more standing around."

She left the room, and I grabbed some shorts and a T-shirt out of the drawer.

It wasn't until I took off my pajama shirt that I noticed the gray blob where I'd wiped Maddie's ashes in my rush to put the box back together.

I pictured Mom's blank look when she'd looked at me.

Even she didn't know what she was talking about. Here was Maddie, on my shirt, just like she said she would be, and she didn't feel a thing and neither did I.

I threw the shirt across my room, where it rolled under my bed.

9

Jack

I overslept and left the house at six in the morning. It was later than I wanted when I motored out to our float, our buying station filled with tanks and freezers behind it.

The building had been falling down when Boon and I bought it when we were first starting out. But we both knew our way around a hammer, and after a few months, chipping away at replacing the floor joists and hanging new drywall, the warehouse started to take shape.

Neither of us took a day off those first years. There was the fishing, the buying, and the selling to get done. And once the shipping business got going, we had to fill orders. Before we knew it, we had a handful of local guys on our payroll.

And the not-so-local guys, like Manny, who was waiting for me on the float now, a yellow bandanna covering the top half of his dreadlocks.

I put the engine in neutral and let the tide inch me until the boat edged against the wooden dock.

Manny reached out, grabbed the line, and tied it off on the cleat. After the boat was secure, I walked to where he was standing and swung a leg over the side.

"Where you been hidin'?" Manny asked me, his accent thick,

a sign that he'd been on the phone with someone back in Jamaica since I'd seen him yesterday.

"It's been too long," I said, stepping onto the gangplank. I walked past him to the stairs leading to the warehouse.

We had a similar exchange every day, just different words. I gave him the finger and he chuckled, his teeth a flash of white in the fog.

Manny had been our bait guy for so long, I sometimes forgot he'd planned to go back to Jamaica when we'd first met him.

He'd been at the Wharf Rat, sitting at the bar in shorts and a pair of flip-flops, even though it was March, and the air was still cold, snow on the ground. He'd told us his girlfriend had lured him to Maine with her blond hair and blue eyes and dumped him, and now he was heartbroken and broke and looking for work, just enough so he could get home.

Boon had asked him what kind of work he was looking for, and Manny looked at him sideways.

"The kind that pays, mon," he'd said, moving his head to the music playing in the background, his dreadlocks bouncing off his shoulders.

We'd hired him, and he'd borrowed an air mattress and a small fridge from Boon and an old camp stove from me and moved into the room above the buying station, making sure the alarm clock he'd bought at the hardware store was loud enough to wake him at three every morning, when he was supposed to meet our bait guy. As far as I knew, more years later than I had fingers to count, he'd never kept the bait guy waiting.

I closed the door to the warehouse behind me now, the bottle of water I'd gone in for tucked in my back pocket. Manny was stacking traps on one corner of the float, reggae music coming from the old radio he kept lashed to the rail.

He'd loaded the bait on the boat already, the bin of herring a flash of silver in the dawn. When he saw me, he said something that came out in a jumble of sounds and words.

"Is that Jamaican for *I quit*?" I asked.

I knew it was patois. He'd slip into the language now and again. He hated when I called it Jamaican.

"It's patois for *you'd be in sorry shape without me*. When I quit, I tell you in plain English."

"How's the crew back home?" I asked.

"You know, everybody missin' Manny. Not enough to go 'round." His laugh tumbled out in smooth waves.

"Too bad you're not as popular here." I stepped on the boat and heard his voice from behind me.

"You lucky I'm here. And the ladies lucky too. None of you locals got what I got. Listen," he shouted, leaning over the railing toward me. "I'm a black marlin swimmin' in a sea of flounder. You get what I'm sayin'?"

I turned the engine, noise filling the air, put her in reverse, and saw his lips moving as he threw me the line.

"Don't wait up," I yelled out. He blew me a kiss, covered his mouth with the back of his hand as if he couldn't contain the emotion.

I put her in gear and headed out to the trawl I was hauling. There was a handful of us that fished all year, moving our traps offshore when the water was colder and inshore when spring came, following the lobsters looking for warmer water.

I motored out, cutting across the channel and heading north, the tops of my buoys barely visible in the distance.

Ten minutes later, I pulled up alongside the first buoy and squinted, thinking my eyes were playing tricks on me. On top of my traps were buoys I didn't recognize. I throttled over, gaffed the line, and pulled it to the rail.

The buoy was purple. A single thick stripe around the center.

In the summer, new buoys always appeared in the water, but they were recreational licenses, with one or two traps in the shallows off the coves where someone might catch a handful of lobsters if they were lucky. But summer folks were usually smart enough to stay far clear of the territories of working lobstermen. Those who weren't smart enough lost their gear, cut loose to tumble on the bottom. Although, there were other methods as well.

The Frazier brothers had a chainsaw stashed on their boat for when they found a trap too close to their own. It was a sport for them, slicing the traps in half and throwing them back in the water.

Hank Bitts, nicknamed Bitty even though he was the size of a linebacker, was the most reasonable in the group, with his miniature beanbag lobsters he stocked up on at the dollar store. He'd give them out to kids at the lobster festival, but they had another purpose on the water. He'd stuff a couple of them in a trap he found too close to his own, but not before he mutilated them, leaving holes where the eyes should have been or cutting off a claw, or disemboweling it, as if to warn whomever found it in the trap that next time, it might be him that got mangled.

I'd never destroyed gear before. The way I saw it, you'd spin your wheels and start a war if you weren't careful. People got shot, boats got sunk, sometimes nobody knew who started it, or over what, but by that time, it was its own thing and it didn't matter.

But these were Finn's.

He'd warned me, after all. As much as told me he was going to mess with my territory. I knew all the colors that fished out of this harbor and these weren't ones I'd ever seen.

And I was going to cut them. That much I knew.

The tightness in my chest was back, not exactly pain, but a heaviness that made it hard to breathe. A heat spread up my neck, a ringing in my ears now. I blinked, swallowed, resisting the urge to slice my knife through the line, smash the buoy on the deck until it came apart in chunks. I had hours of work to do, and traps tumbling on the bottom into my own was not what I needed.

I let the buoy go, watched it drop back in the water, wobble, and right itself.

There were trawls to haul, and nothing was getting done sitting here, stewing in my own juices. I put the warp in the hauler and pulled up my first trap.

An hour passed before I took a water break. Then it was back to work: gaff the buoy; put the warp in the hauler; notch and throw back the punched and undersized lobsters, crabs, and whatnot; band the claws; bait the bags; and repeat. And repeat. And repeat. And repeat.

I'd been doing it so long, the movements were second nature, but the days were never the same. If it wasn't the weather, it was the tide, or something acting up on the boat. Out here, there wasn't time to think about anything but what you were doing, or you'd pay the price.

I'd had my share of days when I was lost in my thoughts and the wind would shift and a wave would crash over the bow, knocking the traps over the rail. Or the warp line would snake around my ankle, and I'd catch it right before I threw the trap over. My adrenaline spiking, the image of my body pitching over the rail and plunging into the cold water snapping me back to what I should have been concentrating on.

Now, I heard the hum of an engine off my bow and looked up to see a boat heading toward me, maybe fifty yards away.

I watched it before it slowed, almost to a stop, then turned right, changing its course to pass me. It was the *Go Deep*, the Miller brothers' boat that ran out of Owl Head, nowhere near their territory. Finn ran with their crew back in high school. I knew he was still tight with one of the Millers. I grabbed the mike off the radio clip.

"Miller, Kelly here. You off my starboard?"

The VHF hummed, crackled. Then nothing.

I turned over the engine, threw her into gear, and throttled after the boat, the diesel engine growling. I was ten feet off *Go Deep*'s stern when the boat stopped. I pulled up, threw out a fender, and stood by the rail.

Keith Miller came out of the wheelhouse, a puzzled look on his face. He walked back to where I was standing.

"Didn't hear me on the radio?" I yelled over to him.

"Don't have it on. What's up?"

Keith was the oldest of the Miller boys. He'd done some time in the state penitentiary years ago after his girlfriend fell off the back of his motorcycle and died. At the time, the girl's father was a district counselor, and he'd lobbied hard for Keith to be charged with manslaughter, even though Keith had been sober and going the speed limit when she fell off the bike. Keith never even got a lawyer, just pleaded guilty and walked into jail, let go early for good behavior. He was a quiet guy, kept to himself. I'd never had a problem with Keith. It was his little brother, Wayne, I was looking for.

"Don't see you over here much," I pointed out.

"Going over to the island to pick up some gear. You need something?" He said it in a way that meant I better need something. And it better be important.

"I thought you were your brother," I explained. "There are traps over there that don't belong. On top of mine."

He looked over to where I pointed, then looked back at me.

"You stop me for that?" he asked.

"I stopped you to tell you I'm cutting them," I told him, the heat rising up my neck. "Tell your brother Wayne and his moron buddy you heard it straight from me."

He stepped back when I said this, pushed his sunglasses up until they sat on top of his head. I saw his gaze flicker to the scar above my eye and rest there for a minute before he looked away. He knew I was talking about Finn.

The week after Finn and his cronies jumped me, Wayne had sported a black eye and a fat lip. I remember landing a punch or two before everything went black, but I knew I hadn't done that kind of damage to Wayne. It got back to me that Keith had done it. When he found out the numbers; four to one, meaning four of them to one of me, he'd beat the shit out of his little brother. For being that kind of guy.

But that had been a long time ago, another lifetime ago. The Millers worked out of the next harbor over, and one of Boon's brothers was tight with Keith, but I hadn't had any dealings with them. For the most part, we stayed out of each other's way.

Now, he cleared his throat and watched me. He was one of those guys who went bald before he was out of high school. I don't think I'd ever seen him without a hat on. Today it was a brown knit cap, pulled low on his forehead. He had a goatee and a tattoo on the side of his neck of an ornate shield. The Miller crest. I knew I was walking a line talking about his brother, but I didn't care. The noise in my head was deafening.

He walked close enough to the rail that he could have reached out and touched me. His eyes flicked over me, came back to my face.

"Kelly," he said, his voice even, controlled. "I'll pretend I didn't hear that."

I leaned forward. "All I'm asking is that you deliver a message. So there's no confusion over who did what."

"Look. We've got a mutual friend, and I heard you've had a shit year, so I'm going to cut you some slack. You're not thinking straight."

"How's that?" I asked, but it came out more like a shout than a question, and his eyes locked on mine.

He put his hand on the rail of my boat. "First of all, you're going to back up. You might have a problem with whoever owns those traps, but that problem isn't me, and I've got about this much patience left in me." He held his thumb and forefinger out in front of me, the space between them so small, only the tiniest sliver of light seeped through.

Even through the noise in my head, I got it. I held up my hands and stepped back, gave him a nod to show I'd heard him.

"Now," he said. "Let's start over. I don't give a shit whose traps those are. And I don't give a shit if you cut 'em. I do give a shit that you're telling me about it. A guy got shot on the island last month over who knew what and who didn't."

He wasn't exaggerating. Two families who'd argued for decades over territory got into an argument out on the water about some traps that had been cut. Someone pulled a gun, and a stern man was shot in the neck. He lived, but barely.

"Either cut 'em and shut up or cut 'em and make it known. But either way, keep me out of it. You start dragging people into it, you're going to start something you don't want to start."

Keith walked back to the wheelhouse and turned on the engine, a thick rattle filling the air. He throttled in reverse. When he was across from me, he gestured for me to lean in.

"Take some advice," he said loudly over the noise of the engine. "You've got a good reputation out here. You know better than this. Get off the water until your head's straight, or you're going to get hurt."

He was right and I knew it. But the buzzing in my head was making it hard to concentrate. I blinked, trying to make sense of what was happening.

I stuck out my hand for him to shake. "Sorry I slowed you down. That was out of line."

After we shook, he looked in the direction of my traps. "Finn's on the booze again. If you're looking for him, check out the Rat. But you didn't get that from me."

He slapped the rail, spun the wheel starboard, and rumbled away, the *Go Deep*'s engines spinning the water into a blanket of white. There was an eerie silence then, only the water lapping against the hull. There was no feeling left in me, the anger I'd felt before faded and gone, leaving only a heaviness in my limbs. I couldn't remember a time I'd felt so tired.

But there were still traps to haul, bait bags to fill, lobsters to crate, a string of traps to cut loose, free to tumble across the ocean floor.

I motored over, gaffed the purple-and-white buoy, grabbed the knife from its mounted sheath next to my leg, and held it to the warp line, the seaweed wrapped around it thick and slippery.

It took me less than a minute to cut Finn's traps.

It was against the law to cut them. Trap molesting was a civil violation. If I got caught, there'd be a mandatory three-year loss of my fishing license.

I looked down at the knife, and the sun lit up the steel blade in a flash of light, blinding me. Dots of silver popped like fireworks in front of my eyes.

There was no air to breathe, the pain in my chest searing.

I slid down to the deck and pressed the heel of my hand into my eye socket, trying to regain my vision.

Keith's words played in my head, over and over, on a loop.

Get off the water until your head's straight, or you're going to get hurt. Get off the water until your head's straight, or you're going to get hurt. Get off the water until your head's straight, or you're going to get hurt.

And then Boon's voice chimed in. *You're not a one-man show calling the shots.*

When I opened my eyes, I was on my back, flat on the deck. The sky had grown dark, a large cloud blocking the sun.

I glanced down at a flash of light and saw the knife on my chest where I'd dropped it. The blade rising and falling with my breath, the tip of the jagged teeth resting inches from my neck.

10

Jess

The breeze off the water fluttered the curtain in the bathroom window at the shop. I was supposed to be up at the counter, stocking the glass case with today's fish. Instead, I was looking out the window at the pier below, where dozens of boats bobbed on the water. It wasn't the view I was looking at. It was Alex, who was down on the dock, loading crates onto the stern of a boat.

I hadn't seen him since I'd called his father a jerk. Remembering it made my cheeks hot.

When he'd told me he was Mr. Finn's son, I'd been speechless, mortified. He'd brushed it off, though. And hadn't said anything about it for the rest of the ride home.

After he'd pulled away in his truck, I'd stood on the sidewalk in front of my house, my head spinning. Had I even said I was sorry for what I'd said about his father? He'd wrapped my foot, given me a ride home. And what had I done? I'd called his father a jerk. A total jerk, is what I'd said.

Now it seemed like I had two choices: hide in here and pretend the whole thing never happened or apologize. I looked in the bathroom mirror. Looking for what I didn't know. Maybe not to see so much brown. Eyes, hair, freckles. Even my shirt was the color of dirt. The yellow fish shop logo on my chest was the only bright thing looking back at me. I stuck out my tongue. I was just some girl who ended up on Alex's street. He wasn't going to care if my hair was brown or green or pink.

I left the bathroom, opened the back door, and stepped out onto the dock. He was still on the pier, holding a cup in his hand, his back to me. I headed in his direction before I lost my nerve.

When I was almost next to him, he turned suddenly. Then his cup was in the air, tossed like a basketball, his T-shirt rising up his middle and uncovering a flash of brown skin. He saw me then, as the cup flew over me, the bottom of it just missing the top of my head.

"Oops!" he said, his arms still extended in the air, his eyes wide. We watched the cup bounce off the rim of the barrel and land on the wooden dock, where coffee splattered in small drops.

"Sorry. I didn't see you," he said as he bent and picked up the cup. He threw it in the barrel and stepped close to me, and there were those eyes. Rings of black and tan and green. He smiled, and I looked down. Looked anywhere but at those eyes.

"Did I get any on you?" he asked.

I held out my arms, looked at my legs. "No. I think I'm good," I said.

"I'm not known for my jump shot." He pretended to shoot an imaginary ball, then looked at me. "Hey. How's the ankle?"

"Good. Fine." I wiggled it. "Back to new. It's actually why I came down here. I mean, I didn't know if you'd remember who I was—"

"I remember. The Jessica otherwise known as Jess." He looked behind me. "Came down? From where?"

"I work there." I pointed to the fish shop.

He raised his eyebrows at me. "I worked in the deli one summer back in North Carolina. Filled in for a guy in the fish department one shift. It's hard work."

It was, but I loved it. With the door open, the breeze coming through the screen, and the smell of fried clams from next door sneaking in, it hardly seemed like a job at all. I'd worked at a summer camp as a junior counselor when I was fourteen, assigned to the six-year-olds. That was work.

"That's not exactly easy either," I said, gesturing to the fishing boat in front of us, the one he'd been loading crates onto.

"Oh, I don't work on that," he said. "I just wanted to get a look and thought I'd give them a hand for a tour." He studied the boat. "She's a beauty."

I looked over at it. It looked like every other boat in the harbor.

He saw my expression and dropped to a crouch and pointed at the bottom of the boat.

"She's got a triple-diagonal mahogany hull." He looked up at me. "Cold-molded construction," he said, and stood up.

"You like boats, then," I said.

"I like boats," he agreed, grinning.

"So, anyway," I said, realizing I had to get back to the shop, "thanks for your help that day."

"It wasn't a big deal. It's not like I have a ton going on here." He waved his hand when he said *here*, and I took it to mean Alden.

"Well, still. And I wanted to say I'm sorry again . . . for what I said."

He looked at me and waited. I felt my stomach drop.

"I called your father a . . . a name," I rambled, feeling my cheeks turn red. "And I—the truth is—I don't even know him."

He looked down, studied his shoes. When he looked up, his face was blank, empty.

"Anyway. With my ankle, you know, hurt, I didn't remember if I apologized. So, um, sorry."

He didn't speak, just looked at me like he'd rather be any-place else in the world than talking to me. Suddenly I wished I'd just stayed in the bathroom with my brown-eyed, brown-haired self.

"I have to get back. Thanks again for the ride," I mumbled.

I walked away from him as fast as I could. The only noise I heard was the sound of my sneakers against the gangplank. I pulled open the back door, stepped in, and shut it behind me, my heart pounding.

I passed Boon's office on my way to the front. He was on the phone and waved at me, pointed to his watch and grimaced.

I went to the front door and flipped the sign to *OPEN*. There was already a line of customers waiting at the door. I went behind the counter, pushing Alex out of my mind.

It was noon when Boon came out of his office and told me to take a break for lunch. After my knives were clean and my area scrubbed, I grabbed my lunch from the freezer and went out the back door.

I walked to the slip where *Hope Ann* usually was. My father was out fishing, and I slipped off my sneakers, sat on the dock, and dangled my feet in the water.

Our small skiff rocked slowly in the water. I put my foot on the edge of the stern and turned my face to the sun, letting it warm my skin. My eyes were closed when I heard Boon's voice from the deck above. I held my hand up to shade my eyes and saw Alex walking toward me, a brown bag in his hand.

When he reached me, he pointed at Boon. "That guy is wait-ing for you to give him a thumbs-up, or he's going to rearrange my face."

I looked at Boon, who was fifty yards away, above us, watching us with his arms folded across his chest.

"Can you?" Alex said, glancing over his shoulder. "He didn't seem like he was joking."

I put my thumb in the air, and Boon waved and went back in the shop.

"Mind if I sit?" Alex asked, pointing to the dock next to me.

I scooched over to make room, and he sat down.

"I work next door. At the sailing camp. I stopped by the shop to see if you had time for lunch, and that guy told me you were here."

"Boon," I said.

"Huh?"

"His name is Boon. And he was kidding about rearranging your face. He's never serious."

"I thought he was your father the way he was grilling me about why I was looking for you."

"He's my uncle. Well, just my dad's friend from forever ago, so I call him uncle. If it was my father, he would have been serious." I rolled my eyes.

"Well, that guy, I mean Boon, puts on a good act." He glanced back again. "I almost didn't come down here."

I looked at him, wanted to ask, *Why did you?* Instead, I concentrated on my lunch, tried not to stare at his legs, only inches from my own. A slug-shaped scar ran across the top of one knee. I looked out at the water, surprised at the urge to reach out and trace the shape of that scar with my fingertip. He opened the bag on his lap and took out an apple, rolled it around in his hand like a baseball.

I thought of Carly and the way she'd go on and on about Griffin Pike, the captain of the varsity hockey team. She'd analyze the way he said *Hey, boss,* to her when they passed in the hallway, or

whether the high five they'd shared at the pep rally was actually more than just a high five. She'd tell me even being near him made her heart race, her palms sweaty. Sometimes she'd catch my look when she said this. You don't *understand*, she'd whine, desperate for me to feel the same way about someone. And she was right; I didn't understand.

Until now.

I concentrated on breathing, tried not to notice that my limbs were suddenly heavy. Maneuvering the grape from my hand to my mouth in one motion seemed impossible. Instead, I closed my fist around it, looked at the water, and waited for him to speak.

Out of the corner of my eye I saw him fidget with the brim of his baseball hat, pushing it up and then down again. He saw me watching and stopped, put his hand under his leg, apparently aware of the habit.

"I wanted to explain about earlier," he said finally. "You caught me off guard."

I turned to face him. He looked as nervous as I was.

"I actually drove past your house a couple of times. I wanted to see if you wanted to hang out. Go to a movie or something. But I chickened out, and then this morning you just appeared out of nowhere, and . . ." His eyes darted nervously at me, and he stopped talking.

I didn't say anything. My head was still stuck on him driving past my house. *To see if I wanted to hang out.*

"The thing is, well, Finn's not my father. Not my real father." He pushed his hat up and down again. "He's my stepfather, my mom's husband. My father died when I was little, and um, I guess I could have pretended that I didn't know him, pretended he wasn't my stepfather, but that seemed weird." He paused again. "And I didn't want to . . . to go there about my father. You know, explain it."

I looked away. I knew that feeling. I still flinched when people asked how many siblings I had. Mostly I said two. She was my sister. Had been my sister. But sometimes I said one. Sometimes it was too hard.

"When you showed up on my street that day . . . I don't know . . . you were nice and normal, and well. Anyway."

I made a face at him. "I was a mess that day."

He grinned. "Well, sure, I mean you were hurt, but still, nice and normal."

"Do you hang out with a lot of people who aren't nice or normal?"

"I don't really hang out with anyone. We moved here last fall, and I was supposed to start school in the spring, but . . ." His voice trailed off.

"But you didn't," I finished for him.

He took a bite of his apple, shook his head.

"You don't like it here?" Maine wasn't for everyone. Just ask my grandmother.

"I love it here." He tossed the apple core into the ocean, where it bobbed and floated under the dock. "I deferred admission until September, but now I'm not sure I even want to go."

"Is that why you moved here? For school?"

"Yes and no. Mom's interior design business got hit hard with the recession. Ryland kept talking about how well he could do in his hometown with his charter business. When I got into Maine Maritime, it was sort of all the push she needed. She's regretting it now, though. I'm not in school, there's no charter business, and her husband fell off the wagon." He glanced over at me, the explanation sounding like an apology. "He wasn't always a jerk."

I blushed. "I only met him once, and that word just blurted out of my mouth that day. It was more the ankle—"

"No. It's fine. There are a lot of words to describe him lately, and *jerk*'s the nicest of them." He said this with a smile on his face, but it faded quickly. "What happened that day? Between the two of you?"

"It's a long story. I have a little sister, and I think your brother is bothering her. She's had kind of a tough year. I was just going to ask him to stop bugging her, and then your stepfather was there, and I don't know. Let's just forget it."

"Elliot's picking on her?" His face colored. "That's just great. Stepfather's a drunk, and brother's a bully. You must think I'm a real winner." His voice was strained, and he shook his head. "Tell your sister he won't bother her again. Okay? Gosh, I'm sorry."

"It's not a big deal. I don't know the whole story. Kat can be, um, well, Kat. She said something about them racing each other, and how she beats him all the time. She's not exactly a wallflower." I smiled, trying to show him it wasn't a big deal, but he looked embarrassed.

"El's a good kid. Ryland's tougher on him than me. Elliot was just a baby when my mom met Ryland, and he sort of raised him. Ryland always talks about how he was a jerk when he was younger. Sort of the high school bully. He doesn't want Elliot to go down that path just because he's bigger than everyone. But now that Ryland's drinking, my mother kicked him out of the house until he stops. I think Elliot's having a tough time dealing with it."

I swallowed, felt my heart lurch. *Out of the house?* I tried not to think of my parents, of my father telling my mother she was killing him.

"I'm sorry," I said. "Is your mom okay?"

"She's pretty tough. Not one to take any crap. She's sort of upset with me because I told her I was having second thoughts about going to school. I said it was because I wanted to stick around until Ryland got his act together. But it's more than that. And she knows it. She's not happy about me waffling on my future, as she puts it."

I thought about this. "Maybe she needs to know plan B," I said, using my father's line.

Don't complain to me about plan A, he'd say, *until you have a plan B.* He said it to Kat the entire season she threatened to quit her softball team. She'd whine and complain about how the other girls were only on the team because their parents made them play and they *always* lost. Finally after the last game, Kat told him that next year, she was going to join the boys' baseball team. *Aha,* my father had said. *Plan B.*

"Is there a plan B?" I asked now.

"I hope," he said. "I applied for an apprenticeship at a boat-building school in Brooklin. Way up north. It's probably closer by boat. Sort of over there." He pointed across the water.

"I know where it is," I said, and he looked at me.

"Right. You're from here."

"From here." I tapped the dock. "The part of Maine you're talking about is like another country. You must really like boats to go up there."

He laughed, his eyes resting on the skiff I had my foot propped up on. "Yours?" he asked, studying it, leaning over until his cheek was almost touching the dock.

"She's my sister's. Mine is a sailboat."

"I'm impressed."

"Don't be. My father wanted me to have her to learn on." I heard my voice petering off, embarrassed that I might have come off as spoiled.

"No. I'm impressed that you called the boat *she,* not *it.*"

"You haven't met my father. I knew what *port* and *starboard* were before I knew the alphabet."

"So, where is the sailboat?" he asked.

"Behind our house, under a tarp. A crack in the hull. My dad keeps saying he'll patch it, but I'm not holding my breath. It's not like he has a lot of free time."

He looked down at his watch. "Time. Oh, crap. I've got to run. My campers will be done with lunch in a minute." He got to his feet and threw the paper bag in the barrel behind us.

"I should get back too," I said, standing up and slipping on my sneakers.

We walked up the gangplank in silence. When we reached the back door of the shop, he stopped and turned to face me. He fiddled with the brim of his hat. Push, pull, push, pull.

"I could fix her," he said finally. "The boat, I mean. I could take a look at the crack. See if I can help. Do something to make up for my family."

"You gave me that ride and everything. You don't have to do that."

"Well, look at it this way. You'll be doing me a favor. I'll fix her and take some pictures. You get a working sailboat, and I get another project in my portfolio." He tilted his head at me, his green eyes bright for the first time since he'd joined me at the dock.

"Yes," I said, the word sneaking out before I could stop it. "I mean, okay. If you don't mind."

"Tomorrow? I'll walk over after work and get you. I keep my truck in the town lot at the fields."

I got out of work at four in the afternoon, right when my father was likely to be motoring in.

"I'll meet you in the lot," I said quickly, relieved that the boat was behind a shed at the Salt House. I didn't have to worry about running into my parents. They never went there anymore anyway.

We said good-bye, and I watched Alex walk away, my heart racing so fast, it felt like it might break loose, push its way through my chest.

Back in the shop, Boon was in his office. I tried to slip past him, but he cleared his throat.

"Nice try. Get in here."

I backed up and leaned against the doorframe in front of him. He was smiling, his dark eyes playful.

"He's cute," he teased. "I think your old man will approve."

I felt my heart skip a beat. "He's nobody. Just a kid from school," I lied, trying to sound casual.

Boon lifted his eyebrows. "Then how come his license said he was eighteen?"

"You made him show you his license?"

"Of course," he said. "His urine's in a cup in the freezer too."

I gave him a look. "Very funny, Boon."

He laughed and shuffled papers on his desk, but I lingered in the doorway.

"Boon," I said, and he looked up. "Can you not mention it?"

He looked confused for a minute. Then his mouth formed a straight line, and I sighed. I'd known Boon all my life. I knew every one of his looks.

"You know what he's like," I pleaded, before he said anything.

"That he's protective? Yes."

"You're protective. He's . . . I don't know, weird about it."

"Yeah, well, he is who he is," he mumbled, half paying attention.

"That's great," I muttered. "Thanks for the help." I didn't know why it suddenly mattered so much. But it did.

Boon looked surprised. He leaned back in his chair and watched me. "What's going on?" he asked finally.

"Nothing. I didn't think it would be a big deal to not mention it to my dad. Forget it," I said, turning to leave. I felt tears form behind my eyes.

"Jessica. Wait," Boon said, and I stopped. "Come here," he said, pointing to the chair across from his desk. "Sit."

I crossed the room and slumped in the chair.

He watched me. "How are things at home?" he asked.

"Home? I don't know. Fine."

"They don't look fine from where I'm sitting."

I waited, didn't answer. This was what my father called Boon's meddling. I didn't think it was meddling as much as Boon just being Boon.

He didn't hold back any part of him. Physically either. Always touching people when he talked to them. An arm slung over a guy's shoulder. A hand on your back.

My father was the opposite. He kept to himself. So much, it seemed he'd muster up as much as he could give and spread it only between me and Kat and Mom. My mother always said it was because he spent so much time alone on the water. That all that aloneness made him that way. I thought it was the other way around. I think my father went to the water to be alone. That he didn't have to pretend to be anyone else out there.

Boon put his elbows on his desk. "I'm not expecting things to be great, with the year you guys have had. But I was hoping for getting better. I haven't wanted to bother your mother with all that's she's dealing with. And your dad, well, let's say he's hanging on by a very thin thread, if you ask me."

His words came out loud when he said this, unable to keep his frustration with my father out of his voice.

He paused, his voice more controlled when he continued. "I've been accused of meddling, so I'm trying to stay out of it. Just keep tabs on you and Kat, and let you all know I'm here if you need me. And you've seemed okay, Jess. Not perfect, but okay. You've always been pretty even, ever since you were a baby. Sort of un-flappable, actually. But you've never asked me to lie for you."

"It's not *lying*. I mean, if he asks you, that's one thing, but . . ."

"You don't believe that," he said.

"What?"

"By that definition, a lie is something you say, not something you don't say."

My head felt light all of a sudden. "Look. Whatever. You're making a big deal out of nothing."

"You mean out of nobody."

"Huh?"

"You're asking me to not mention that you had lunch with no-body. The eighteen-year-old-friend-from-school nobody."

"Boon—"

"Fine," he said, going back to his papers.

I eyed him. "Fine as in yes?"

"Fine as in I won't mention it. Only because I wouldn't have mentioned it anyway. Not because you're asking me not to. But"—he held a finger up, pointed at me—"behave yourself."

I gave him a salute and went back to the front of the shop.

We had a steady trickle of customers for the remainder of the day. When my mind wandered to Alex, I told myself to stop it. Stop replaying the way he said my name. Stop picturing his kiwi-colored eyes. Stop tracing the slug-shaped scar on his knee. Stop all of it.

But my mind kept drifting back to him. Finally I let myself stay in the thought.

My insides felt stirred up, alive again. I couldn't remember the last time I'd looked forward to something, been *excited* about something. Maybe keeping Alex a secret from my father wasn't the best plan. But I wasn't willing to lose this feeling inside of me. It belonged to me.

It was my plan B.

11

Hope

It was Peggy who suggested we walk.

She said after her first husband died, her walks on the beach in those first weeks kept her sane. She'd put Alex on the bus for school, get right into her car, drive to the long stretch of beach across town, and walk until her legs ached. Not even her pregnant body, with her swollen ankles and huge belly, eight months at the time, slowed her down.

It saved her, she said. All that vast blue spreading out next to her and the crashing of the waves pushing the fog from her head.

And it gave her someplace to go instead of back inside the house, where a hospital bed sat in the living room and pill bottles lined the kitchen counter.

Her husband had wanted to die in the house they'd built together. But the cancer had taken even that from them and his last weeks were spent in a hospital room, his body pumped full of so much morphine, he looked at her and Alex like he didn't know them.

Like they were strangers.

Peggy and I walked in the mornings after we dropped the kids at camp. Our hair tucked under baseball hats or pulled back messily. Our bodies thrown into mismatched shorts and tank tops, sometimes stained, usually wrinkled, as if we knew the words we'd say out loud would somehow seep into the clothing.

I learned that she'd met Ryland at an AA meeting several years after her husband died. She'd volunteered to go with a friend who was nervous about attending her first meeting. Almost a decade had passed, and she'd never seen Ryland drink. Until now.

Now Peggy said, since moving to Alden, she never saw him sober.

I talked about how I couldn't write anymore. Or make love. Both acts a form of automation, a feeling of being outside of myself, watching from a distance, detached and robotic, my movements generated from memory instead of desire.

It's lonely, I told her, feeling the thickness of those words roll off my tongue.

We were walking on the hard-packed sand by the water when I admitted this. The ocean was flat, motionless, small waves running over our feet. When I said it out loud, the skin on my arms puckered into small goose bumps, as if my body wanted to rid itself of this information.

"What's crazy is that I miss doing both," I said. "Even in the middle of having sex now, I'm aware that I miss how we used to make love."

"I don't think it's so crazy," she replied, her pace slowing as she took a sip of coffee from the cup she was carrying. "Both of those things require you to be present. Maybe you're just taking a break. An emotional hiatus."

I sighed. "For over a year?"

Peggy raised her eyebrows. "Yeah," she said.

"Do you remember that feeling?" I asked. "After you lost your husband?"

"Do I ever." Peggy sighed. "I remember not being able to

breathe whenever somebody mentioned his name. We were high school sweethearts. Bought a house in the same town we grew up in. That was the hardest part. Seemed like every coffee house, restaurant, park, and beach had a memory of him. Of us."

"You must have wanted to move," I said, thinking of the Salt House, how all those memories made my chest heavy, my legs weak.

"Disappear is more like it. But Alex was just a boy, and then Elliot was born. I think that forced me to deal with it. I had to drive to school, and to the park, and all of those places that had all those memories. Little by little, it just got easier. Then one day—and I remember it so well—it was maybe a year later, or more, I don't know. That's not important. Anyway, I was in the car with Alex, just driving—I don't even remember where we were going— and we passed this family. A man and a woman and a little boy. They were riding bikes on the path near the beach, and this picture popped into my head. Like a snapshot. And I turned to Alex in the passenger seat and said, 'Do you remember when your dad tried to learn how to Rollerblade? He kept falling off the path onto the sand, and then he got going too fast and ran into the trash barrel and tipped it over and it spilled and he ended up in a pile of trash in the dune?' and we both laughed about it. And I mean, I *really* laughed."

She looked over at me, still surprised, it seemed. "Anyway. Now I'm desperate to *remember* the memories. I write them down sometimes, so I can tell the kids about him. A way of keeping him alive, I guess. There's no sadness anymore when I think of him. If anything, it's the opposite. I miss him, sure, but I always smile when something reminds me of him."

"Thanks for telling me that," I said. "Some days I think I'm there, and then suddenly, I'm at the not-breathing part again."

She was walking next to me, close enough that our elbows bumped occasionally. I looked over at her, thankful for her friendship. It spurred me on, her fortitude. These same words hurt Jack, worried my mother.

I thought back to when Peggy and I first met, remembering I'd been unable to breathe on that day as well.

I'd taken Orange Kitty for his annual appointment at the veterinarian's office. When I was returning him to his carrier after the doctor had finished, I noticed a tiny baby sock in the corner. Flakes of catnip seeped through the holes in the cotton. Orange Kitty had scuttled in to retrieve it, and it was clear why he'd gone in the carrier so willingly at home. The girls must have used the makeshift toy to lure the cat into the carrier for his appointment last year. I kept a bag of catnip in the pantry, and the girls had used a sock to hold the catnip. A small sock. Maddie's sock. The sight of it made my hands shake.

I paid for the visit and made it outside to the parking lot before the tears came, fast and blinding down my face. It had been brutally hot out, the AC in my car broken, so I'd walked around the side of the building. There was a small courtyard in the back with benches and a scattering of small animal statues. A plaque on the ground dedicated the space to *Our Beloved Friends*. I sat down on the bench, pressed a tissue to my eyes, and tried to breathe.

I don't know how long I sat there before I realized a woman was sitting across from me, also with a small carrier, yet hers appeared to be empty. It was obvious she'd been crying too, and she gave me a small nod when I looked up at her.

"My carrier had a guinea pig in it from my son's class," she said. "I only had to keep it alive through Columbus Day. Three days. Then in comes a heat wave. In October. I didn't even know Maine got heat waves. And apparently guinea pigs are prone to heat stroke. *Prone* to it. So not only is my son the new kid in town, but his mother has just murdered the class pet."

Despite myself, I laughed. She looked surprised, and then laughed too.

That was almost a year ago, and although we'd become good friends, we'd avoided the tough stuff until now.

I'd told her about Maddie when we first became friendly, of course, but we didn't dwell on it. It was one of the reasons I enjoyed her company. Alden was a small town, smaller after Maddie died. After the story of her death made the papers, I felt like I had eyes on me wherever I went.

With Peggy, I could just exist. Just be.

Now, I raised my face to the sun, felt the heat spread over my forehead and tickle the tops of my cheeks.

"How are things?" I heard Peggy ask, and I looked over at her. "I've been meaning to ask," she continued, "you know, between you and Jack?"

"He wants to finish the Salt House. He wants to scatter her ashes. He wants to make love more than once every couple of months. He wants us to be . . . us again. All things I can't begrudge him." I felt the words release something inside of me as they left, a lightness of sorts. They'd felt heavier unspoken.

"How were you guys before you lost her?" she asked quietly.

"Good," I answered, knowing this to be true. "I mean, we had our stuff, like every married couple. But sex wasn't an issue, if that's what you mean." I smiled at her, a tight-lipped smile that didn't reveal how much it hurt to admit this. I was the one who'd made intimacy in my marriage an issue. This I knew.

"You and I talk so much, but I don't know Jack at all. I mean, we met that night at your house, but we didn't talk much."

"No," I agreed. "Sorry for that. He was against the dinner

party from the start. Social things have never been high on Jack's list."

"Ah," she said. "Well, I'm happy you guys were good . . . I mean, before all this stuff. . . . I'm relieved to hear it's just a rough spot."

It wasn't so much what she said that struck me as odd, but how she looked after she said it, as if she'd been contemplating it for some time and was glad to put it to rest.

"Do we seem doomed?" I asked. "I mean, is that why you're asking?"

She waved her hand at me, brushing the question away. "Of course not."

"I do *love* Jack. I hope you know that. I am trying to get back on track with my marriage." I heard the strain in my voice, and my face colored.

Peggy stopped and grabbed my arm. "Oh shit, Hope. Of course I know that." She sighed, dropped her face in her hands. When she looked up, she was a deep shade of red.

"God, I'm an idiot. I should have never said anything. Look, it's just me trying to get a handle on this new Ryland that's appeared since he started drinking. And last month . . . when I asked him to come to your dinner party with me, he, um." She paused. "Sort of said some things."

"Things?"

"Well, it's nothing, just . . . it's been bothering me." She made a groaning noise and looked away.

"Peggy, please!"

"Oh! It's stupid! I shouldn't have brought it up, but I don't know Jack at all, and we've become so close that I felt strange not telling you . . ." She rambled until I put my hand on her shoulder.

"Tell me."

Peggy took a deep breath. "The gist of it was that Jack was not, well, not such a nice guy . . ." Her voice faded.

I thought of the fight I'd had with Jack that night; his comment about Ryland flirting with me.

"Look, Peg, if it's worth anything, Jack had a similar sentiment about Ryland. They both grew up in this town. Maybe they didn't like each other in high school. Who knows?" I gave her a jab with my elbow. "We don't have to be couple friends."

She breathed in again, and breathed out slowly.

"I told Ryland to move out," she said.

"Oh, Peg. I'm sorry." I put my hand on her arm.

Peggy shook her head. "He's been coming home late, or not at all. He came in after midnight the other night with some story about fixing a pipe. He's been doing some plumbing to make ends meet. I was actually going to let it go until I noticed his toolbox in the corner, right where it'd been sitting all day. It was obvious he was drunk—his eyes were glassy and he was slurring his words. I asked him what was wrong with the pipe, and he looked at me like I was nuts and told me not to worry about it. But in the nastiest tone of voice, you know? I could've dropped it, but it just made me furious. 'No, really,' I said to him, 'How'd you fix it? With your bare hands?' He just stared at me and then turned and looked over at the toolbox. Like he could feel it watching him."

"What did he say?" I asked, holding my breath.

"Nothing. I just sat down in the chair and said, 'Leave.' And he did. Up and left. Just like that." She snapped her fingers. Then turned and started walking again. I jogged to catch up to her.

"Are you sure he was lying?" I asked, thinking that her reaction sounded a little extreme.

"It's not about the pipe. You know, he used to tell me he was a different person when he was drinking. And it's not that I didn't believe him. I did. I just never imagined *how* different. I know this year has been hard for him. Not finding work and then knowing we're all unhappy about where we live. We were only supposed to rent that house for a month, two at the most, until we found something we wanted to buy. It's been over a year now. The walls are basically falling down around us, it's in such poor condition. I know he feels bad about that. About all of it. Which is probably why the drinking started in the first place. I know he was counting on getting his fishing business off the ground here. And that obviously hasn't happened. He was successful in North Carolina. . . . And now, well. I know he's struggling. But I can't allow him to be around the boys like this."

I didn't want to say it, but fishing around here wasn't the same as fishing in North Carolina. I'd lived with a lobsterman for more than twenty years. I knew how protective they were of their territory. And if Ryland thought being an Alden native meant anything, he was wrong. It wasn't like once you were a Mainer, you were always a Mainer. Once you moved away, you were an outsider. And that applied to everyone. Local fishermen had even stricter rules. And all of them involved being born here, staying here, and working here, every day.

"If Ryland grew up here, he knows how territorial it is," I said. "He must have known getting back into it was going to be hard."

"Well, I think there's more to it. After the party at your house, he was talking in circles about how Jack had traps where he used to fish. On and on about how that territory was his from the beginning. I didn't mention it because I was too embarrassed."

I put my hand on her arm, stopping her.

"Did he say that to Jack at the party?"

"I don't know. He passed out that night, and when I brought it up the next day, he brushed it off as guys being guys."

My mind went back to that night, to Jack telling me *I don't want him here again.* I felt my pulse quicken. He'd seemed off the entire night, now that I looked back on it. The people we'd had over were old friends we'd met in a birthing class when I was pregnant with Jess. They all lived in Alden, and Jack watched football with the husbands most Sundays in the fall. He liked everyone that was there, and yet, he'd been on edge.

Now I wondered if Ryland had said something to him at the party.

"I hope Ryland understands that's serious around here," I said, trying to mask the concern in my voice. Her expression told me I hadn't.

"Believe me, I know. Seems like every time I turn on the TV, there's something on the news about someone getting hurt, or a boat being destroyed, all over someone's territory. Crazy," she said, shaking her head.

"Not so crazy if you see how hard these guys work," I told her. "The news highlights the bad stuff, but mostly everyone is just like Jack . . . hardworking people trying to make a living."

There was a protectiveness in my voice, and my words hung in the air. We were quiet then as we walked. I heard a beep, and Peggy held up her wrist, pointed to her watch. We turned, walking back in the direction of the cars.

I looked over at her. "I'm sorry. I didn't mean to overreact," I said. "I don't always like the hours that Jack works, or that he refuses to work with anyone, but I love him for it all the same. He doesn't treat it like a job. It's his living. I knew that when I married him."

"You didn't overreact," she said, her arms pumping now. She picked up her pace, and I did a little skip jog to keep up with her. "I'm the one who isn't reacting enough. Ryland's going to get an earful tonight about what's going to happen next. Not only is he going to rehab, but I'm looking for a new place to live. For me and the boys. I didn't even tell you that Alex was talking about delaying admission to school again. I don't know if it's that he misses Amy or if he's just miserable here, but everyone better start getting on the Peggy train, if you know what I mean."

She was a tiny woman, small and lean all over with ankles and wrists that looked almost porcelain doll–like in their daintiness, but now, with her legs reaching out in long strides, and the muscles in her upper arms flexing with each pump, she looked powerful, unstoppable.

"I don't envy them," I said, huffing along next to her.

"Neither do I," she said, her eyes blazing and focused on a point in the distance, as though seeing the path ahead clearly now.

We said good-bye in the parking lot, and I watched Peggy drive away.

I sat in the car, the engine running, and thought about what she said, the look on her face when she insisted everyone better start getting on the *Peggy train*.

A feeling of shame washed over me, thinking about the problems Peggy was dealing with compared to my own.

She had an alcoholic out-of-work husband and a house that was falling down around her. An interior decorating business that was struggling even though she put in sixty-hour workweeks.

And me?

What were my problems?

An emotional hiatus, Peggy had called it. She made it sound normal, expected even. And maybe it was.

But my head felt heavy, and I pressed my forehead against the steering wheel, my shoulders bending under the weight of something I hadn't told Peggy.

Something I hadn't told anyone. Not my mother or the girls. Certainly not Jack.

The day she died, we'd spent the morning at the Salt House. Just Maddie and me.

It had been a beautiful June day: sunny but cool enough for a sweatshirt—a perfect day to weed the sunflower garden at the Salt House. We'd gone over for a few hours before we went to the grocery store.

I hadn't meant to keep it a secret from anyone at first. It just never came up. And before I knew it, months had passed, and there was no reason to bring it up.

And now, I knew I would never tell anyone. It seemed cruel to me. It was Jack's family home—a house the girls adored.

But I also knew it was one of the reasons I hadn't been back to the house.

I thought of what Peggy had said about her husband's death. How visiting the places they'd been together had forced her to deal with her feelings.

I closed my eyes. Making myself go back to that day. I wasn't ready to physically go to the Salt House. But I hadn't even let myself think about that morning.

The sunflower garden had been wild, stalks reaching past the gutter line, the yellow-topped heads bobbing in the breeze.

Weeds covered the ground below them. I pulled open the small white gate and stepped in. A path bordered the flowers, the dirt cool on the soles of my feet.

I lowered to my knees, bent over, and breathed in the earthy smell, small specks of pollen swirling in front of my face. I pulled out a weed, then three more, making a small pile in front of me.

Then she was there, crawling next to me, dirt covering her hands and knees, picking up one of the weeds and bringing it to her mouth, throwing it to the ground, a scowl on her face at the taste of it.

I stood, and she stopped at a sunflower, grabbed the thick stalk and pulled herself up, her legs splayed wide for support. I heard my voice. *What a big girl.* Her giggle. I felt the sun on my back and pressed my face into the brown of the sunflower.

In the car now, I forced myself to relive it. I stopped us from getting in the car. I didn't let my mind wander ahead to our trip to the grocery store. I didn't jump ahead to putting her down for a nap.

I stayed with her. I felt her small hands grasping my legs for support and listened to the sound of her chatter, the smell of salt and flowers and earth swirling in my head.

When I opened my eyes, I was still in the car. But in my mind, I was in the garden, surrounded by the sunflowers. I looked up at their round faces and saw them looking back at me. A crowd of yellow petals rippling in the breeze.

Waving to me. As if to say, *There you are.*

12

Jack

I was on the boat, hauling my second string, a trap balanced on the rail, pressing the brass gauge against the carapace of a lobster, when my cell rang. I'd been out on the water all morning with almost nothing to show for it.

Seemed like the only things I was pulling this morning were bugs too small to keep. I threw the lobster back in the water, let the empty trap rest on the deck, and fished the phone out of my pocket.

I needed the break anyway, with the way my lungs were on fire.

I'd thought I'd slept off the cold I was battling by crawling into bed before dinner last night. But I wasn't on the water one hour this morning before the ache came back, like someone had taken a sledgehammer to my back. And not just once. Again and again.

Jess sounded almost as bad when I answered the phone, her normally lively voice sullen. "I'm sick," she said. "A cold or something. I want to go home, but I can't find Boon."

"Do you have a fever?" I asked, worried. Jess was never sick. She was the type of kid who kept track of her attendance at school, who insisted that her runny nose wasn't a cold, just allergies, so she wouldn't fall behind and miss any classes. There wasn't typically time in Jess's schedule to be sick.

"I don't think so," she said in a tone that wasn't convincing. "I would've called Mom, but she's in Boston all day. I know you don't like to be bothered when you're working." She said this like she called often and I ignored her. I couldn't remember the last time Jess had called me on the boat.

"You're not bothering me, Jess," I said gently. "I'll come in and take you home."

"No," she said loudly. "I mean, I'm fine to get home. I have my bike. I'm just going to bed anyway, so it makes no sense for you to be there." There was an urgency in her voice. "Okay, Dad? Don't come in."

"Are you sure? Because, I can be there in ten—"

"Dad. Seriously. I'm not five. I can get home on my own. Don't be like you always are."

She was quiet then. I wasn't very good at picking up on the subtle stuff. I knew this from living with a house full of girls. I'd been told this repeatedly by my house full of girls. But Jess's voice wasn't subtle. The tone of it was sharp, the words thrown at me.

Don't be like I always am? I held the phone away from my ear and looked at it. When I put it back, she was talking.

"Can you just call Boon? That's all I called for. I'll lock up the shop, and he can open it up when he gets back here. I think he just went to the warehouse where cell service stinks, so I can't reach him. Okay?" She sounded exasperated.

"Okay. Are you sure you're all right—"

"Wait." She cut me off. "Boon's here. He just walked in. I'm leaving. Can you talk to him?"

She didn't wait for me to answer before there was a rustling on the other end, and then Boon's voice, muffled and confused.

"Hey. What is this, a hot potato?"

"Boon?"

"Yeah. What's going on? She left."

"She's sick. Going home to bed."

"Does she need a ride? I can go get her."

"No, just let her be. Close up if you have to. I don't know what's on your plate today."

There was a pause, and then he said, "You know what? I'll go pick up Doris. She'll love it. She's still pissed we fired her." Doris was Boon's eighty-year-old mother, who worked behind the counter one season until the summer tourists complained that the usually fast service was now slow because Doris had fifteen-minute conversations with every local that came in to buy fish.

"You fired her," I said. "I was fine with making the tourists wait."

"Which is why you're out there and I'm in here."

"Boon, I'm out," I said, done with the small talk. "These traps aren't pulling themselves."

"Wait a sec, now that I have you on the phone. I was just over at the warehouse with Manny. He said Bitty came over for bait this morning and told him he's missing some strings."

"Missing how?"

"Missing as in he can't find them. He thinks they got caught out in the storm that came through a while back. They'd have to travel quite a bit to get to you, but keep an eye out. He's blue and white."

Like I needed him to tell me Bitty's buoy colors. Like I wasn't the one in these waters every day.

"Tell Jess I hope she feels better. You should be home with her," Boon said. "Manny said you were coughing up a lung this morning."

"You're breaking up, Boon."

"You can hear me fine."

"Didn't catch that. Hanging up now."

"Catch this. You're an asshole," I heard him say before I ended the call. The last thing I needed was Boon and his Clara Barton act. Plus, I wanted the line free in case Jess called. I hoped I hadn't given her whatever I had.

Not that I'd seen her lately to pass on anything to her.

She used to wait around for me after she finished at the shop in the afternoon. I'd motor in and see her lounging on the pier near our skiff, her feet in the water. She'd come on the boat and talk to me, or help me clean up, coiling the lines, or wiping the deck. Then we'd throw her bike in the bed of the truck and head home.

Now she was never around. It was mostly my fault, with my not getting back to the dock until after five or six. But even the days I was in by four, I'd duck in the shop, and Boon would shrug and tell me I just missed her. Then I'd get home, and she was either not there or locked in her room with the door shut.

Thinking about home now reminded me of Hope. I wondered if she was still angry about last night.

I hadn't meant to sleep through dinner. But when I got home after work yesterday, Hope had been cooking, and she'd taken one look at me and said go lie down before we eat. So I had, and the next thing I knew Hope was shaking me awake, telling me to change out of my work clothes.

I remember the toothpaste against my teeth was ice, the heat from my fever lighting up my face in the bathroom mirror.

I told Hope not to kiss me when I climbed into bed, that I didn't want her to catch my cold. I didn't want her to feel how hot I was either. She'd been on me to go to the doctor, even made an appointment two weeks ago that I'd skipped. I didn't have the energy to argue with her about it. I'd had colds before. They ran their course. I didn't need a doctor to tell me that.

When I'd climbed into bed, Hope had started talking about Peggy. I couldn't follow it. I had my back to her, half-asleep, and

I heard her say she'd been waiting *all day* to talk to me about this and I'd slept right through dinner.

Are you awake? she asked, and I mumbled, *Mm-hmm.*

She kept talking, and then she was shaking me, and I turned my head and said, "Jesus, Hope. What?"

"Why won't you talk to me about this?" she demanded.

"We need to talk about this right now?" Not that I knew what *this* was.

"Why didn't you tell me you knew Peggy's husband?"

I craned my neck at her. "Who?"

"Ryland, Jack. Ryland Finn? The guy you picked a fight with me about after our party?"

"I told you I knew him." I turned over, closed my eyes.

"You told me he was an asshole. That was it."

"He is an asshole."

"Well, he told Peggy the same thing about you."

"Okay."

"Okay? That's it? Why? Why would he say that?"

"Maybe he doesn't like my cooking," I said into the pillow.

"That's not funny, Jack. I'm serious."

I didn't answer because Ryland Finn was the last thing I wanted to talk about. I hadn't thought about him since I'd cut his traps more than a month ago.

"Peggy said he told her your traps are in his territory."

I pushed up on my elbow and looked at her. "Hope. Peggy's your friend. I get that. Keep me out if it."

"I know you don't like her husband. But I'm asking you why he would say that."

"And I'm saying it has nothing to do with you."

"What has nothing to do with me?" she said, standing up, her voice getting louder.

I turned over, pulled the covers up to my shoulders.

"Jack. Wake up. Sit up." She leaned over and shook my shoulder.

"Go to sleep, Hope."

"I'd like to know what happened between the two of you."

I stayed quiet. She didn't want to know what happened. But I couldn't tell her this. I couldn't tell her any of it.

"So that's it?" she asked.

When I didn't answer, she sighed. I felt her eyes on me. It was a moment before the bed dipped and she got in.

I felt her fingertips on my shoulder. I reached back and grabbed her hand, pulled it across my middle.

"I'm on your side, Jack. Whatever it is. I'll be on your side."

"I'm sorry," I said.

She leaned her forehead against my shoulder, and I felt her nod.

I was sorry. Sorry about the side of the story she knew nothing about. Sorry about the side of *me* she knew nothing about. Hope turned off the light, and there was darkness, overtaking me. A thick black oil spreading through my body, heavy and suffocating, making it difficult to breathe. I wondered if I had brought this year to us; if losing her was payback for my mistakes; the universe handing me what I deserved.

They say the sea hates a coward. That it finds out everything you did wrong. That sooner or later, the sea will catch up to you. Demand of you. Make you suffer the truth.

13

Jess

I didn't tell Alex that I faked being sick to get out of work just so I could go with him.

He'd patched the crack in my sailboat and wanted to take it out for a test sail on the river behind the Salt House, where the current was calm and the riverbank just a short swim in case the repair didn't hold.

He thought I had the day off from work, and we'd left it that he'd pick me up at my house just before noon, when the tide was almost high.

Mom was supposed to be out of the house first thing with Kat and Grandma for their trip to Boston. My plan was to call in sick after they left. But Mom slept through her alarm. And Grandma took forever on the phone with Roger. Then Mom kept popping her head in my room to see if I changed my mind about going with them. I thought about faking sick right then, but I knew Mom would cancel their plans and stay home if she thought I wasn't feeling well. I finally left the house to avoid talking about it anymore.

Which is why I had to go to work and *then* pretend to be sick.

It was a foolproof plan until I got on the phone with my father and acted the way that I did. I hadn't planned on getting angry with him. But hearing his voice made me furious. I wanted to shout into the phone, *See—your ridiculous rules are making me sneak around like a child.* But he wouldn't see it that way. In his eyes, I was a child.

When Dad said he'd motor in to take me home, I thought I'd blown it. But then Boon had walked in, and I'd used the moment to duck out.

And my plan had worked.

I'd raced home on my bike and changed my clothes. I left a note on the table for my father that I'd felt better and had gone to Betsy's house and would be home after dinner.

Alex had picked me up, and we'd launched the boat from the dock right at high tide, and spent the afternoon taking turns tacking.

Alex was just as good at fixing the boat—the repair held up great—as he was sailing it, and we got her moving a couple of times. We tied up to the mooring in the river and spent the rest of the day lounging on the boat, dipping in the water when it got too hot. We stayed on the boat until the tide started to ebb. My father and the shop a million miles away. This morning a lifetime ago.

Now we were parked in the lot at Breakwater Light, eating clam chowder from to-go cups and watching tourists take selfies atop the rock cliff; the ocean spread out in the background.

The Clam Shack at the base of the lighthouse was famous for its lobster rolls. But I'd suggested it for dinner because it was at the end of a long road up on Elk Point, almost the end of the earth, and one of Alden's busiest tourist spots because of the view.

I wouldn't run into anyone I knew. And by anyone, I meant my father.

In front of us a handful of picnic tables sat overlooking the water. The sun was still hot, even though it was almost dusk, so we parked in the shade and rolled down the windows. The ocean breeze cooling us off, but forcing us to jam our napkins under our legs so they didn't fly away.

Alex was sitting next to me, a lobster roll balancing on his leg, and the empty chowder cup on the seat between us. I'd opted for a hot dog, and Alex insisted I was just being polite since he was paying, refusing to accept that lobster wasn't one of my favorite foods. He hadn't let it drop since we started eating.

"I just don't get it," he repeated again, taking a bite of the lobster roll, pausing while he chewed. He wiped his mouth with his napkin several times before he spoke. "I mean, is it that you think it's too much work to get it out of the shell, or you just don't like it?"

"We serve fresh lobster at the shop. Getting it out of the shell is part of my job. It's messy, but not hard."

"But you secretly hate it. Of course. A lobsterman's daughter—animal-rights advocate at heart—is forced into butchering the lowly crustacean and becomes a vegetarian, taking a moral stand against cruelty to animals. That's it, isn't it?"

My mouthful went down the wrong way, and I chugged my soda to swallow it. "I'm eating a hot dog," I pointed out when I could finally talk. "I'm all for animal rights, but there's a food chain, and I'm okay with that."

Alex shrugged, apparently out of theories.

"I guess I'd eat it if it was, like, the last thing left on Earth to eat. But I don't love it. Not like you do," I offered.

"Not even when it's like this?" He held up the remainder of the lobster roll. "Buttered and toasted. Open on the top. Perfect amount of lettuce. Not too much mayo."

I shook my head. "Maybe one a year. Definitely not like you eat it."

He eyed me suspiciously, as though I'd just told him an elaborate lie. "All right, then," he said after a minute. "What is your favorite food?"

I shut one eye, thinking. "Cheeseburgers."

"Drink?"

"Um, Diet Coke. No wait. Lemonade. But only the kind they sell at fairs—fresh squeezed, with lots of sugar, and if you order a large, you get the oversize plastic cup with the lid and the straw. I'm a sucker for a good cup."

"Dessert?"

"My grandmother's date nut bread," I said, and laughed when Alex's nose wrinkled. "Just kidding. Probably ice cream. Black raspberry. But it might be a tie with crème brûlée. My dad makes a mean one."

Alex gave me a funny look. "Really? I can't picture that."

I shrugged. "He just likes using the torch."

Alex gazed out the window and nodded, as though this made perfect sense.

"Now you," I said. "Favorite food. Drink. Dessert."

He breathed in, looked up. "Lobster. Root Beer. Tapioca pudding," he said in one breath.

I stared at him. "Ew," I said finally.

"Ew to which one?"

"All of them. Pudding? Out of all of the desserts in the world, you choose pudding?"

"Have you ever had homemade tapioca pudding?" he asked. "It's delicious."

"I can't say I've ever had tapioca pudding, never mind homemade."

"Well, then you are not qualified to judge. Someday we'll visit my hometown, and we'll sit at the counter at the Corner Café, and you will have the homemade tapioca pudding, and you will be a changed woman," Alex said with satisfaction. He pointed at me and gathered up the empty bowls, napkins, and spoons. He piled them on the disposable tray and got out of the truck. He shoved the door closed with his foot, balancing the tray in his hands.

I watched him walk to the trash barrel on the other side of the parking lot. He'd been joking, of course. But the thought swirled around my head. Us. Together. In his hometown. My elbow was on the door, and I put my chin in my hand, covering my dopey grin in case Alex happened to look back at the truck.

We'd spent the last several weeks having lunch almost every day on the hood of his car in the town parking lot.

We talked about movies. Books. His family. And mine. His friends. And mine. We talked about the future. How he wanted to start a boat-building company. How the smell of a bilge on an old wooden boat, the mixture of cedar and salt water and pine tar was one of the best smells on Earth.

I told him I had my eye on Emerson, my mother's alma mater, but my home would always be in Maine, where the seasons changed just when you got used to the one you were in. We talked about everything.

Everything that is, but us.

The truck door opened, and Alex slid in next to me. I was turning to face him when I felt something vibrate against my thigh. I shifted my weight forward and reached behind me. Alex's cell phone was wedged in the crease of the bench seat. I dug it out and held it out to him, the word *Amy* flashing on the screen in white letters.

"It's ringing," I pointed out casually. He took it with a blank look, and silenced the phone, mumbling something about a friend from back home.

"A girlfriend?" I teased, and he blushed, a dark crimson coloring the top of each cheek.

A heat crept up my face in response. I hadn't been digging for information—he'd already said he'd dated a girl in high school, but they'd gone their separate ways after graduation—but his reaction to my comment made my stomach flip.

The phone was still in his hand, and instead of putting it in the pocket of his board shorts, where he usually kept it, he reached across me and shoved it in the glove compartment. When he snapped the door shut, his wrist brushed against my leg, and I thought I saw him flinch.

There was an awkward silence between us for a moment— a first for us.

When we'd gone to the Salt House weeks ago to see the crack in the boat, I'd been nervous. But after just minutes on the ride over, my nervousness simply vanished. It wasn't anything I could put my finger on. . . . It was all just . . . easy. I couldn't even remember how we seemed to fall into the habit of having lunch together. It just happened. Like it was the most natural thing in the world.

Out of the corner of my eye, I watched Alex fidget with his hat. He was focused on something outside of his window, his face turned away from me. I shifted to see what held his attention, but there was only a row of parked cars.

He turned suddenly, looking down at his watch, and then up at me.

"I should get you home," he blurted, starting the engine before I answered him. He waited for me to fasten my seat belt, and we reversed out of the spot. "I don't want you to be late," he called over the noise of the engine, and I nodded, resisting the urge to point out that it was barely seven o'clock, and I hadn't said a word about needing to be home.

We were quiet then. I told myself it was because the windows were open and it was loud in the truck. But the tips of my knees almost touched the glove compartment, where Alex's cell phone was tucked away and out of sight. I wondered if our quick departure had something to do with the call he'd refused to take.

When we pulled up in front of my house, Alex put the truck in park but kept the engine running.

Every inch of me wanted to stay in the truck with him. But my father's truck was in the driveway, and I was praying he didn't look out the window so I could avoid making up a story about why Betsy was dropping me off in an old beat-up truck instead of her shiny VW Bug.

I got my things together quickly and said good-bye to Alex, hopping out of the truck and shutting the door behind me, waving as I walked away.

"Hey, Jess," Alex called out through the open window. "Wait a second."

I hurried back and leaned in through the window, anxious to have him pull away from the curb before the noise from the truck engine made it up to the house.

"I'd feel better if we took her out for a sail one more time," he said. "There was some moisture on the bottom when I was putting her away. It's going to bother me until I know for sure it's safe. Will you come out with me again?"

I nodded, glancing at the house as I backed away from the truck, gesturing that I'd call him. He watched me, leaning forward as I backed away, a puzzled look on his face at my hasty exit. I jogged up the steps and went in the foyer and quickly switched off the outside light. I let out my breath when I looked out and saw his truck finally pull away from the curb.

The house was quiet, and I didn't see my father until I turned on the light in the living room. He was asleep on the couch, his coat and work boots still on. Like he'd literally walked off the boat and collapsed on the couch.

"Dad?" I said, shaking his shoulder. He opened his eyes and sat up. It always amazed me, his ability to go from asleep to awake in one second.

"I was waiting for you," he said.

He coughed then. It came out a bark. There was a crease on the side of his face from where it had been pressed against the arm of the couch. "How did you get home?"

I frowned at him. "I got a ride. Your cough sounds bad."

"I'm glad you feel better," he said, ignoring me. "I was worried about you. You didn't sound like yourself on the phone this morning."

"I'm fine," I said. "Was your day okay? You look tired." I didn't know why I said this. My father always looked tired lately. His face was naturally angled, but now in the dim light, it looked gaunt.

"Whatever you had, Manny got too. He went home sick, so after I was done hauling, I had to work the weigh station."

"What about Boon? Couldn't he do it?"

"Boon was covering the shop. Turns out Doris was mad that we fired her. She wouldn't come in." He gave a weak smile.

I knew how much work the weigh station was—and Manny was younger than my father. Whenever Boon had to cover for Manny, he complained about being sore for weeks.

"Did you eat?" my father asked. "I picked you up some of the soup from Herbert's that you like."

Herbert's Turkey Farm sold chicken soup that tasted and smelled like it was made right at home. But the farm was on the edge of town, nowhere near anything. A long drive for a bowl of soup.

"I left a note that I was eating at Betsy's. Didn't you see it?" I said, feeling awful.

"I didn't get it until I got home. I put the soup on the stove just in case you wanted some. I'll eat with you if you're still hungry." He gestured to the table. He'd set the table with two place mats, a bowl on each next to a napkin and spoon.

I followed him into the kitchen. I wasn't hungry. I wanted nothing more than to go in my room and shut the door. But I knew he hadn't eaten a thing, and he wouldn't if I didn't sit there with him. He looked so thin to me lately. His belt had been hanging on the back of the bathroom door the other night, and I saw that he'd made a hole in it to make it smaller.

I filled the bowls, brought them to the table, and sat across from him.

He dipped his spoon in the soup, brought it to his mouth, wincing when he swallowed. Then he placed his spoon on the napkin and sat back in his seat.

"Don't you like it?" I asked.

"Not much of an appetite lately. I'm glad you're feeling better. You had me worried all day."

I swallowed hard, thinking of him working a long day on the boat and lifting crate after crate for hours after that, and then getting in his truck and driving a half hour in the other direction from home just to bring me the soup he knew I liked.

He worried all day while I was sailing. Sailing in a boat he'd given me years ago when I'd asked him to teach me to sail. We'd stayed in the river at first because I was afraid of the dark water, fearful of how far it stretched in front of the Salt House.

But after a month, my father convinced me to go out in the bay, reassuring me that we were just fine. That he wouldn't let anything happen to me. That it was his job to keep me safe.

We sailed in the harbor all of July. By August, we were past the breakwater. The last sail we took that summer, we were so far out in the Gulf of Maine, I couldn't see land.

Across the table, my father caught my eye and winked. The bowls of soup between us. The air around us filling with the smell of home.

14

Kat

Grandma was going back to Florida in a couple of weeks and moving in with Roger, and Mom was saying that she hadn't heard anything as ridiculous as that in a long time. They were in the kitchen, and when Mom said this, Grandma patted my arm, in a soothing sort of way, like I was the one getting spoken to.

My cereal was getting soggy, but I didn't want to crunch too loud and miss something. I hadn't seen Mom this fired up since that night she fought with Dad.

"Tell me you're not serious," Mom said.

"Why would I say it if I wasn't serious?" Grandma gave her a puzzled look.

"You've only been dating for a year!"

"We've been dating for a year and a half, and I've known him for ten. Longer than I knew your father before I married him. For the record."

I'd never met my grandfather. He died when mom was Jess's age, but this seemed to make Mom even madder.

"What's that supposed to mean?"

"It means time is irrelevant when it comes to love. I knew your father ten minutes, and I wanted to marry him. And we'd still be going strong if he was here."

"But why now? I mean, it's sort of out of the blue." Mom squeezed the bridge of her nose and closed her eyes. It was a habit she got from Grandma, but I didn't think it was the right time to point that out.

"Well, because he asked," Grandma said. "Just last night. He asked and I said yes." She took a sip of her coffee, winked at me over the rim of the mug. "I've lived alone for thirty years. A lot of those years I spent missing your father. There wasn't room for anyone else. And now I feel that there is. And you know what I always say. So much of life is just finding that balance. The balance of holding on and letting go."

Mom put her chin in her hand. "You do say that. All the time, you say it."

"Well, I say it because it's true. Those words helped me enormously after your father died." Grandma looked at me. "Did your mother ever tell you this story?"

"Here we go," Mom said.

"She was sixteen," Grandma said to me, pointing at Mom. "And dead set on not moving out of Alden, away from her friends. I didn't have a job, any family of my own up here. My parents were livid that I wasn't coming back home to Alabama with their only grandchild. Livid! My father could have bought and sold Alabama twice over with his money, and he told me he wouldn't give us a dime unless we moved back. It didn't matter to them what was best for you. Or me. I was almost forty years old by then. Can you imagine moving back home after you've had a husband and a child. A *life*!"

I didn't know if this was a question, but she was looking at me, so I shook my head. I heard Mom let out a long breath.

"So one day the phone rings, right in the middle of this whole mess, and it was your uncle Pete, Petey we called him, your grandfather's brother. He died soon after in a car accident. Anyway, he was asking how I was holding up, and I just lost it. I mean, crying and carrying on, talking about how I was tired of fighting with my parents, exhausted of explaining why I needed to do what I was doing. Finally when I was done, he just said in the simplest of ways into the phone, 'Then stop.' And I said, 'Well, stop what?' and he says, and I'll never forget this, 'Well, stop explaining, Barb. It's your life, after all.'"

Grandma got up from the table and poured herself another cup of coffee from the pot on the stove, held it out to Mom, who covered her cup, shook her head.

"So anyway," Grandma continued after she sat down again. "I hung up speechless. Just speechless. I was a forty-year-old woman asking permission to live her life." She stopped talking, and I waited, but when she looked up at me, she smiled, finished with her story.

"I don't get it," I said. "What does that have to do with that thing that you say. About balance or whatever."

"Oh. There was a book of poetry on the table that I was reading at the time, and it was open to that page. Sort of a sign, I think."

Mom lifted her eyebrows at me, and then looked at Grandma. "Are you getting married too?"

"Oh, I suspect," Grandma answered. "But one thing at a time. I don't want to get overwhelmed."

"No, that's prudent," Mom said.

"You make Jess go to her room when she's sarcastic," I told her. I didn't know what *prudent* meant, but the way she said it was definitely sarcastic.

Mom groaned. "I'm sorry for being sarcastic. I'm just surprised. I know you told me a few weeks ago that you were serious about Roger. I just love having you here. I thought maybe you might reconsider moving back. Even spend half the year here. Lots of people do that—"

Grandma held up her hand, interrupting her. "I love spending time with all of you. But I despise Maine. You know this. Your father loved it here, so I lived here. And I visit for all of you. But that's where my ties end."

"You're so dramatic," Mom said.

"And you hate change," Grandma said, folding her arms across her chest.

"Can we go now?" I asked.

"Go where?" Grandma asked.

"My fun day," I told her.

She looked from me to Mom.

"I told Kat we'd spend the day together," Mom explained. "Do whatever she wants. Her choice."

"Anything?" I asked.

"Anything that is within driving distance and not dangerous."

"Well, then. Where to?" Grandma asked me.

"I wanted to go to the water park."

I looked out the window at the rain, the sky bright from a flash of lightning.

"Dangerous," Grandma said.

"How about a movie?" Mom asked.

"Can I get gummy bears? The big box?"

She never let me eat them because they stuck to my teeth and caused cavities, or so the dentist said. Her mouth twisted, but she nodded glumly.

"Okay," I said, and hopped off the chair while Mom went to get dressed.

Grandma motioned for me to come over to her. "After the

movie, tell her you want to go to Bert's for ice cream, and then to the Salt House," she whispered.

The Salt House was my favorite place on the planet. Well, besides the water park, but that was out anyway because of the rain.

"But she's says no every time I ask her to go there."

"It's within driving distance and it's not dangerous," she said, then looked back to her newspaper, as if she hadn't said anything at all.

"Why doesn't she like it there anymore?"

"Oh, she likes it plenty. Now, go. Your fun day awaits."

Mom was quiet in the car, and when I asked her from the backseat if we could stop by and see Daddy, she looked at me in the rearview mirror like she was surprised I was sitting there.

"He's on the boat, Kat," she said.

I looked out the window at the rain coming down; the fog was so thick, I could see only the outline of the stores as we passed them.

"He doesn't usually go out in the rain."

Mom shook her head. "He shouldn't be out there today, coughing like that last night. I argued with him this morning when he went to leave, but he went anyway."

"He said he feels okay. I asked him last night when he was reading me a book. But then he fell asleep, and he was making weird noises like he was having a bad dream."

"Your father doesn't know how to admit he doesn't feel well. He thinks it makes him look weak."

"Daddy weak? That's crazy. His muscles are like BAM!" I flexed my arm and held my hand up to where Dad's muscle would be.

Mom smiled, and I thought it would be a good time to bring up what Grandma said.

"Remember you said we could do anything I wanted today?"

"I think I did say that."

"So we'll go to the movies."

"On our way as we speak," she said.

"And then we'll get ice cream," I added.

"Of course."

"And then we'll go to the Salt House." I held my breath after I said it.

She looked at me in the mirror.

"Please," I begged.

"Kat, no."

"Why?" I asked.

"Well, to start, it's not open."

Every summer Mom spent an entire weekend "opening" the Salt House.

The trunk of her car would be filled with cleaning supplies, clean sheets, towels, and grocery bags. Dad stuck to the outside, putting the screens on the windows and cutting the grass.

I knew this because I begged them to take me one year, and it was the most boring day of my life.

Mom kept kicking me out of the house because she was cleaning it, and Dad said he had special jobs for me, but what he really meant was yard work. I spent most of the day swinging on the hammock by the water wishing I'd gone with Jess to the town pool.

"We can still go and just see it. We didn't even go at all last summer."

"Yes, we did. You remember we went and took pictures in the beginning of the summer when they tore out all the walls and put new ones up?"

"I mean after that," I said.

"Well, you know, it was a busy summer . . . with everything that happened." Her voice faded away.

I could tell by her face that she meant Maddie. She died the day I got out of school for summer. After that, Mom didn't want to do much of anything. Dad brought me to the house once after that. It looked the same on the outside, the yellow shingles still chipped, but the grass around it was so overgrown, it looked like you could get lost in it.

Dad had mowed the lawn while I walked from room to room. The walls were gray, and it just looked lonely and empty. All of our stuff was packed in boxes in the front hall, and the first one I opened had all of Maddie's cups, with scrapes on the part you drink out of because she was just getting teeth and liked to chew on them. I closed the box and went down to the hammock until Dad was done.

But that was a year ago. It seemed like more than a year ago. It seemed like forever. And I told her that now.

She looked in the mirror and sighed. "Okay. How about this. I'm not ready to go today—"

I started to argue, but she held up her hand.

"But soon. I promise."

We were in the parking lot of the movie theater, and she pulled in a space and turned off the car.

She gestured to the front seat. "Come up here."

I climbed over, and she pulled me against her, her arms around my middle. I felt her chin on the top of my head.

"Question for you," she said.

I tilted my head back and looked at her.

"There are a lot of memories for us in that house." She played with a piece of my hair. "Of lots of things."

She swallowed hard enough that I heard it.

"I mean lots of memories of your sister. Of Maddie," she said in a voice that was loud, louder than it needed to be in the small space we were in, like she was forcing out the words before they slipped away.

"Isn't that a good thing?" I asked.

She gave me a little smile. "It is a good thing," she agreed. "I want to make sure you're ready."

"Ready for what?" I asked.

"Well, sometimes memories can make you happy. And sometimes, they can make you sad." Her fingertips touched my cheek when she said this. Like she was brushing away invisible tears. "I just want to make sure you're ready, that's all."

"I'm ready." I nodded fast to prove it.

She didn't look convinced. And then she looked out the windshield at nothing and started to get the faraway look that meant she was going to get very quiet. I pulled my knees underneath me so I was taller in the seat and stuck my head in front of where she was looking.

"Mom? I'm ready," I said loudly.

Her eyes focused on me and she let her breath out, like she'd been holding it.

"Well, then. I think I need to be brave like you."

"You're brave, Mommy," I told her, resting my head on her shoulder. "The bravest mommy in the whole world."

When I looked up, she was smiling down at me. It wasn't a happy smile, but it wasn't sad either. We sat like that for a minute until Mom said we should go to get a good seat.

We were walking through the parking lot, holding hands, when I realized we had talked about Maddie.

And for the first time in as long as I could remember, Mom hadn't cried.

15

Hope

In the kitchen, Jess was on the phone.

"I'll see you soon," she said before she hung up, her voice chirpy, a sparkle in her eye when she turned around.

"Alex?" I asked her.

The cordless phone bobbled in her hands, slipped and clanged against the counter. She smothered it as though it were a football tumbling in the grass. After she placed it securely in the holder, she looked at me. I was smiling, but a look of panic crossed her face. I felt my smile fade.

"It was Bets. She's home for the weekend."

"Oh. That's nice. I know you've missed her."

She watched me warily.

"So, Alex," I said. "I heard you know each other."

I didn't tell her it was Kat who told me about them. How she'd seen them having lunch on the hood of Alex's truck in the parking lot in front of her camp. Kat and Jess got along great for the most part. But when they argued, it was usually Jess telling Kat to mind her own business. Now, I didn't want Jess to be angry with Kat.

She shrugged. "He works at the sailing camp next to the shop."

"And you met how?"

She rolled her eyes. "I don't remember. I think I was riding my bike and I hurt my ankle. He gave me a ride home."

"You were riding your bike way over there?"

"I just said I don't remember. It was, like, forever ago. Why does it even matter?"

"I'm just surprised you never mentioned him."

"Maybe I didn't mention him because I knew you'd act like this," she accused.

"Act like what?"

"Like this. Like me hanging out with a boy is this huge deal."

"Well, it is sort of a big deal. I mean, you haven't had a boy-friend before."

"He's not my boyfriend. Even if I wanted him to be, since Dad treats me like I'm two years old."

"Jessica. Come on. I'll admit he's a little overbearing when it comes to you and boys, but you can always talk to me."

She scowled at me. "Maybe I didn't want to. I wasn't aware that I had to report everything that happens in my life. I mean, it's not like you don't have your own stuff."

"Stuff? What kind of stuff?" I was baffled, taken back by her anger.

"Things you keep to yourself. Things you don't say."

"Can you give me an example?"

"I don't know. Like yesterday. You told Grandma that you liked her date nut bread even though I saw you cover most of it under your napkin. Then you threw it in the trash when she left the room."

"There's a difference between saying something to spare some-one's feelings and willfully withholding information." My voice was strained now, my patience dwindling.

"Okay. Then what about Kat? You *withheld* information from

her," she said. "Is that different from me *withholding* telling you about Alex?"

It took a minute for the words to process in my head. It was as if I'd been expecting to hear them all along—how could I *not* have expected to hear them!—but they still came as a shock. They rippled through my body. The hair on my arms stood up. Time stopped.

Suddenly I was back in Maddie's bedroom, the police officer holding my arms, gently guiding me out of the room, repeating that we needed to give the paramedics space. From between the tangle of legs and arms, her pudgy arm, the necklace tangled in her fingers. Then Jess in the doorway, just off the bus, earlier than usual, earlier than Kat. It was her last day of school, only a half day to give the PTO time to get the gym ready for homecoming that night.

She'd missed the dance, of course, spent the night with Kat, waiting for us to return from the hospital while Boon and his girlfriend tried to keep them distracted by playing cards. Everyone flinching, I'm sure, when a car passed outside.

Everyone on edge, waiting, hoping.

Later, when we were home, Kat had asked, "Mommy? What happened?"

"She stopped breathing," Jack had whispered, and pulled the girls against him. Jess had put her arm around Kat and closed her eyes. I wondered if it was to block out the image of Maddie, the necklace around her wrist, the locket that hung off it gone.

I couldn't go back and remove the necklace from Kat's neck so it wouldn't drop in the crib while she and Maddie played. I couldn't pause the moment Maddie decided to taste it and rewind it, record over it like the mixed tapes I used to make in high school. I couldn't stop time and make Jess come in the house five minutes later, time enough for me to unwind the necklace from around Maddie's wrist.

Time enough for Jess to not see it.

But she had seen it.

And the week after Maddie died, when Kat asked if I'd seen her necklace, I lied and told her the store I bought it from called, and the necklace caused awful rashes on several people, and they asked for it back.

Jess had looked at me wide-eyed, startled at my overly elaborate lie, and I turned away, ashamed that I didn't have a better answer.

But when Kat searched for the necklace, I saw it on Maddie's wrist. And when she asked me if I'd seen it, I pictured the locket in Maddie's mouth.

Months ago, Kat begged me over and over to replace the locket, and I knew she was disappointed in the one I'd brought home, a miniature version of the original. I'd chosen the smallest one I could find. So small, I was surprised she managed to get a picture inside of it.

"Mom?" Jess's voice broke the silence. I blinked, her face coming into focus.

I heard the door open, and Kat walked in, my mother behind her. They were holding ice-cream cones, a stream of chocolate running down Kat's arm.

"We should have got cups," my mother said, wetting a paper towel and running it up Kat's arm. She looked over at us, from me to Jess then back at me, and quickly threw the paper in the trash.

"Missy, you need a good cleaning. Come upstairs with me, and I'll run a bath with some of that fuzzy salt stuff everyone is so fond of giving old ladies."

She turned Kat toward the door. Kat skipped out and up the stairs. My mother patted my shoulder before she crossed through the living room and closed the door behind her. I waited a moment before I spoke.

"I didn't know you felt this way. Remember we talked about it after? You said she would blame herself—"

"I remember," she blurted. "She would have blamed herself. I never said she wouldn't."

"But you think I was wrong for not telling her the truth."

"I didn't say that."

"Well, what are you saying? You're obviously upset."

"I'm not upset. I'm just stating a fact. You withheld information from Kat. I withheld information from you. I guess that makes us both liars."

A look crossed her face when she said this. I saw that her anger was a surprise to her, as if the words had come from some unknown place inside of her.

I kept my voice steady, calm. "You're not a liar, and neither am I. Your sister stopped breathing. That is the truth. That is what we told Kat."

"But not from SIDS like you led her to believe. Likes she believes now."

"I never mentioned anything about SIDS. She heard that at school and told me about it."

"You didn't tell her that it *wasn't* that," she accused, her voice growing louder.

I didn't tell her to speak in a quieter tone. I could hear the bath running upstairs. I knew Kat couldn't hear us. Most of all, I knew that I wanted Jess to keep talking. That she needed to keep talking. It seemed to me that what she was saying had been eating at her. I saw that it had sat inside of her and festered.

"No, I didn't. You're right. She told me that she liked to think that Maddie just went to sleep and stopped breathing. She said thinking that made her feel better."

"And you said she should think that. I heard you. I was there."

"I did say that," I agreed. "And I'd say it again. I want for all of us to think of things that make us feel better. Don't you?"

She shrugged, scowled.

"Can I ask you something?"

She didn't speak, but she looked at me out of the corner of one eye.

"Do you think I should have told her? Is that what this is about?"

"No." She rolled her eyes as if this was the most absurd thing she'd ever heard. "It's not what this is about. You're the one talking about being truthful. All I'm saying is that it's not black-and-white."

"It's not black-and-white. I agree. But that doesn't mean that you were right to not tell us about Alex. I want you to know you can talk to me, Jess. I know things have been—"

"Can we not talk about it? I said it wasn't a big deal. He's going to college and I probably won't ever see him again, so it's not worth talking about. Okay?"

Her face was blotchy. She was on the verge of tears from the pitch of her voice. I wanted to put my arms around her. Erase the past year for her. Undo all the sadness that was etched in her face.

When I stood, she walked to the doorway and put her hand on the doorknob.

"Can I go? Bets is expecting me."

I nodded, and she was gone, her footsteps heavy on the stairs.

I sat in the chair and looked at the door. I'd been foolish to think that Jess wouldn't have struggled at some point with what we told Kat. In some ways, I felt that I'd let the fact that Jess had always been so mature, so levelheaded, convince me that she'd come to me if she needed to talk about it.

Or maybe it was that we'd always been so close.

Jack thought it was all those years Jess and I had alone together. Eight years before Kat was born.

Not that we'd planned it that way. Jack and I tried for another child when Jess was three. It took more than two years, and then I miscarried in the tenth week. We took a break after that.

After Kat was born, we thought we were done having kids. We'd had such a hard time conceiving Kat, and the doctor said my chances of getting pregnant were slim—so slim, we didn't even bother with birth control—and then years passed, and there was that hot, humid night at the Salt House when Jack had pulled the mattress down to the screen porch and we made love. And Maddie had come along.

I walked over to the phone and called Peggy.

"I have some news," I said when she answered. "It seems as if Alex and Jess have met."

"Oh, I know," she said breezily. "I saw them talking outside the house in the beginning of the summer. Jess was riding her bike or something. I wanted to go out and formally introduce them, but I didn't want to be the uncool mother."

I cleared my throat. "I think they have moved past just meeting."

"Huh?"

"They might have even moved past just friends."

There was a pause. "Hope, I'm confused," she said. "What are you talking about?"

"I'm not entirely sure," I admitted. "I just found out. Jess has a little sister who adores her—a little sister who also happened upon some information that her sister had a boyfriend."

"A *boyfriend*!" Peggy shouted. "I've never heard him mention her name!"

"Apparently they have lunch together every day in the parking lot near the camp. Kat saw them."

"Every day!"

"I'm sure they're just friends. Honestly, Jess is not exactly experienced with boys. Jack is strict to the point of crazy—it's something we fight about, and he's never been able to explain it. I actually told Jess last year to come to me if she ever wants to go to the movies with someone. But she's never mentioned Alex, and she was defensive just now when I asked about him. The only thing I got out of her was that it's *no big deal*."

"I'm sure they're just friends," Peggy said. "Alex has been serious with a girl back home for ages. But I'll talk to him and get the scoop, I promise."

We hung up, and I dialed Jack's cell. It rang once before I changed my mind and ended the call. There was no sense in bringing this up with him now. Jess didn't need him asking her about it. Jack could never explain to me why he had such an issue with her dating. I should have pushed the issue with him. But she'd never shown much interest in dating anyone specific until now. If she was even interested in dating Alex, for that matter. It wasn't clear from our conversation.

Plus, if I called Jack and he answered, I had a feeling I'd hear him cough, and I didn't think I'd be able to stop myself from lecturing him.

He'd been hot to the touch last night again. I'd asked him to stay home when he was getting dressed for work this morning. But he'd insisted that he was fine, just run-down from the hours he was putting in. I dropped it and turned over and went to sleep. Because the hours he was putting in was another argument we'd had over the last year that we'd silently agreed to stop having. By this I mean we avoided the conversation.

How many times can you argue about something before you decide that the argument is more destructive than the thing you're arguing about?

It went the same every time, this fight. Jack went to work when things were difficult at home, and I resented it. That was a boiled-down version. But there were valid points on each side. Every good fight that has the ability to last more than twenty years has validity.

Jack argued that working the hours he did was justified because he liked to work alone, without a stern man. It took him longer to do what he needed to do because there was only one of him.

It wasn't true, I'd counter. Over the years, he'd cut back the number of traps he fished, and it was only in the last year that he'd been putting more in.

But that would lead to his argument that since I wasn't working, he was picking up the slack.

And there were the two mortgage payments. And that was a whole different argument.

So we didn't argue about it anymore.

Now, I went into Maddie's old room and closed the door.

I pulled open my desk drawer and took out the stack of letters that were addressed to me, care of *Parent Talk Magazine*.

Josie had handed them to me months ago when we'd had lunch. She'd looked sheepish, explaining that she'd opened them, even though they were addressed to me.

"I wanted to make sure they weren't from nutcases. Read them," she'd said, pushing the stack across the table. "Maybe they'll silence those other voices in your head."

I'd read each of them several times by now.

There was a letter from Janet scrawled across ten pages, about her teenage son's suicide. How she blamed herself for the longest time.

And Pam, a breast cancer survivor, who recently lost her young daughter to leukemia, writing to tell me how she would never step foot in her church again. No longer able to pray to a God that would allow such a thing to happen.

And Graham, who lost both his wife and daughter in a car accident that he somehow survived. The list went on and on. The letters were all varied in tone. Some angry. Some accepting. Some eloquently written, and others short and blunt, punctuated by exclamation marks and capital letters.

But all of the letters had one thing in common. In one way or another, they all said this: *You are not alone . . .*

16

Jess

Today at lunch, Alex suggested we might want to cancel our sail, with the tide not high enough until dinnertime, and the potential rain, but we'd been trying to get over to the Salt House for weeks, and we finally agreed that we'd take a short sail, downriver and back at the most, just long enough to check the repair.

I'd met him in the parking lot after work, and we'd grabbed sandwiches from the sub shop and pulled up at the Salt House just before six, when the tide was at its highest.

But by the time we took the tarp off the sailboat, and carried it across the marsh to the water, the first drops of rain tapped lightly on our foreheads. The weather report said there was a chance of a thunderstorm in the evening, but later, after midnight. By the look of the clouds forming above us, the storm had arrived six hours early.

The wind had picked up even in the short time it took us to get the boat to the water. The river was dark under the overcast sky. Alex motioned for us to head back to the shed just as the sky opened, rain pouring down on us, the rumblings of thunder in the distance.

We grabbed the sailboat and hurried toward the house, the boat slipping from my grip and knocking against my shins. Lightning flashed over the water behind us. Alex dropped his end and grabbed the bag out of the boat, holding it out to me.

"Go inside," he yelled. "It'll be quicker if I drag it."

I took the bag and sprinted to the house, my shorts and T-shirt drenched through, drops of rain slipping off my nose. There was a small cluster of rocks by the front steps, and I turned them over, forgetting which one the key was hidden under.

When I finally unlocked the door and stepped in, the smell of the house made me stop where I was. The house didn't look the same because of the renovation, but it had the same smell—briny and musty mixed together. The way you'd expect an old house at the ocean to smell. I breathed in deep and closed my eyes, realizing how much I'd missed this place.

In the back hall, there was a raincoat, and I grabbed it and brought it out to Alex, but he was stripped down to his board shorts, apparently unfazed by the rain with the way he was taking his time with the tarp, smoothing down every gap. He laughed when I held out the jacket and told me to go get warm while he finished covering the boat.

Inside the house, I lit a candle in the kitchen and left a towel in the front hall for Alex so he could dry off. Upstairs, I took a quick shower and slipped on jeans and a long-sleeve shirt that were packed in a bin in my bedroom. They were from last year, tighter than the clothes I normally wore, but when I looked in the mirror, I didn't mind what I saw.

There wasn't a hair dryer, but there was a fan in Kat's room, and I dried my hair in front of it. Then I rifled through the box on my mother's bureau to see if there was some perfume to dab on.

I heard Alex open the front door, and I retraced my steps, cleaning up after myself so I didn't leave a trail for my parents. Then I walked down the stairs and turned into the kitchen.

Alex was at the window, looking at the water in front of us. He'd draped the towel over the faucet, where it dripped into the sink.

"You'd never guess this was the view from the front," he said, stunned.

I walked over to where he stood. "Yeah. It's pretty great. I used to hate it when I was younger, though. The water at high tide seemed like it might come in the house."

As soon as I said it, I wanted to take it back. I thought of Alex's house on the train tracks. How the view from his house was a chain-link fence and steel rails.

But he was looking out at the water, nodding to himself.

"My father and I used to go fishing before he died. I was young. Six. Seven, maybe. My uncle came with us once, and he wanted to go out deep, so my father motored out until we couldn't see land." He rolled his eyes, shook his head. "It was just this crappy dinghy, and the water was so black. As far as I could see on every side was just water. And there was this leak in the boat, so my father had to keep bailing to keep us afloat."

"What happened?" I asked, and he looked at me, his eyes going down the front of me and quickly back up.

"Wow," he said, and coughed, flustered it seemed. "I mean, wow, you're all showered and everything. Um, what was I saying? Oh, nothing happened. They fished for a while until they realized I was petrified. Then we went in." He shrugged. "Probably why I got interested in boats, though. Or fixing them, I mean. All those nightmares about that leak."

"You don't talk about your father a lot," I said.

"Well, he isn't alive, so . . ."

I cut my eyes at him, and he tried to keep a straight face, but it didn't last long, a smirk pulling at the corners of his mouth.

"Don't give me a hard time. You know what I mean."

"What do you want to know?"

"I don't know," I said, thinking, *Everything*. When I looked at his face, I saw that he was serious. So I said it out loud. "Everything."

He tipped his chin to the screen room and grabbed the bag off the table. I followed him to where our couch was covered with a blue tarp. Outside, the rain had stopped, and orange streaks split the sky. Alex pulled the tarp off the couch, and we put the bag on the seat between us. The sandwiches had miraculously stayed dry, and we ate them from paper plates on our laps.

It turned out Alex telling me everything about his father took less than ten minutes. He'd died when Alex was eight, and his memory of him was vague. He repeated the things his mother had told him—that his father loved black licorice and his job as a school counselor and hated spiders and hiking—but since they were his mother's memories, they somehow seemed empty to him.

"So what about you?" he asked when he was done talking.

I looked at him. "What about me?"

"You don't exactly talk about your father either. And he's alive."

A persistent fly buzzed around us, hovering over Alex's plate, now empty. Alex put our trash in the bag and put it on the floor in front of us. He sat back against the couch, turning so his body was facing me, his arm resting on the back of the couch. I'd put the candle on the stack of boxes in the corner, and the light from it was a soft glow on his face.

He was looking at me, waiting for me to answer.

"He's my father. There's not much to say."

"He's good with me fixing the boat, right?" he asked. "I felt kind of funny being in the yard, working on it, you know, without having met him."

"It's my boat. It's not like I needed to get his permission."

And he has no idea you're fixing it was what went through my head.

The boat had been sitting with a hole in it for three years. I was betting that my father wouldn't notice it was fixed for another three years.

"I know. But I should've checked with him just the same. What if he had shown up here when I was working on it? 'Boy, eighteen, has his face rearranged after found trespassing.'" He said this in a voice of a news reporter.

"You're still hung up on that? I told you, Boon was kidding. He's harmless."

"He might be. But your father isn't. He's got kind of a reputation."

I screwed up my face at him. "As what?"

Alex look surprised. "As, um, intense. You do know that I work with half the boys in your grade."

"You work with five of them. And one of them is my best friend's brother. So he's getting it secondhand. Not because I dated any of them. Dating isn't exactly allowed in my house."

Alex looked like he wanted to say something. But then he looked away, picked at the fibers on the back of the couch, looked back at me. He pushed the brim of his hat up, pulled it down. I knew what that meant.

"What?" I asked, perplexed.

"I wasn't going to say anything, but my mother sort of lit into me about us. I guess your mom didn't know we were hanging out. You know, having lunch."

"Was she mad at you?" I asked. "That you didn't tell her about me?"

"No. But it's not like she keeps tabs on who I hang out with. She was mad because, well, you're younger than me and she thought your mother was upset, and she was embarrassed that I didn't introduce myself."

"She's fine," I lied. "It wasn't a big deal."

"Well, still. She's right. I should've gone down to the docks and introduced myself to your dad. I mean, you are only sixteen. And I'm in his house right now. With his daughter."

"First of all, I'm seventeen in a couple of weeks. And second, don't say anything to him. I'll tell him. He's got this weird thing about me and boys. If he finds out about us, that we've been together, it'll just be a million questions."

Alex was quiet, then, and when I looked at him, he was staring at me, his mouth open. The words ran back through my head. *That we've been together.* My face flamed.

"I don't mean together as in we've been *together*. Like that," I said quickly, breezily. But repeating it just made it worse. Alex didn't smile, and I swallowed.

The words were out there, and the picture of us together was in my head. Even though I hadn't meant it like that, I couldn't erase the image.

I was aware suddenly of how close we were sitting next to each other. He barely had any clothes on. Board shorts, no shirt. I kept my eyes on my lap. I knew if I looked at his body, lean and muscular and tanned, and that scar on his knee, the one I dreamed about tracing with my fingertip, my face would give me away.

His hand touched my shoulder, his fingertips grazing the skin on the side of my neck. I looked at him, and those green eyes were looking straight into me. Neither of us moved. I stopped breathing. I didn't look away from his gaze. Underneath me, the couch dipped and Alex leaned forward.

My whole body tingled. I felt his breath on my cheek, then his lips on mine. My hand reached out, and I ran it down the front of his chest, and he shivered, his lips pressing harder against my own. When our tongues slid against each other, he shifted and pulled me closer.

The way he touched me told me he'd been thinking about it as much as me. He pulled my legs over his lap, our bodies pressing against each other, his hand running up my leg, under the back of my shirt, his thumb grazing the side of my breast. I'd thought of this moment so many times in the last month. But in my mind, I didn't feel the softness of his lips, the stubble on his jawline, the heat of his skin under my hands.

Now I didn't want him to stop. My hand found the back of his neck. My fingers running down his bare back. He made a noise and pulled away, his hand gently holding my face, his fingers in my hair, keeping me still. He was breathing hard, his skin on fire.

"Jesus," I heard him whisper, his head down. He breathed out. I leaned forward, tried to kiss him again, but he pulled back.

"No, Jess. Stop," he said. "I've got to stop."

I didn't move. He pressed his forehead against my own, let out another breath. I ran my fingertips down the smooth skin on his back, and he shifted, tightening.

When he picked his head up, he looked bewildered, frightened almost.

"I didn't know you wanted this," he whispered.

I leaned in to kiss him again, but he stopped me. Then he stood up and walked over to the other side of the room and leaned against the wall. As far away from me as he could get without leaving the room.

I stared at him, stunned. "What's wrong?" I asked.

"It's just—" He paused, avoiding my eyes, his gaze on the floor. "I don't know. You're only sixteen."

"Almost seventeen." I smiled. "We're a year apart. It's not like you're Mr. Maturity over there," I joked, but he pressed his lips together in a grimace.

I felt the smile leave my face. "I'm just saying a year difference is not a lot."

"It's not. . . . That's not what I meant."

"Well, what do you mean?"

"I don't know. I wasn't expecting this. I guess I thought, well . . . you're you."

I crumpled my face. "Huh?"

He sighed, shifted from foot to foot. He looked uncomfortable, pained. "I mean with your father, you know, with the whole no-dating thing. You haven't dated a lot of guys. Anyone, from what it sounds like. So I just got it in my head that we were friends. That we were just friends. Nothing more."

"Okay," I said slowly, trying to understand. "We started as friends. But we can move past that. I mean, it was just a kiss."

He snorted. "That wasn't just a kiss, Jess," he said quietly.

I folded my arms across my chest, covering the side of my breast his hand had just touched, feeling my face grow hot. Now I stood up, moved to the doorway, trying to sort out what he was saying. I heard him say it again in my mind. *You're only sixteen. You haven't dated a lot of guys.* My face burned.

"So would it make a difference if I had dated a bunch of guys?"

"That's not what I mean," he said, pressing his fingers in his eyes.

"What, then? Afraid you'll have complaints?" It slipped out before I could stop it, but I was frustrated, angry now, that he thought my dating history, or lack thereof, was any of his business.

He cocked his head at me. "Yeah, Jess. You could tell by my reaction I had complaints," he said sarcastically. "Look. I'm trying to do the right thing here, and you're making it impossible."

My jaw dropped. "I'm making it impossible? If I remember correctly, it was you who leaned over and kissed me."

"I know I did!" he shouted. "I told myself that we were just friends. That being here alone with you was nothing. And then you said that, about us being together, and the way you looked at me, I just kind of lost it and kissed you. I just wasn't expecting you to kiss me back. And it changes things, Jess. Believe me, it does. And now you're telling me you want this, and my head is about to explode. And I can't kiss you right now. Okay? I can't kiss you."

I felt rejected. Like a silly girl with a crush. *The way I'd looked at him.* Like he hadn't looked at me the same way.

Or maybe he hadn't. Maybe it was all in my mind.

I'd lit a candle, put on perfume, spent hours thinking about tracing that slug-shaped scar on his knee, dreaming of touching him, kissing him. And all along he was thinking of me as a friend. That being here alone with me was *nothing*.

I walked over to the candle, picked it up, and blew it out. He was standing in front of me, the only light in the room from the moon above.

"Well, let's be just friends again," I said quietly. "Then you won't have to worry about kissing me anymore."

He dropped his head back against the wall, closed his eyes.

I waited for him to tell me that's not what he wanted. That he wanted to kiss me. That he wanted to run his hands all over me. But he didn't say a word.

I grabbed the bag and went into the kitchen to make sure everything was back in its place. I put the glasses in the cabinet. The candle back on the table.

Alex came out after a minute. I took his keys from the table, held them out to him, and he took them without a word, his face invisible under the brim of his hat.

We were silent on the ride home.

Alex looked at the road ahead with a vacant stare. There was a lump in my throat, and my whole body was tight. I tried not to look at his hand on the steering wheel, the muscles on his forearm. I tried not to think about the way his tongue felt on mine.

But it was impossible. In my mind, I replayed all of it.

The words he'd said at the house didn't match up with the way I'd caught him looking at me when he thought I wasn't watching. The words didn't sync with the way he'd touched me on the couch, with the look in his eye when he kissed me. None of it made any sense.

And it hadn't been just today either. I'd felt something between us for weeks. And it hadn't just been one-sided.

Now something occurred to me, and I turned to face him.

"What did you mean by this changing things between us?" I asked, the sound of my voice suddenly loud as it pushed past the lump in my throat.

"What?" Alex looked over at me and then back at the road. I saw the veins on his hand pulse, his grip tightening on the steering wheel.

I eyed him, my stomach suddenly turning over as the thought in my head became clearer, remembering the phone call from a girl named Amy that he'd ignored, the awkward silence after he'd put the phone in the glove compartment.

Now I cleared my throat. "At the house, you said what happened between us changes things. *Believe me, it does,* is what you said."

Alex sighed, rolled down the window as far as it would go, and leaned away from me, as though he wanted to jump out of the truck.

"Can we not talk about it, Jess?" His voice was soft, pleading, but I was back on that couch, seeing the look on his face when he leaned into me. There was no mistaking how he felt about me. I was sure of it. And then he'd walked across the room and made some lame excuse about my age, my inexperience.

My insides boiled, the heat on my cheeks returning.

"Did you say that about someone specific or is it just your advanced maturity talking?" The thought tumbling out of my mouth. The words came out angry, and he flinched, but I couldn't pull back from it now.

We were in front of my house now, and he pulled the truck over to the curb.

Alex looked out the window at the house. "Someone's home, right?"

The streetlight lit up one side of his face, and I saw him fiddle with his hat. Push, pull.

"You're not going to answer me?" I asked.

"I wasn't sure there was a question in there," he said, finally looking at me.

"You know everything about me—that I haven't had any boy-friends, and I'm not allowed to date—but we never talk about you. Then we start kissing and you stop and say you can't kiss me any-more and give me a bunch of reasons that make zero sense and I guess what I'm asking is did you stop kissing me because of an-other girl?" I blurted out in one breath.

Alex took off his hat and tossed it on the dashboard, leaned over, and pressed his forehead against the steering wheel, a grunt of frustration coming out of him. When he sat up, he glanced over at me, but he didn't look me in the eye.

"It's not like that, Jess."

"That's not an answer," I said.

"It's complicated. Okay? It's not a yes-or-no thing."

The inside of the truck was suddenly cold. I swallowed, pulled my bag up between us on the seat. My voice was caught in my throat, a sob lurking somewhere behind it.

"It kind of is, Alex. Did you stop kissing me because of another girl? Yes, or no?"

He didn't answer, and in the dim light, I saw the look on his face. Sometimes his face was a city storefront, alive and full of light, and then suddenly closed for the day. A metal security gate rolled down and locked into place.

This was Alex now. Closed and locked up.

I opened the door and got out, pushing it closed behind me. I turned and walked up the stairs. I felt his eyes on me, felt them with each step I took.

The house was empty, but I went straight to my room and shut the door. My bag was filled with the trash from our sandwiches, but I dropped it in the corner and plopped on my bed, not caring that I still had sand on my feet from walking barefoot on the driveway at the Salt House.

After we'd kissed, I'd left the Salt House without slipping on my flip-flops, ignoring the sharp stabs on the soles of my feet from the crushed shells on the driveway. I'd walked to Alex's truck as fast as I could, thinking Alex was far behind me. Maybe even waiting for me to come back in.

But Alex had been right next to me. Right on my heels. He pulled out of the driveway quickly. Anxious, it seemed, to leave the house.

But no. That's wasn't it.

Now, lying in my bed with my eyes closed, it occurred to me that Alex hadn't been anxious to get away from the house. That wasn't it at all.

He'd been anxious to get away from me.

17

Jack

Hope didn't budge when I kissed her on the forehead. I'd hoped this morning would be like yesterday, maybe a smile, a kiss, something that would send me off with her touch on me. Yesterday, I'd leaned over to kiss her good-bye, and she turned her head so my kiss landed on her lips instead of the cheek I'd been aiming for. She'd put her hand on the side of my neck, her fingers tickling the hair on the back of my head.

She'd slipped her shirt over her head, and I'd sat down on the bed to take off my boots, but she'd tugged at the back of my shirt, whispered to just get in. I'd slipped in next to her, fully dressed, boots and all. It was the first time we'd been together since the night we'd fought. Not that I hadn't tried. At night in bed, it was as if a cold front was trapped under the sheets with us. I didn't move after we finished, just wrapped my arms around her. I was an hour late getting on the water, but I was in that bed all day in my head.

Last night she'd been quiet again, though, distant and preoccupied. This was how we were now. All or nothing.

The rain came down all afternoon, swirling in gusts and then petering off to a drizzle. Once, the sun thought about coming out, but then the wind picked up and the rain came in sheets. Not that it mattered. Once you were wet, it was all the same. I didn't feel it after a while. The fever that seemed to come and go was back again. I went through the motions, keeping warm, hot almost, even though my shirt was soaked through.

The sun was low in the sky when I pulled up to the float. Manny was getting the crates ready to be hoisted up to the warehouse. He was bent over, and when he glanced up at me, he straightened and put his hands on his hips.

"You're as red as these bugs get when you cook 'em," he said, pointing to the lobsters in the crate.

"Fighting a cold," I said, climbing off the boat. A cough went through me, and it was a minute before I got it under control.

He was saying something about how I should get that checked out when I waved him off, walked up the stairs, a heaviness in my legs.

Inside the warehouse, I went in the bathroom and rummaged through the drawer until I found the pill bottle I was looking for. The pain in my back was getting worse, and I was burning up, even though I was soaked through. I shook one of the pills out of the bottle into my palm and swallowed it, the chalky taste coating my mouth. I didn't know if it would help—the date on the bottle said they'd expired last year—but I was desperate. There was a towel hanging on the back of the door, and I rubbed my head and face with it before I went back outside.

Manny was gone when I got back to the float. Up above, I heard a door shut and saw him on the side stairs to the old room that he now used as an office. He walked to where I was standing and held out a glass jar filled with a reddish-brown liquid.

"Drink it," he said. "It's tea with a somethin' special in it. A family recipe."

I took a sniff. It smelled like cherries and something I couldn't place.

I held it back out to him. "What's next? You going to tuck me in?"

He took the jar, leaned over, and put it on the deck of the boat. "Trust me. Make you sleep like a baby."

I climbed on the boat, slipped the jar into the cup holder next to the wheel, thinking I'd toss it out later.

"Maybe," Manny said, untying the line and throwing it over the rail, "you won't be such a *battyhole* if you get some sleep."

I flipped him off, and he blew me a kiss as I throttled forward. I left him standing on the float, the water churning up behind me.

Calm Cove was just around the bend. I was at the wharf when the sky opened up, the rain pelting the boat as I tied her off. I took the jar out of the cup holder and went below to wait it out. I stepped out of my Grundens and pulled my shirt off, the flannel so wet that when I draped it over the faucet, a puddle formed below it and trickled down the drain.

There was a dry sweatshirt in the crate, and I pulled it on, sat on the edge of the cushion. The rain drummed against the boat, and the wind had picked up, rocking her from side to side. I thought about getting up and going back to the house, but I wanted to fix the drip from the faucet that I'd been ignoring. Might as well take advantage of the rain and get it done.

But my body refused to move. The jar was on the table in front of me. I reached out, unscrewed the cap, and brought it to my lips. I took a sip and winced, the alcohol masked by the cherry smell sliding down my throat, settling like a small fire in my stomach. It wasn't exactly good, but it wasn't bad either. My head felt lighter in two sips. By the third, the ache in my back was just a tingle. I hadn't eaten all day, and the warm liquid made my limbs feel weightless. My legs stretched out in front of me, my head tipping back.

I closed my eyes, rested the jar on my chest, and sipped from it until it was gone. There was a thud, and I opened my eyes to see the glass jar rolling on the floor. I thought I'd only dozed off for a moment, but when I looked at my watch, two hours had passed.

I dug my phone out of my pocket and called Hope to say I'd be late, and she was quiet on the other end.

"Just come home," she said, but whatever Manny had put in the tea had my tongue thick, my vision blurry. Not drunk exactly, but numb. *I can't,* is all I could manage to mumble before I hung up the phone. I thought of shutting my eyes again, just for a second, and before I could muster the energy to stand, my body slid down on the bench and my eyes closed.

I woke to the sound of an engine revving, slow at first, up to full throttle, then down again. I had no idea how long I'd been sleeping, but it was dark, and the fever was back by the way my eyes were burning.

I looked at my watch and swore. It was almost one in the morning. My mouth was dry. I thought of the painkiller I'd taken at the shop. Apparently it hadn't expired. Add in the alcohol in the tea, and the combo had knocked me out for hours.

I pulled on my boots and went up to the boat deck, still half-asleep. Calm Cove was a working dock during the day, noisy and full of boats. But at night, after the Wharf Rat closed, it was typically quiet, even on a Friday night.

The Wharf Rat was dark except for a faint light in the back window, most likely Eddy closing up for the night. The noise was coming from the other end of the dock. I followed the sound to a boat that sat in the last slip, its dual engines rumbling.

The boat was dark, not a light on that I could see. I yelled out, but my voice disappeared, lost in the noise. I walked toward the engines. It wasn't until I was standing with the full moon behind me, giving light to the wheelhouse, that I saw a man in the captain's chair, sitting with his head down.

I yelled again and stood so close to the boat that it bumped my thigh.

I considered walking away, but whoever was in the chair seemed to be asleep, with twin engines churning up the black water.

I slapped the side of the boat, two hard whacks with my open hand. The boat rocked, and the man turned, but in slow motion. I saw his hand fumble with the key, and the engine went silent. He turned in his seat, and I caught the shadow of a woman in front of him, standing between his legs, her arms around his neck.

Her long hair shielded her face, but her shirt was open. I backed up from the side of the boat. The light in the wheelhouse went on, and when the captain's chair swiveled to face me, I was looking at Ryland Finn. A drunk Ryland Finn. His eyes tiny slits in the dim light.

"Caught in the act, Chief," Finn slurred, giving me the thumbs-up. The woman in front of him fiddled with the buttons on her shirt, but she swayed from side to side, too drunk for the task. She seemed to realize it and settled for pulling the sides of her shirt closed and crossing her arms across her chest.

She had an angry patch of acne on her chin. She was young, maybe in her early twenties. Her eyes were wide and vacant. Pink lipstick was smudged halfway across her cheek, and when she moved away from Finn, she stumbled and went down on one knee. She used the seat next to her to pull herself up, but it was a slow, clawing process, as if she were climbing out of a deep ravine instead of merely standing up.

"Go wait in the truck," Finn said to her, and she stumbled over to the side of the boat. She threw a leg over the rail and almost toppled back into the boat. I grabbed her wrist before she fell. Finn didn't move, just sat in the chair, his chin resting on his chest, his eyes barely open.

She managed to get her other leg over, and when she slid from the boat to the dock, she stumbled into me, her polka-dot bra crushing into my arm. Now that she was in front on me, she seemed even younger.

"Did you come with him?" I asked, bending to look at her face. She pulled her arm away, but I stepped closer to her. Her wrist was tiny in my grasp. I loosened my grip but held her there.

"I'm not letting you go until you tell me you came here willingly with him," I said.

I glanced at Finn out of the corner of my eye to see if he would react to this, but he sat in the chair, his legs out in front of him. His shirt was unbuttoned and a black tattoo ran the length of his hairless chest.

"Yeah, daddy, I did," she sneered, a smile pulling at the corners of her lips.

I dropped her arm, and she walked backward, still facing me, not bothering to close her shirt. She waved her fingers at me, turned, and weaved down the stretch of dock. When she reached the gangplank, she used the railing to pull herself up the steep incline before she disappeared into the darkness of the parking lot.

The dock dipped, and Finn's shoulder grazed me as he stumbled by. It was a slow, halting walk, as if he knew he might end up in the water with one misstep.

When he reached the *Hope Ann*, he paused, his body swaying from the sudden stop.

I was twenty feet behind him when I saw him climb over the side, the boat rocking when he boarded her. My body tightened.

"Ah, the famous *Hope Ann*," he said when I reached the boat. "Your wife's namesake."

"Get off the boat, Finn." I stepped over the side of the boat onto the deck.

He ignored me and leaned against the railing, pulled a cigarette pack out of his shirt pocket, fished one out, and lit it. He took a long draw on his cigarette before he stuck the pack out, offering me one. I crossed the distance between us and slapped the pack out of his hands. The lighter hit the floor and skidded across the deck. He followed it with his eyes, then looked at me.

"Relax. You're the one that interrupted us. I thought maybe you were lonely, looking for some company."

"I was sleeping before you ran your engines at one in the morning. Idiots like you shouldn't be allowed to own boats."

"Simmer down. She asked me to start her up." He raised his eyebrows at me. "And who am I to say no to a lady?"

The light from the tip of his cigarette glowed in an arc. He almost missed his mouth when he brought it to his lips. He was beyond drunk, his eyes red and watery under the glow of the dock light above.

"But you know what I mean. You never knew how to say no to the ladies either." He chuckled, his eyes closing for a moment, then his head jerked, and his eyes opened again.

I felt my fist close. "You have two seconds before I help you off the boat."

He held up his hands, looking amused. "Ah, Kelly. Always serious. I'm just screwing with you."

"Go home and sleep it off. Last warning."

Headlights from up above in the parking lot flashed. Apparently, the girl was still waiting for him.

It looked as if he might take my advice. He arranged himself, one leg at a time, into a standing position. I stepped aside to let him pass, but he stopped in the center of the boat and turned, pointing at me.

"I meant to tell you Hope's pretty. Your wife. And smart. I can tell. One smart, pretty woman." His words were jumbled, his eyes pinched.

His breath hit me, reminding me of the last time he'd been on my boat. How he'd woken me up that night too. Him and three other morons, drunk and throwing punches at me before I was even standing, before I was even awake.

Maybe it was the burning in my back, or the pounding in my head, but suddenly there was a rage inside of me.

He'd forced my hand, putting his traps in my water. If I'd been thinking straight that day, his traps would have been empty, the door left open. A warning. The smart way to handle it. But I'd cut them. Stupidly. Like an amateur. All because of this asshole. Now he was on my boat, drunk, talking about my wife. How smart she was. How pretty.

I put my hand in the pocket of my pants, slipped my middle finger through the thick brass key ring, and closed my fist in my pocket.

He didn't see me coming. His eyes were closed when I grabbed him by the collar and tugged as hard as I could. He grunted, and stumbled forward, my fist slamming into his nose. There was a crunch of bone, and my hand lit up, the key ring cutting into my knuckle, but it did what I wanted: the bridge of his nose exploding under my fist.

He dropped to his knees and moaned, cupping his face in his hands, dark blood pouring through his fingers. The sight of it should have stopped me. But I felt my leg pull back and shoot out, my boot connecting with his side. There was a thud, and he rolled across the boat. He didn't move then, his body a lump in the corner. I walked over and nudged him with my foot, and he held up his hand, as if to ward me off.

"Get up," I said, grabbing the fillet knife from the sheath fastened to the rail behind him. He rolled onto his knees and tried to stand. But he was either too drunk or too hurt or too stunned, and he stayed on his hands and knees, blood running down his face onto the deck.

"You're bleeding all over my fucking boat." I yanked him up by the back of his shirt, but his enormous body just wobbled, his hand slipping in the blood. I leaned over and pressed the knife against the side of his neck. He felt it and froze.

"Get. Up. Now," I said, and he reached up with one hand and grabbed the rail, hoisting himself up on one leg, then the other. When he stood, he looked at the knife and took a step back.

"Jesus," he sputtered, his eyes wild, blood splattering against the deck like raindrops.

I grabbed the front of his shirt and held the knife against the side of his neck again. He put his hands up. I pointed the knife at the dock, and he threw a leg over the side, climbed off, and stared at me.

"That was a warning punch. You mention my wife again, I won't be so gentle. And you come near my water again, I won't just cut your traps. Next time, I'm coming for you."

He was pressing the sleeve of his shirt to his nose, and when he heard this, I saw his face contort. He seemed confused, as if the blows had stunned him.

When he let go of the shirt, a thin line of blood still ran out of one nostril, and he tilted his head back, looking at me out of the corner of one eye.

"Whatever traps you cut aren't mine," he said. His hand touched the side of his ribs. He winced and swayed on his feet.

"These are my waters. And I know every buoy in them. So you can deny it all you want. Be a man and own up to it," I said.

"A man like you? You get Boon to fight your fights or you wait until I'm shitfaced." He leaned against the piling for support, slack jawed and blinking furiously, throwing his head back now and then to staunch the blood dripping from his nose.

"You came on my boat once without an invitation. Now you know what happens if you do it again."

"You got a screw loose, Kelly. I heard about that kid of yours. That baby. I didn't know about that when I came to your house. Peggy told me after. And you know what? I decided to not mess with you. Let you have my water. Figured, you know, you probably got enough on your plate."

"Leave," I said, pointing to the parking lot with the knife.

"That's why I brought up your wife. How pretty she is. That's all I was trying to say. That you still got a lot of good stuff. But I can't get it out of my mouth before you haul off and break my nose. Probably a rib too."

The headlights from the parking lot flashed again, and he backed up, not taking his eyes off me.

"You know what, Kelly? You deserve everything that's coming to you."

He disappeared into the dark, and a few minutes later, I heard tires crunching against the gravel up above.

There was a large circle of blood on the deck. I put the knife back in the sheath and felt my head spin. I heard the crunch when my hand hit his face. I stumbled to the side of the boat, and leaned over, my stomach heaving, the brown liquid burning as it came up and hit the water with a splash. I grabbed a rag and wiped my mouth. Then I leaned over, dipped it in the ocean, and pressed it against my knuckle, expecting the salt to light the gash on fire.

But I didn't even feel it, just felt the pounding in my head. The way it seemed to pulse even with my heartbeat.

18

Kat

The new thing that happened this summer was Jess got a boy-friend. She didn't think I knew, but I did. And she was a traitor. This she did know, because I whispered it to her every time she got close to me. This morning she got the milk out of the fridge for her cereal, and when she sat next to me, I said it to her, long and drawn out, traaiiittoooor, with a dip in my voice at the end for what my teacher, Mrs. Whitley, calls *emphasis*.

Jess looked up at me from her cereal, so I knew she heard me. She waited until Mom left the room to hiss at me.

"What are you whispering?"

"Like you don't know."

"That's the point. I *don't* know."

"You're such a liar."

"That's what you've been saying to me? That I'm a liar?"

"No. That goes without saying. What I've been whispering is that you're a *traitor*." I rolled my eyes. Sometimes she was so dense.

She drank the milk out of the bottom of her cereal bowl, took it to the sink, and walked out of the room.

I followed.

"You said you'd tell me what happened at Smelliot's house, and you didn't. So you are a liar," I said to her back.

She turned and folded her arms across her chest. "I did tell you what happened. Which was nothing. I saw the kid you were talking about, but that's it. I don't know why he told you Mom and Dad were getting divorced. Case closed."

"Case not closed. You left out that you met his *brother*. And you also didn't mention that he's your *boyfriend*. Friend of the enemy. So that makes you a *liar* and a *traitor*."

Jess walked past me and shut the bedroom door. When she turned around, her face was pink, and she had a crazy look in her eye.

"Who told you all of this, Kat?" she asked.

"Told me what?"

"About Alex. That he was my boyfriend?"

"No one you know." I hated that she never told me anything. I told her *everything*.

"Kat. Cut it out. Tell me how you know about Alex."

"So he is your boyfriend," I said, pleased that I had the right information.

"First, he is not. And second, tell me what you know about it."

I looked out the window, yawned, like this was all very boring. See how she liked having secrets kept from her.

But I also wanted to know about this Alex person. And I could tell by the way she was staring at me that whoever he was, whether she called him her boyfriend or not, he mattered to her.

"You promise to never not tell me something again?" I asked, hoping this moment would at least buy me something in the future.

"No." She scowled at me. "Why don't you promise to not be so nosy?"

"Okay." I shrugged. "Well, my nosiness just so happens to know something that you don't about your *boyfriend*. Namely, that you may not be his only *girlfriend*."

That did it. If I thought she had a crazy look before, this made her even crazier. What Boon called batshit. She grabbed my forearm and yanked me into her bedroom and slammed the door behind us, locking us in.

She led me over to the chair and sat me down and leaned over me, her arms on either side of my chair.

"Talk," she said, her eyes drilling a hole into my face.

"Jeez, relax, will you?" I pushed the chair back, rolling on the wheels, but she grabbed my arms and pulled me back to her.

"Now," she growled at me.

Jess had the brownest eyes, and long lashes, like Mom. Dad always said they were like a pair of does, the two of them. Now her eyes were mean looking. I brought my knees up to my chest and pressed my face into them. What started as me teasing her had turned somehow, and I was sorry I'd brought it up at all. I pushed her hands away.

"Kat," Jess said, softer now. "I'm sorry. I didn't mean to pull you." I felt her hand on the back of my head, her fingers patting my hair.

"I know you were just fooling around. But it's important to me. How about this?" she said, tugging my hair playfully where her fingers intertwined in the back of my head so my face came off my knees. She was calmer now. "You tell me everything you know, and I'll tell you everything I know. Deal?"

"Everything?" I asked. She nodded, but it was a side-to-side movement that let me know she was lying. But it was something. Something was better than nothing.

"Okay," I agreed, hopping off the chair. "I was at camp, and the counselors always make us have snack time all together on the picnic tables. And they usually sit under the big willow tree—you know the one near the parking lot." I glanced at her to make sure she knew the tree, and she nodded.

"But I won first place in the relay race, and the prize was that I could choose where to sit and have ice cream. So I chose to sit with the counselors under the tree because they're always giggling and fooling around, and I always wonder what they're talking about."

Jess motioned with her hand for me to hurry to the good part.

"So we're sitting under the tree, and my counselors are all standing together under the long branches looking at this guy who is sitting on the hood of his truck. I didn't see what the big deal was—he was just some guy with a baseball hat on looking at his watch every two seconds. But Abby, my counselor, was going on and on about him. She said she'd seen him around town but didn't know his name or where he was from. She goes, 'Oh my God, he is so cute,' and Alyssa, my other counselor, says, 'So, so, so cute!'"

I mimicked them, my voice high, hand movements and all, thinking Jess would laugh. But her face was stone.

"My ice cream was dripping down my hand, so I had better things to do than care about what they were talking about, but then Smelliot next to me, who got to eat at the tree because he came in second in the race—well, he said he tied me, and then cried like a baby when I told him he didn't, so they called it a tie, but it wasn't, not even close—"

"Kat!"

"Okay! So Smelliot says, that's my brother and points to the kid that they're talking about. And Abby and Alyssa go nuts, swarming all over him, asking a million questions about how old his brother is, where he goes to school . . . blah, blah, blah."

"He pointed at Alex?" Jess asked.

"Are you even paying attention? Yes, Alex. Who do you think?"

"Well, what did he say about him?"

"He said his brother's name was Alex and he was eighteen and they moved here from North Carolina, and he's going to college somewhere up here."

Jess closed her eyes, and when she opened them, I could tell she was putting two and two together.

"And then I walked up," Jess said slowly, her voice a whisper.

"Yup. I almost dropped my ice cream when you climbed up on the hood next to him. And I almost threw up when he scooched over until he was as close as he could get to you."

"He wasn't that close. I was just sitting next to him."

"Your legs were touching."

"Our shorts *may* have been touching. It's not a big deal."

"Dad would think it was a big deal."

Jess's face colored. I wrinkled my nose at her.

"Is he your boyfriend?" I asked.

"We're just friends, Kat."

"How do you even know him?"

"I met him the day I went to talk to that kid. I hurt my ankle, and he drove me home. He came to the dock after that, and we just started talking. Anyway, what about the girlfriend part? You said you knew something about a girlfriend."

I'd only seen them together for five minutes that day. Our snack time had ended right after Jess showed up, and my next activity was across the field. When I came back to the tree later, they were gone. But I'd seen her face when she climbed on the hood next to him. The way she looked at him. They hadn't touched, really. I was just digging for more information. But they had sat close to each other, close enough that Abby, my counselor, had asked if that girl was his girlfriend. I didn't offer up that that girl was my sister, mostly because my mouth was still on the ground.

But Smelliot had shook his head.

"I don't know who that is," he'd said, pointing to Jess, "but my brother has a girlfriend in North Carolina. Her name is Amy, and they're getting married someday."

I told Jess this part of the story, and she starting pacing up and down the floor of the bedroom, her thumbnail in her mouth, chomping away. I raised my eyebrows.

"So, um, who is Amy?"

"Huh?" Jess looked at me from a million miles away.

"Amy . . . the girlfriend? The one he's going to marry?"

Jess sat on the bed, stood up, and started pacing again. This was what she meant when she did the little side-to-side nod, the nod when she agreed to tell me *everything*. Apparently *everything* meant nothing.

"Sounds like a *love* triangle," I said. Emphasis on *love*.

Jess screwed up her face at me. "Where did you hear that?"

"I know things, Jessica. I'm almost ten. Double digits." I held up one finger and made a circle with my other hand to show her the number.

"You're eight, and you don't know things. Where did you hear it?"

I sighed. "Abby said it when Smelliot told us about Amy. She looked right at you two and said, 'Well, it looks like the new boy in town has a little love triangle.'"

"That sounds like Abby." Jess made a disgusted noise. She sat on the bed and stared at the wall. She stayed that way while I watched her. Jess was hard to read, like Mom, always quiet when they got upset. I hated how it changed the mood in the house. Dad and I had the tempers, but at least the upset didn't sit in the house, make it hard to breathe or move. That's how it felt now. Like a wool blanket was on top of us.

I slid over on the bed next to her until my shoulder rested against her side. She didn't look at me, but I felt her lean against me. I knew she was thinking about Alex. Alex who hadn't told her about his girlfriend. Alex who wasn't her boyfriend. I hoped he just went away, back to North Carolina, along with his brother and his lies about my parents getting divorced.

19

Jess

The week had been busy, and I was glad for it. It was August, and the tourist season in Alden was in full swing. The shop was closed on Sundays, and I had Saturday off, but Monday through Friday, my alarm went off at seven in the morning. I showered at night and let my hair air-dry. Most mornings it was still damp when I pulled it into a ponytail. I tried not to think about how Alex said my hair was a color he'd never seen.

I tried not to think about Alex at all.

I hadn't seen him since we argued last Friday. I'd spent the rest of the weekend with Bets, catching up with her now that she was home. When she asked me what I'd been doing all summer, Alex's name was on the tip of my tongue. But I didn't mention him. I was afraid once I said his name out loud, I wouldn't be able to stop talking about him. To stop thinking about him.

Monday took forever to arrive. And then at lunch, Alex wasn't there. I'd walked over to his truck to have lunch in our usual spot in the parking lot, and the space was empty. I'd wanted to talk to him about what happened. To tell him I knew about Amy. To ask what it meant. I'd sat on the curb next to the spot, bit into my apple, and waited. I left when fifteen minutes had passed. When I knew he wasn't coming.

He wasn't there on Tuesday or Wednesday either. On Thursday, I went back to my spot on the deck where I always used to eat before I met Alex. I figured if he wanted to see me, he knew where to find me. Then again, he would've known where to find me all week.

Now, it was Friday. A week since we'd kissed.

The alarm had pulled me out of a dream, a good one, although I couldn't remember it, only that Alex had been in it. Then slowly, detail by detail, the past week trickled into my head. The argument we'd had at the Salt House. The look on his face when he'd shouted, *I can't kiss you.* The empty parking space.

I got out of bed and dragged myself to the bathroom, getting dressed in a daze, wishing I could crawl back into bed to my dream.

In the kitchen, my mother was sitting at the table. Kat was lying on the floor on her stomach in front of the TV, a cartoon flashing on the screen in front of her.

My mother smiled at me over the glasses resting on the bridge of her nose, a pad of paper in front of her. She was holding a pencil in her hand, but the page was blank, just tiny doodles in the corner of the paper.

"Writing?" I asked.

"Eh. If that's what you call staring into space."

I opened the refrigerator and grabbed my lunch to take with me.

"What do you want for breakfast?" she asked, getting up from the table.

"I'm not hungry."

"How about cereal, then?"

I shook my head, and she put her hand on her hip. "You need to eat, Jess."

I gave her a look. She'd dropped at least two dress sizes in the past year, and she hadn't needed to lose weight in the first place.

Although, these days, she did seem more like her old self. She was almost back to her normal size, and most days, if not all, she was dressed when I came home. I should have commented on it, recognized it. But I was tired of thinking of her, tired of worrying about her.

"Do you feel okay? You look a little pale." Her hand reached out to my forehead, and I moved my head to the side, dodging her touch. A flash of hurt crossed her face, making me feel worse than I already did. I felt my eyes well up.

"What's wrong?"

I shook my head. I didn't even know if I could explain it. "I'm just tired, I guess."

"I was worried about this being too much for you—you were only going to work three days, four at the most. Why the jump to five?"

"I don't know. I like the money," I lied. What I liked was having lunch with Alex every day. I didn't say this, though.

"If you need money for something, let's talk about it. You're only sixteen, Jess. You can ask us if you need something."

"I'll be seventeen in two weeks," I reminded her. "In case you forgot."

"I didn't forget." She crossed her arms. "You seem angry."

"I'm not angry," I said, even though I knew it wasn't true. I grabbed my backpack off the table and stuffed my lunch inside, yanking the zipper closed.

She raised her eyebrows at me but stepped back, away from me, as if she sensed I needed the space. "Okay. Well, can I give you a ride, then?"

"I have my bike," I said, already walking to the door.

"What's the matter?" Kat peered up at me as I stepped over her.

"Mind your own business," I mumbled, and she crossed her

eyes at me, held them there. It usually made me smile, but not today.

"Grump," she said, and put her chin back in her hand and looked at the screen.

I opened the door and slammed it behind me as hard as I could, satisfied at the loud noise it made. My grandmother was in the hallway of the foyer, her hand on the brass knob of the heavy front door, and she gasped at the noise and put her hand to her chest.

"Jessica Barbara Kelly, you almost took that door off the hinges." She patted her heart, breathing out dramatically.

"Sorry, Grandma," I said, feeling ridiculous. "I didn't mean to scare you."

She was wearing a flowery short-sleeve top over cotton elastic-waist pants, the dark panty hose beneath them sagging at her ankles, peeking out from under the straps of the sandals on her feet. In her arms was a polka-dot yoga mat.

"I thought you hated to sweat," I said, looking at the mat.

"I don't hate to sweat. What I hate is exercise. But this is just for old-lady yoga at the Y. We put the mats down, and stand on them, lift our arms to the ceiling a half dozen times, and then we eat coffee cake." She grinned at me, her pink lipstick bright against her heavily powdered face. "And then I'm not a liar when I tell my doctor that I enjoy fitness."

"You shouldn't worry about exercising," I said. "You're too thin as it is."

"Oh, you know doctors these days. Pay them enough, and they'll find something wrong with you. Apparently, I have high cholesterol. You know what my nutritionist told me after she did some fancy body analysis on me?" she asked, looking down at her body, her clothes loose on her petite frame. "She said I was skinny fat. Can you believe that? She didn't mean it as a compliment either. I left her office and called Roger right away and said, guess what, honey? We're two skinny-fat people. And he laughed. Like it was the funniest thing he'd ever heard. It's one of reasons I love that man. His idea of exercise is an after-dinner stroll for ice cream."

She pointed her finger at me. "Speaking of cake and ice cream. Somebody has a birthday coming. Seventeen!" She shook her head and whistled. "When did I get so old?" she asked. "You know, I remember being your age like it was just yest—"

"I have to go, Grandma," I said, interrupting her, pointing to the door she was blocking. "I'm sorry. I don't want to be late."

"Well, look at me. Going on and on. Hop in. I'll drive you," she said, hurrying out the door and down the steps to her car.

"I have my bike," I said, walking out the door behind her. I'd driven with my grandmother before, and it wasn't an experience I wanted to repeat. I had a better chance of walking to work and getting there on time. "Have fun. I'll exercise for both of us," I called to her.

"And I'll eat cake for both of us," she said over her shoulder, waving both her hands in the air as a good-bye.

The day was cool, the air gray and thick. The wind was salty against my face as my bike picked up speed down the long, winding road into town.

At the shop, I brought my bike in and got to work. The fish case needed to be filled, the ice replenished, the planters out front watered. By midmorning, there was a line of customers, locals getting their fish before the parking lot filled from the Wharf Rat.

Still, the morning crept by.

In between customers, I scrubbed the counters, cleaned the bathroom. Boon was out of the office for the day, and I organized his desk.

At noon, the door jingled. I was at the register, arranging receipts, and suddenly, there was Alex, standing in front of me, fiddling with the brim of his baseball hat.

"Hey," he said.

My mouth was dry, and I didn't trust my voice. I held up my hand as a hello. I dropped the pile of receipts I'd been arranging in the drawer and closed the register.

He was quiet while I did this, and I saw through the glass case that he was wearing khaki pants and a white button-down shirt. When I looked up at him, he smiled nervously.

I wanted to say: Where have you been? Who is Amy?

Instead, I crossed my arms, cleared my throat, hoping the thickness that had settled there would disappear.

He fiddled with the brim of his hat again. He didn't seem in any hurry to speak. I looked down at my watch, then back at him.

"So what's up?" I finally asked.

"Oh, nothing. I mean, well . . . I hadn't seen you. I mean not that we planned to, but, you know, during lunch, we usually . . ." He stopped talking, and a dot of pink appeared on the top of each cheek.

"I walked over to your truck on Monday, but you weren't there," I said.

"No," he agreed. "Sorry about that. I should've called. It was a busy week. It just got away from me." His face went from pink to red.

Got away from him? He worked at the sail camp. I'd been a camper there years ago. You had to wait for the tide to be almost high to go out. The rest of the time was spent watching movies and waiting. Playing dodgeball and waiting. Tying knots and rigging sails. And waiting.

I didn't say anything. Just opened my lunch and took out my sandwich, unwrapped it.

"Anyway, I'm actually heading to the airport. I have to go home for the weekend. I mean, back to North Carolina."

"Is everything okay?"

He nodded, but it was more of a shrug with a halfhearted tilt of his head. Maybe, I don't know, it said.

He opened his mouth to say something and then closed it. There was a long silence between us, and he seemed to be waiting for me to speak. The fact that I was quiet was surprising even to me—there was so much I wanted to ask him. But I was suddenly aware that I'd given as much as I was willing to give. I could have asked about Amy. I could've asked him to explain. But he was standing in front of me and hadn't explained. And I could see he wasn't going to.

All week I'd gone to the spot in the parking lot and felt my heart sink when it was empty. That seemed to be all the explanation I needed.

"I'll be back next week," he said. "Can I see you then?"

"You know where to find me," I said, keeping my voice steady. "Have a safe trip."

He fiddled with his hat again. Then he turned and walked out the door, the bell jingling as it closed.

Through the large glass window in the front of the store, I watched him leave, shielding my body behind the wall. He walked to the curb, stopped, and turned around, as if he might come back. But then he walked to the parking lot. When he faced me again to get in his truck, he was biting his bottom lip.

Long after he pulled away, I pictured him biting that lip. I knew the texture of that lip, the softness of it.

I wondered if a girl named Amy did too.

20

Hope

I didn't hear Jack come home, but he was next to me when I woke up. Sunlight crept under the window shade. The red numbers on the clock read 7:00. I sat up, put my hand on Jack's shoulder. His eyes opened. They were glassy, disoriented.

"Jack," I whispered. "You overslept." It was Saturday. A work-day for Jack.

He put his arm on my hip and closed his eyes. He pushed the sheet down until it was bunched around his middle. I pressed my hand to his bare chest. His skin was hot to the touch, slick under a thin film of sweat from his fever.

"I'm getting up," he mumbled, but his eyes stayed closed.

"That's it, Jack," I said. "I'm calling the doctor. We're going."

He shook his head. "I need sleep. That's all."

He patted my hip, and I saw there was blood covering the back of his hand, dried and flaky, a deep gash on his knuckle.

"Jack. What happened?" I touched his wrist, and he glanced down, shut his eyes again.

"I banged it on the engine. It's fine."

"It's not fine. It's deep. You need stitches."

"I need sleep, Hope. Let me sleep."

I sighed. "Let me clean it, and you can sleep. But if you're still hot later, we're going to the emergency room."

He groaned and turned over, and I left to get a washcloth.

He was breathing deeply when I returned. I cleaned the blood off. If it hurt, he didn't show it, not even a flinch when I swabbed some ointment in the cut, covered it with a bandage and wrapped it with gauze to keep it in place.

I climbed back into bed next to him, and looked down at him. He'd called last night to say he was working late, and I heard the weariness in his voice, the drained edge of it. Come home, I said, and he whispered, I can't. And I thought of the last argument we had. And the one before that. I knew when he said I *can't*, he meant I *won't*.

Now, with his long body stretched out next to me, I reached out and put my hand over his heart, felt the rise and fall of it. He was leaner than I'd ever seen, muscular still, his shoulders and arms thick from years of heaving heavy traps out of the water, but the slight softness that had formed over his belly in the last years was gone, a hollowness in its place. I knew every inch of this body. Every nick, every scar, the shape of every limb and joint. His breath was ragged, his eyes clenched in pain even in sleep.

I put my head on his chest, turned until my lips were pressed against the wisps of dark hair. I felt the tears come, silently, swiftly. They trickled down my check and slid down to the hollow of his belly. I don't know how long I stayed there, but when I sat up and wiped my face, an idea was forming in the back of my mind.

In the kitchen, Kat and my mother sat at the table, a puzzle between them, half-done. I said it before I could change my mind, before another day of living in the past slipped by.

"I think we should have a girls' day at the Salt House today. You know, have lunch and go swimming. Spend the day together."

Kat stood up so fast, she knocked her chair over. "Are you serious?"

My mother looked up at me, startled. "Well, now," she said.

Kat jumped up and down, and my mother put her hand on her chest at the noise it made. Kat had been begging me to go to the Salt House for months, but in the last week or so, she asked almost daily, sometimes two or three times a day. So much so that it seemed to border on an obsession. But when I asked her why it was so important, she was vague, just saying she missed it.

Now, while my mother went upstairs to get ready and Kat went to her room, I called Boon and told him that Jack was sick and not to worry when he didn't see him.

"I was just going to call you," he said. "I was worried when I saw his boat still here. Manny said he was sick as a dog yesterday."

"I didn't see him, but he's been fighting something for weeks. You know him, too stubborn to slow down."

There was a pause then. It seemed as if Boon was on the verge of saying something, but the line was quiet.

"Boon? You there?"

"So Jack didn't come home last night?"

"He came home late. Said he had to fix something on the boat."

"But he's home now? He didn't just call to say he was sick, right?"

"What? No, he's here."

After a moment, he said, "You've seen him? I mean, put eyes on him?" There was a hesitation in his voice. As if he had to ask but wasn't sure he wanted to hear the answer.

"He's in bed. What's going on?"

"Oh, good. That's good."

I waited for him to explain, but there was silence on the phone.

"Boon. What's going on? Tell me what's going on."

"I don't know, Hope." He paused. "There's some blood on his boat. On the deck."

There was silence on the phone while I thought.

"Oh. It's probably from the cut. He has a cut on his hand. He said he hit it on the engine."

"A cut?" he asked. "That's it?"

I frowned. "Not like a paper cut. His knuckle is split open."

"His knuckle? On which hand?"

"I don't know. The right, I guess. Why?"

"It's just, well. It's not a drop or two. It's probably the cut, though," he reassured, but he sounded doubtful.

"Is there a lot of blood? I don't understand."

He paused again. "Don't worry. You know how blood mixes with water and it looks like a lot. More than it is. That's all. Keep him in bed. He sure as hell needs the rest."

He said he had to run, that he was swamped, but I knew he was rushing me off the phone. I hung up and went back to the bedroom. Jack was still sleeping, and I pulled back the sheet, uncovering his body, my eyes searching for another injury. Boon's voice in my head. *Blood mixes with water and it looks like a lot.*

There was nothing on him out of the ordinary. Bumps and bruises that were always there, with his line of work. Two large bruises on each shin. A rope burn on his forearm. A gash on his knee that had scabbed over already.

I pushed gently on his shoulder, once, then again, and he turned on his side, snoring, pulling the sheet with him, the back of him now uncovered.

There was the mole on his left shoulder, and the scar that ran from the back of his knee to his ankle from a clumsy stern man who'd dropped a trap on him years ago.

I sighed and took the sheet from under his arm, snapped it until it spread out in the air and landed over him. I smoothed it out and looked at the bandage on his hand. The cut had been deep. It would have bled. But how much?

I walked to the dresser and dug out my swimsuit, slipped it on, and threw a T-shirt and shorts over it. I moved slowly, telling myself that it was because I didn't want to disturb Jack.

But every inch of me was dreading going to the house. I thought of the last time we'd been to the Salt House as a family. Last June. Not long before we lost her.

Jack and I had decided to stay at the Salt House for a few days before the girls got out of school. The kitchen needed to be packed up, and Jack had a list of things he wanted to work on. But by lunch every day, we'd end up on the beach in front of the house with Maddie, lounging on the blanket, watching her crawl to the water as fast as she could.

Jack would leave in the afternoon to pick up the girls from school, and I'd spend the hour he was gone rocking with her in the chair on the porch while she napped.

I hadn't wanted the week to end, with Jack around as much as he was with the week he'd taken off of work. But I remember feeling worried that we were behind on renovations. That we wouldn't be ready to move into the house by September.

Looking back now, it's hard to believe this was my only concern. My biggest fear.

Now I went to the kitchen, and Kat skipped over to give me a hug. Her excitement filled the room. I saw that she was dressed, her bathing suit strap peeking out from under her shirt. She had her backpack on her shoulder, and when I reached to take it, she stepped back, away from me.

"We have things to do before we leave, Kat. That's going to get heavy."

"I don't want to forget it. Besides, Grandma's ready. And Jess is kind of grumpy because I woke her up, but she's getting dressed too."

"I need a cup of coffee. And there's breakfast too."

"Can we just eat there?" she whined.

There was a bagel shop on the way. It was probably just as well to get out of the house. With Kat jumping around like she was, I was afraid she'd wake Jack.

It was a half hour before we were finally in the car. I'd packed us lunch, and Jess and Kat had loaded some cleaning supplies in the trunk. Jess was quiet, but less sullen than she had been all week. I knew that Alex was away for the weekend. Peggy had mentioned that he was going back to his hometown, but she'd been busy in the last weeks with looking for a new place to live, and the one time we'd managed to talk on the phone had been cut short when the Realtor came up on her call-waiting.

I hoped visiting the house today would be a good thing for Jess. She'd always loved our summers there. But unlike Kat, she hadn't said a word about how much she missed it.

Kat, on the other hand, could barely contain herself, fidgeting in the seat. I smiled at her in the rearview mirror, and she waved at me, giggling. Even though her excitement was contagious, my stomach flipped.

There'd been days in the past year when I'd pointed the car in the direction of the Salt House and told myself to just go. Get it over with. But I'd change my mind and end up turning around.

But there was no backing out now. There couldn't be anyway.

Lying next to Jack this morning, I'd felt him slipping away from me. Maybe it was the hollow spot where my hand had rested on him that made me feel that way. Or the thought of his blood on the deck. But there was something else. Something in his voice last night. *I can't.* It wasn't just the words. It was his voice when he said it. How it sounded empty. Indifferent.

Now I was thankful for my mother's company in the car. She turned in her seat, the seat belt cutting across her hip, and played the alphabet game with Kat, each of them picking out things they saw outside of the car, working their way down to *Z*. Jess joined in eventually, and the chatter kept my mind occupied.

We were barely stopped in the driveway at the Salt House when Kat clambered out, her sneakers crunching the crushed shells as she ran to the front door. Jess followed, her long legs striding across the lawn.

My mother looked at me, rested a hand on my forearm. "Take your time. I'll get the girls to help me drag the picnic table out of the basement. We can eat outside."

I handed her the keys, and she joined Jess and Kat on the front porch.

I waited until they were inside the house before I got out of the car and looked at the front porch.

I let the moment wash over me. Months ago, I would have fought the flood of emotion, pushed it away, let it overwhelm me.

The rocking chair on the front porch was in the basement now, put away since Jack had closed up the house last year.

But I looked at the spot where it sat, remembered the last time we'd rocked in the chair. I felt the weight of her in my lap, felt her hand snaking up to curl a strand of my hair as she drifted off to sleep. I didn't move until the memory of it faded enough that I could breathe again.

I walked across the lawn toward the backyard, the ocean spreading out before me. The grass was short, and I wondered when Jack had stopped over to cut it. I knew he came here often. He didn't ask me to come with him anymore. The answer had been no so many times this past year, he'd stopped asking.

To the right was the hammock, the worn rope stretched between two tall elms. I saw the girls swinging lazily in the morning, Maddie nestled between them.

Inside the house, I heard voices in the kitchen. My mother's laugh, and then Jess's. There were boxes stacked against every wall. My mother had opened the windows to air out the chalky smell of dried plaster. I climbed the stairs, turned left down the hall, passing bedrooms. Some walls were flat gray: the ones we hadn't plastered. Trim board lay stacked on the floor.

A project abandoned for more than a year.

The nursery was the only room that was finished. We'd insulated it before she was born, and the girls had helped me decorate it. I walked to the wall, remembering the day the girls picked out the wallpaper.

We'd spent an hour tucked inside a nook in the design store surrounded by stacks of sample books. You choose, I'd said, she's your baby sister. They agonized, picked one, found another they liked, then another. They finally settled on a thick yellow paper with a border of butter cream, sage, and lavender hearts. It took us two days to wallpaper the room. Jack popping in every so often, telling the girls to call him when they gave up, with a wink to me, my belly large—eight months pregnant—wallpaper glue stuck to my hair. The girls shouted for him to get lost. He'd bet them twenty dollars they'd be begging for his help after an hour. They shoved him out the door, and he caught my eye before he shut it. The look on his face said he was lucky. He knew we were lucky.

I moved to where the crib once was. Next to it there was a window, and I opened it, glanced down to the sunflower garden below.

There was a noise from the hallway, and then my mother was in the doorway, out of breath.

"Is Kat up here?" she asked quickly.

"No. Why? I thought she was with you."

"She was with me. Right next to me and Jess in the basement, and then she said she forgot something in the car, and now I can't find her. I told Jess to check by the water and I'd look in the house."

I looked out the window at the ocean. The sun shining off the blue water. The tide was out, and a dark stretch of sand was uncovered. Something yellow caught my eye, and I squinted, not able to make it out.

Then there was Jess, running across the lawn to the flash of yellow, to the water. Not jogging. Sprinting. As if every second mattered.

I flew past my mother, out the bedroom door, my mother following me, calling absurdly from behind me to be careful on the stairs, the yellow finding its place in my mind—Kat's backpack that she'd insisted on holding on her lap on the ride over.

She knew better than to be at the ocean by herself. It was a rule. One she'd never broken. Until now.

The lawn ended at a stone wall with a four-foot drop to the beach below. But the flash of yellow I'd seen wasn't at the wall. Or on the beach. It was farther out, at the water, where the ocean began and stretched for miles and miles.

In front of me, Jess reached the wall and disappeared over it, out of my view. I ran after her, my legs pumping as fast I could get them to move, my lungs burning. There was panic. Then anger. What the hell did she think she was doing? Low tide would have the water thirty or forty yards out, but when it came in, it came fast.

Kat knew this. Her father was a fisherman. She didn't need to be told the sea had its own set of rules. She'd heard the stories we all knew by heart. Boats sunk or damaged. Men hurt or missing. Sometimes found. Many times not. She knew better than to be out there alone.

It was only five minutes before I reached the wall, but time moved in slow motion. The girls were two dots in the distance, the sun flashing off the water, blinding me. I ran to them, the only sound my breathing and the slap of my soles against the packed sand. Somewhere in the sky above, a seagull let out a shriek, a shrill cry filling the air.

When I was closer, I saw that the girls were standing in the water, the yellow backpack floating between them, the ocean lapping at their feet, the tide already making the turn in.

Jess was holding something. Holding it the air, away from her body.

It was another minute before I reached them. Kat was crying, her face red and tearstained, a scowl on her face. The backpack was at her feet, open and on its side, water filling it with every wave. Next to it was a wooden brown box, half-submerged.

Jess's face was blank, her arm straight out in front of her. In her hand was a bag full of ashes. It took me a moment to register. Maddie.

"Take it," Jess said to me urgently. "She was trying to dump it in the ocean."

I reached out, dumbfounded, looking from the ashes, now in my hand, to Kat, to the box tumbling in the water at our feet.

"I wasn't dumping it," Kat screamed through her sobbing. She bent down and took the box out of the water. "You made me drop it, and now *look*." She grabbed the bottom of her T-shirt and frantically rubbed the cotton against the wood, trying to dry it even though water streamed from the corners.

Jess hadn't moved, her expression a mixture of emotions that I knew mirrored my own: confusion, shock, disbelief.

My fingers were curled around the plastic bag, my other hand supporting it from the bottom. I hadn't blinked since Jess thrust it at me, hadn't breathed, it seemed.

There was a noise behind us, a shout, my mother in the distance, standing on the lawn, the word *okay* making its way out to us. I held up my hand, signaling that we were, and she put her hand to her heart to show her relief.

I turned back to the girls. Time stopped. No one moved. No one spoke. There was just the sound of the ocean. And Kat's sniffling.

I wondered how long Kat had hidden the ashes. When had she taken them from my closet? How had she even known they were there?

I thought back to this morning, picturing them in the closet. But I hadn't seen them, I realized.

I'd looked at what I always looked at: her baby blanket, the one I wrapped around the wooden box the first day I'd brought it into the house and placed it on the shelf in my closet. I hadn't taken it down from the shelf once the entire year.

I couldn't bring myself to touch it, knowing the smell of the blanket would gut me. The softness of it against my cheek would bring me to my knees. The thought of her wrapped in it, fresh and clean out of her bath, would put me on the floor.

Now Kat looked over at me, her face flushed. Her voice was hoarse, choked. "She's supposed to be in her favorite place. So I brought her," she said.

I swallowed, choosing my words carefully. "This is something important, Kat. Something we should do together. As a family."

"You told Dad you didn't want to. You fought about it. I heard you."

"I meant that I wasn't ready. Not that I didn't want to."

"Well, that's not fair. Dad's ready. I'm ready. And Jess is ready. Aren't you?" Kat asked Jess, whose eyes were still on the ashes.

"Where has that been?" Jess asked. "How did you even get it?"

"In Mom's closet," Kat said. "Way up on the shelf where it's

pitch-black and scary. She would have never wanted to be in there."
Kat looked at the ashes cradled in my arms. "I brought her here because she loved it. Remember? She'd crawl right to the edge of the
water, and you'd chase her and pick her up, and she'd cry and kick
her legs and make you put her down. Then she'd just crawl around
at the edge all day, slapping at the water, splashing it everywhere."

Jess looked at where Kat pointed, a faraway look on her face
that seemed to say, *Yes, I remember.*

Her words sunk into me, and I shut my eyes, desperate to block
out the image. But there she was, scurrying across the hard-packed
sand. And there was Jack, standing guard in the shallow surf, de-
livering her to higher ground now and then, carrying her under
the arms, and holding her out from his body to avoid her flailing
limbs. *Want a water baby?* he'd say, placing her on the blanket next
to me, where she'd abruptly turn and crawl to the water again.

I didn't open my eyes. I didn't speak. If I did, my voice would
fail, and the girls would hear me sobbing. They'd see my anguish.
My despair.

For a full year, they didn't know their sister was on a shelf in my
bedroom closet. I'd kept her there. Away from them.

Away from Jack too.

And now he was sick from working all those hours on the water.
Hours he worked so he didn't have to be home, fighting with me
about spreading the ashes, or selling the Salt House, or arguing
over the contents of the bank statements on my desk. Statements
that I refused to open, as if by ignoring them, I could pretend they
didn't say we were out of money. Pretend they didn't say, *See.*
Look what you *did.*

I swallowed, steadying myself against the urge to grab the
ashes, put them back in the box, bring them home, and wrap them
in the blanket again.

I hadn't been prepared to do this today. Not in a million years could I have imagined this moment, how it would unfold. I thought of the last time I'd talked about spreading her ashes, my mother's words. *Sometimes in life what you think is going to happen is nothing like what actually happens.*

I hadn't believed her. I'd been afraid of this moment, afraid of everything I would feel, afraid of everything I had lost.

But that fear had robbed us. Robbed us of talking about her, of sharing our memories of her.

My daughters were waiting. There was no turning back from this moment. The last year had been leading up to this. Somehow we'd managed to survive losing her, each of us in our own way.

But now we had to figure out how to live without her. Together.

With the ashes pressed against my chest, and the cold Atlantic rising, and my daughters surrounding me, I thought of the letters Josie had given me from our readers. Every one of them telling me: *you are not alone.*

I took a deep breath and opened my eyes. The sun was radiant, the light off the surface sparkling the water, blinding me.

I blinked the girls into focus. The water was now waist deep on Kat. I held out my hand to her and she took it. I looked at Jess, not speaking, but she saw my face, and nodded, as if agreeing.

We waded through the surf to the beach. Kat put the backpack on the sand and gently placed the box on top of it. When she turned to me, I held the bag of ashes out to her.

"You're right," I said. "She doesn't belong in my closet. And this was her favorite place. So let's spread them together. Just a little, though. Because I think the next time we should be together as a family. Okay?"

Kat reached out slowly, and took the bag, then paused, holding it in midair. "We can save some for Daddy," Kat said. "And for

Grandma. There's a whole bag, you know." She held it up, offering proof.

Kat put the bag on the sand, and one by one, we reached in and took out a handful of ashes. Then we stood side by side, our toes at the edge of the ocean, the water in front of us shimmering under the bright sun.

"Ready?" Kat yelled. I heard Jess call back that she was.

I looked down at my hand, my fist full of ashes. Tears blurred my vision. But my mouth opened and the air filled my lungs, and I was calling the girls to me, finding my voice, yelling that I was ready.

We formed a circle, the shallow water under our feet clear and calm.

We held our hands out, opened them, and the ashes stirred, but our bodies blocked the wind, a cocoon shielding what was left, protecting the perfect circles of ash in the center of our palms.

We turned and faced the water. A moment later, out of the corner of my eye, I saw arms swing and ashes billowed out before us.

The sky in front of us was awash with a film of silvery white, sparkling and luminous above the sunlit ocean. Gusts of ocean air, salty and thick, grabbed hold of the opaque cloud, and suddenly it was alive and swirling. A life of its own, rising and falling with each tug of the wind. I felt my daughters lean against me, one on each side, their arms circling around me, our faces turned to the sky.

"Bye, Maddie," Kat whispered, waving her small hand.

A quiet good-bye as the last of her ashes scattered soundlessly in the gasps of salted air.

21

Jack

Monday started out bad and got worse. I was soaked through when I woke up, feeling like I hadn't slept in days, even though I could count on one hand the hours I'd been awake since Saturday. Awake wasn't even the right word. Alive was more like it. Breathing. Existing in a state of fever and delirium and pain.

I'd slept through Sunday. Or most of it. When I was awake, I was convincing Hope it was just the flu. She'd made soup, and I'd had a few sips of it, my appetite gone. It was raining outside, and Kat was watching TV. She asked me to sit next to her on the couch. I must have fallen asleep again, because then it was dinnertime and Hope was pushing more soup at me.

Later in bed, Hope was talking about the Salt House, but my eyes wouldn't stay open. My head roaring as if a train was running through it again. And then suddenly the clock read six in the morning.

I got out of bed quietly, trying not to wake Hope. It was still raining out, but I had traps to pull. They'd sat Saturday as it was. I got my stuff together and left before Hope woke up. I had to stop in the shop to get some bait I'd put in the freezer and was surprised to see Boon's truck in his parking space outside the shop.

I was more surprised to see him sitting behind the counter,

straight-backed, a cup of coffee in front of him. He didn't get up from his seat when I came in, just looked at me, as if he'd been watching for me in the parking lot.

"You look like you're waiting for a kid who's blown his curfew," I said.

"What I'm waiting for is a guy who should be home in bed."

"What?" I asked, walking past him to the freezer.

I opened the door, flicked the light switch, and walked into the cold air. The bait container was on the bottom shelf, and I knelt to grab it, my legs burning from the small motion. When I stood, Boon was in the doorway.

"Hope called on Saturday. Said you were sick."

"It's just a cold. Flu or something."

"She said you'd say that. She also said she knew you'd be here this morning even if you weren't better. She asked me to speak to you."

"Well, consider me spoken to." I popped the lid off the container to make sure I had the right one, and I heard him clear his throat.

"Where were you on Friday night?"

"Boon. I don't have time for this. I'm dealing with enough shit as it is."

"So I hear," he said, flat voiced.

I pressed the lid back on the container, and a sharp pain shot up my arm from the split knuckle that I'd wrapped before I left the house.

"What happened?" he asked, his eyes on the bandage.

"I cut it."

"On what?"

"I don't know. The engine."

He waited as if he expected me to elaborate. When I didn't, he massaged his temple with his finger. "I ran into Eddy when I got

here on Saturday. He was asking for you. Said some weird shit was
happening down by your boat Friday night."

I felt my jaw tighten when he said this, and tried to keep my face
from showing it.

"Said some girl with her shirt half off came running up the dock,
right near your boat." His voice was low, halting. I couldn't tell if
it was because it was early and he was still waking up or because he
didn't want to be having this conversation in the first place.

I raised my hand to stop him. "Don't worry about it. It was a
misunderstanding."

He lifted his eyebrows at me. "Before he left, he went to your
boat and there was blood on the deck. Not just a little. A pool of it."

The cold air of the freezer gave his voice an edge, even though
he was speaking in a tone I'd heard him use with Kat or Jess when
he was explaining something they didn't understand. I pressed the
palm of my hand into my eye socket, pushed against the heaviness
that had settled in my head.

"I said it was a misunderstanding."

"Well, help me understand the misunderstanding," he said, his
voice tight.

"It's the none-of-your-business type of misunderstanding."

Boon tossed the clipboard he was holding on the shelf, and it
skidded across the steel bars. He turned and kicked the door of the
freezer so hard, it bounced off the wall. When he turned, his face
was bright red.

"What the fuck is going on?" he growled.

I didn't want to talk about the other night with Boon, for more
reasons than I had fingers and toes. It was my problem, and it was
my problem to fix.

"Nothing you need to be involved in," I told him.

"Let me make that call. Your head's up your ass lately."

He was quiet, waiting for me to speak. He stared at me for a long moment, then shook his head back and forth.

"You think screwing another woman is going to help? Is that it?" he asked.

"What the hell are you talking about?" I looked down at my watch, frowning at the time.

"A woman gets off your boat in the middle of the morning with her damn tits hanging out, and you want to tell me you're playing Parcheesi with her?"

He was in my face now, and I felt something rise up inside me, all the yelling and words from the other night swirling inside my head and making me dizzy. The fact that he thought I'd cheat on Hope hit me somewhere deep inside, somewhere I hadn't expected. I wanted to slam him up against the shelves and make him eat his words. I wanted to beat the words back into his mouth, to smash the thought from his head that I was the kind of man who would cheat on his wife and kids.

"Is that what you think? You think I was fooling around with the woman on my boat?"

"No, I don't," he said quietly. "But now I have your attention. So talk to me about what's going on."

"There's nothing going on. How many different ways can I say it?"

"You can say it six ways from Sunday, and I'm telling you don't bullshit a bullshitter. I put the word out on Saturday that I was looking to find out what happened on your boat. And you know who called me? Keith Miller." He waited for my reaction, tilted his head at me.

"Keith said you two met out on the water a while ago, and he was worried because you didn't seem good. He wouldn't say how that went down, given that you work out of different harbors and neither of you are exactly friendly. Which tells me something right there," he said accusingly.

I kept my expression blank, trying to push that day out of my head. How I'd chased Keith's boat and told him I was cutting Finn's traps. I felt the back of my neck turn hot, embarrassed by the memory of it.

"You know what else he said?" Boon continued. "He said you might be messing with Finn again. Did you know he's back in town? That he's got his boat in one of the slips? Did you know that?"

I could tell from the way he asked that he knew the answer. I nodded, and he attempted a grin, but it just looked like he was baring his teeth at me.

"Yeah. I thought you might." He chuckled. A sweat broke out on his forehead, even though the air in the freezer was frigid.

"So is he part of the nothing that's going on here? The none-of-my-business type of *misunderstanding*?" He reached out and yanked my arm up, holding my bandaged hand in the air. "You cut your hand on the engine? Give me a fucking break. Go take a look at your boat. The blood's gone, but the stain is still there. Unless that engine was running in the middle of your deck, and you walked in here cut up in ribbons, that blood didn't come from this."

I pulled my arm from his grip. "I'm going to say it one more time, Boon. Leave it alone." I couldn't involve Boon in this. Cutting those traps had been my fight. My mistake. Not his.

"You know, I may not be their real uncle." His finger pointed to the door, gesturing I assumed to the picture of the girls in the hallway. "But you're a fucking brother to me. You know what this year's been like? Having to watch the people I call family fall into a million pieces and there's nothing I can do about it?"

I stepped away from him, the emotion in his voice making me uncomfortable. He looked as worn-out as I felt. For a moment I considered telling him what happened. But Boon knew too much, and his temper was unmanageable. I didn't trust that he'd let me handle it. There was no way in hell that if Boon knew, he'd stay out of it. Not after the year he'd been through with us. And by cutting those traps, I'd put myself on the wrong side of Boon. It wasn't who he was. It wasn't even who I was. Or who I had been. Now he grabbed the clipboard off the shelf and shoved it against my chest so hard, I stumbled backward.

"Eddy needs two dozen oysters. Leave them in the front case with the yellow copy of the slip." He stomped away. "Maybe that half-naked woman will magically appear on my boat," I heard him mumble before his office door slammed shut.

By the time I got to the boat, it was late. I started the engine, my hand on the throttle, when I heard someone shout from the dock. I turned to see Gwen Arden walking toward me from the other side of the pier. I shut the engine and waited.

Gwen had grown up a street away from me. We graduated the same year from Alden High School, and she was the owner of Arden Fisheries, one of our top competitors. She was a tall woman, with a face as pale as a scallop shell and a head full of carrot-colored hair. After graduation, Gwen moved west, worked as a ski instructor at one of the big resorts. When her father died, she came back and took over the family business. A rumor went round that a lobster-man from the next town over went to Gwen's buying station a week after their tryst, and she'd sent him packing, said the lobsters were too small, not up to her standard, with a nod to his middle section.

Gwen and I had ended up at the same table at a wedding of a mutual friend a few years back. Hope and Gwen had sat next to each other, chatting away. At some point, with the band playing loud and more than a few drinks in, Gwen had offered up that the rumor was true . . . and she'd made it known on purpose. Turns out she got tired of being hit on by every Tom, Dick, and Harry who sold to her.

"Try being a single woman in this business," she'd said. "I used to get harassed and ogled all the time. Now guys go out of their way to keep it professional unless they want to sell their catch somewhere else."

"Was it that bad?" Hope had asked.

"Mostly the married ones, unfortunately. You landed one of the good ones here," she said, jabbing her thumb at me.

I stayed out of the conversation, but I heard what she was saying. I'd worked in this business my whole life, been down on the docks since I was a boy. I tuned it out now, didn't even hear it anymore. But now and then, over the radio, a guy would go too far, and I'd bark out to take it somewhere else. I had my own girls at home. I had a new respect for Gwen after that night. It was a tough business, and she'd found a way to hold her own.

Now Gwen reached the boat and walked over to the gunwale to where I stood.

"I'm glad I caught you. Thanks for waiting," she said.

"What's up?" I asked, hearing the impatience in my voice. I wanted to get out on the water. I had a bunch of traps to pull.

"Maybe nothing, but I wanted to give you and Boon a heads-up." She looked behind her and lowered her voice. "I had someone call me yesterday, a girl, called herself Bess, or Tess, I don't know, it was hard to hear her—sounded like she was calling from a pay phone. Anyway, she was trying to sell me a couple hundred pounds of lobster." She paused for a moment and looked around.

"And?" I asked, glancing at my watch. Almost seven fucking o'clock. Jesus.

"She was evasive about what boat she was off of. Said it was her boyfriend's boat, and he was sick in bed. She gave me a name I never heard of. Now, I know everyone in this area. You're pulling a couple hundred pounds of lobster, I know your name, if you know what I mean." She had her hands on her hips and seemed to be getting riled up talking about it.

"Did you meet with her?" I asked, trying to figure out what she wanted so I could get to work.

"I tried. Believe me, I tried. Oh, no, she wanted nothing to do with meeting me. One excuse after another of why this couldn't be a face-to-face deal. She wanted me to come get the lobsters . . . she couldn't be there . . . had to tend to her boyfriend. But I could leave the cash in the boat . . . in an envelope in the cabin!"

"What'd you tell her?"

"I told her she was out of her flippin' mind," she screeched. "I mean, what the hell kind of business does she think I run? We've got a coastline of lobstermen trying to off-load their catch, and I'm going to schlep on down to some mystery boat carrying a boatload of cash. Wacko." She took a deep breath, and I looked at my watch, then back at her.

"Gwen. Tell me what you need." I was done being patient. I had my own lobsters to haul.

"Did Boon talk to her? Did she call you guys to sell them?"

"I have no idea."

"He didn't mention anything?"

"No. But he wouldn't. I catch; he buys and sells. End of story. Plus, you know Boon. Boon likes women. If a woman invited Boon to a boat by himself, he'd go."

Gwen nodded. "I get your point. But keep your ears open. My guess is the lobster was stolen."

I gave her a doubtful look. That was a death sentence around here. "That's not just one or two traps; that's a trawl, maybe more."

"I hear you, Jack, but I'm telling you this girl wasn't right. She sounded high, drugged up. And she didn't have a clue about lobsters. I asked her to give me her boyfriend's buoy colors, and I could tell from the silence that she had no idea what I was talking about. She hung up on me when I pressed her on where she got the catch."

The sky was white now; a dull stretch of gray darkened the edge of the horizon. Gwen turned to see what I was looking at, then tapped her hand on the wash rail, a quick rap of her knuckles.

"Go. Weather's coming. Tell Boon what happened, and keep your ears open."

"You got it," I said, turning the key to start the engine.

"Tell Hope I said hello," she yelled.

I raised my hand to signal I'd heard her as the *Hope Ann* pulled away from the dock.

Once I was out of the cove, the sea turned choppy. Waves slammed against the hull and sent a cold spray over the bow. I kept her at twenty knots, a good clip to get me out there in a hurry.

Turner Point was a narrow slab of rock jutting out into the water. I rounded the tip, followed the curve, and slipped in closer to shore, where massive walls of jagged rock sprung up from the ocean, a dense wall of trees settled on the edge. On a sunny day, the cliffs looked as if they were on fire, the light turning the reddish-brown slabs of granite into a blinding wall of orange flame. Today the granite face of the cliff was dark, the water below it an inky dark blue.

The ache in my back had turned to flat-out pain. The fever was back. I felt it in every inch of my body. It was hard to concentrate. The choppy water had turned to five-foot swells by the time I pulled alongside my strings, cranking the wheel until I was next to the buoy. I put her in neutral and pulled off a couple of layers, stripping down to a T-shirt and Grundens. I was burning up as it was, and looking at a full day's work. I'd pulled almost three hundred pounds from this patch of bottom last week, and now the soak time had been more days than I'd planned with missing Saturday. Plus, I needed the traps to be full, needed to pull at least three hundred pounds. Or more, for that matter. The bank had called again, looking for this month's payment on the Salt House. They'd left a message reminding me it was a week late. As if I needed a reminder of the money I didn't have.

I leaned over, gaffed the buoy, and put the warp in the hauler. When the trap came to the surface, I pulled it up, balancing it on the rail. I stared at it, squinted, not sure I was seeing things correctly. The door was wide open, the trap empty except for a few crabs and some kelp.

I moved the trap off the rail and set it on the deck, examining it to see if the closure had somehow failed. But there was no damage to it.

I'd repaired these traps in the beginning of the season, replacing all the J clips and rigging new cord for the mesh hooks that secured the trap. The white clips still looked new, not one missing, and the hook was intact.

There were only two ways for a door to open: either the door failed or someone opened it. And this door was brand-new.

I turned and flicked on the hydraulics, pulling up the second trap. The whir of the hauler matching the buzz in my head, my body tighter than the line rising out of the water. The trap cleared the surface. I didn't reach for it, just shut off the hydraulics, and watched as the trap twirled, suspended over the water, the door swinging wildly.

Water poured out of the empty trap. Not even a crab in this one. Just a dead dogfish, its mouth slack, hanging open, almost as if it were laughing at me, mocking me.

I looked at the water, trying to think clearly through the pounding in my skull, a deafening drone in my head. I pressed my hands against my ears, pushing back at the pain, the noise swirling inside, growing louder and louder until I felt my mouth open and a shout spill out. I kicked at the trap on the deck, sending it sliding to the stern.

By the third trap, I knew before it was fully out of the water that the door would be open, the trap empty. That the lobsters had been taken out, stolen. I didn't need to pull all of them to know what I was going to find. Every trap on this trawl would be empty, as would the ones on the trawl twenty yards off my port side.

The conversation with Gwen earlier at the dock ran on high speed through my mind. Her voice slamming into me, *she sounded high, drugged up.* I looked at my hand, felt it split against Finn's nose, and saw the girl weaving as she left the dock.

I threw the traps back in the water, tossing the buoy over the side. I turned the boat and headed in, pushing the diesel engine as hard as she would go through the swells. I kept my hand on the throttle, my full weight pushing against it, the gash in my knuckle opening against the pressure, a circle of red appearing on the bandage. The hull pounded against the sea, water slamming into the windshield and over the rails with each wave.

The radio cackled above me, and I heard Boon's voice, saying *Kelly, pick up, Kelly, pick up.* I turned the radio off, tried to concentrate on keeping the boat from taking a wave sideways at the speed I was going.

I turned the corner into the cove at full throttle. I slowed at the No Wake buoy, looking over at Finn's slip, but his boat was gone, the slip empty. The roar of the diesel engine matched the thunder in my head. I came in too fast and threw her in reverse to avoid hitting the dock. I shut her off, jumping over the rail before the boat came to a stop.

I tied the bow line in a quick figure eight and took the gang-plank in two strides, heading to the parking lot. I heard my name, once, then again. I kept walking, reached the truck, climbed in and reversed, the tires kicking up small stones under the tires. I pulled out of the space and saw Boon, in the doorway of the shop, less than fifty yards away, his mouth forming my name. I put the truck in gear and drove off.

Drops of water rolled off the bibs I was wearing, and the windows fogged as soon as I pulled into traffic. I turned west off the main road, my foot itching to slam down on the gas pedal.

The streets just outside the center of town were a maze of narrow, tree-lined roads with cedar-planked houses, one resembling the next. Widow's walks sat perched on rooftops high above the tree line, and cobblestoned sidewalks hemmed the road. Every inch of me wanted to drive as fast as my mind was racing, but I kept to the speed limit.

It wasn't until I crossed the railroad tracks onto Route 45, the street opening wide and flat, that my leg gave in to the tension, my foot pressing the gas pedal until it touched the floor of the truck. I wasn't even sure I could find Finn, but I remembered Hope had said something about Peggy hating the house, with the train tracks right on top of her. There was only one neighborhood where the tracks ran through, a large cul-de-sac of duplexes known as the circle when I was growing up.

There was a new sign at the entrance of the circle with *Magnolia Hill* written on it—even though the street sat at the bottom of a listless stretch of road, and the only trees that rimmed the pavement were a handful of scruffy, overgrown pines. It was adjacent to the town dump, and when I turned into the circle, a whiff of decay seeped in the crack of the window.

I pulled over at the first duplex with a car parked in the driveway. An old guy wearing nothing but a bathrobe over his basket-ball-sized stomach answered the door and didn't know Finn, but his wife came up behind him and pointed to a house farther down the street.

I pulled in the driveway next to an older truck, hopped out, and was up the steps in two. The doorbell didn't ring when I pressed it, so I opened the screen and used my fist to bang on the wooden door. The sound of it echoed, bouncing around the semicircle of houses.

The door opened, and a boy wearing a baseball hat looked out at me. A look of surprise washed over his face, or it struck me at first as surprise. I waited for him to ask who I was, what I wanted, and I realized the look on his face wasn't so much surprise as rec-ognition. He knew who I was. That much was clear.

He stepped back from the doorway, and I could've easily stepped in, but I backed up down the stairs.

"Come out here," I said.

I thought he might hesitate, but he stepped out of the house quickly, followed me down the steps, and stood across from me on the front walk. He took off his hat and held it in his hands. It struck me as strangely polite, considering the circumstances.

"You know me," I said, more of a statement than a question.

"Yeah, I mean, yes, sir."

I studied him. He was a boy, about Jess's age, I guessed. I won-dered how he'd gotten himself into this mess.

"And you know why I'm here?"

He nodded, his cheeks coloring.

"I meant to come talk to you. I mean, I should've come to talk to you," he said.

If it'd been Finn standing in front of me admitting to stealing my catch, I don't think I could've stopped myself from lunging at him, but this was just a kid, half my size. And he didn't give the impression that running away was an option. It struck me as too easy, too *cordial,* this confrontation.

I'd expected teeth knocked out, possibly even mine. I'd been itching for it, to let go of everything, funnel the past year out of me, through my fist and straight into Finn's face. Now this kid with his wide eyes and baby face was standing here instead of Finn, offering up some sort of apology?

"You're lucky I have a kid your age, because my first instinct is to knock your block off."

He took a step back and folded his arms across his chest, a look of distaste appeared on his face, and then left just as quickly, as if he knew enough to hide it. But I saw it, and it fueled me.

I stepped closer to him. "Does that surprise you? You look surprised."

He stepped back again. "I don't know."

"You don't know?"

"I mean; I know you deserve an explanation."

"An explanation? You think that's what I'm here for?"

"And an apology," he said quickly. "I mean, that goes without saying."

I felt my neck tense. He seemed to sense that he was making things worse, and he backed up another step, until he was standing several feet away from me on the small patch of grass that pretended to be a front lawn.

"Look, Mr. Kelly. I know I was wrong, but . . ."

"Wrong?" I took a step forward and grabbed the front of his shirt and pulled him to me. Not hard, but enough that he tripped forward a step.

"Whoa," he said, his eyes wide and his arms in the air, palms outstretched.

"Stand up," I told him. I gave him a frustrated shake, and dropped his shirt.

"I was standing," he said, a look of disbelief on his face, "before you dragged me over to you."

"You're lucky I'm not dragging you down the street by your neck, you little shit. That was mine, what you took," I said. "Wrong doesn't even come close to describing it. Around here, people die for doing what you did."

He looked bewildered, which made me even angrier.

"What the hell did you think was going to happen when I found out?" I asked. "A slap on the wrist?"

I grabbed him by the collar again, his shirt bunched in my fist. He didn't resist, just kept his hands at his sides, making it clear he was going to let me beat him to a pulp without defending himself.

"I didn't take anything," he said quietly.

"What?"

"It wasn't like that." He shook his head at me, and gave me a look that suggested I'd let him down in some way.

I let go of his shirt and stepped away. "What the hell are you talking about?"

His face was as red as the Sox cap on the ground. "Look, I don't know why you'd think that. But I promise there was no . . . taking . . . I mean doing . . . with Jess," he stammered and then stopped, looked me in the eye. "Whatever you think happened didn't. Not even close."

I squinted at him. "Did you just say Jess?"

He looked at me sideways. "Um, yeah."

"Jess, as in Jessica? My daughter?" I asked, dumbfounded.

He nodded slowly, as if now he wasn't so sure either.

"You've got two seconds to talk."

"I don't know what to say." His words came out fast, desperate. "I'm sorry Jess is upset—it was my fault. And I was going to say sorry to you and Mrs. Kelly—I promised my mother I would apologize for not introducing myself to you, but I only got home last night . . ."

His words swirled around my head, clogging my ears, blocking the air from my nose. I blinked at the kid. He was standing in front of me, but he seemed to be getting farther and farther away.

I bent over, put my hands on my knees, felt a tightness in my chest.

"Mr. Kelly? You all right?" I heard him say from miles away.

I felt his hand on my back, then his arm on my elbow, leading me to the front steps. I sat down heavily, leaned against the railing.

"Shit," I heard the kid whisper.

The pain in my back had turned sharp, searing, and the air seemed to be thick and cumbersome. The roaring in my head was back, as if that train that ran through their backyard had suddenly rolled in and taken a left turn straight through my skull. I tried to stand, but my legs gave way until I was sitting back on the step. I blinked and forced myself to take a deep breath, and the kid's face came into focus. He was on one knee in front of me, a cell phone in his hand.

"Mr. Kelly. Should I call for help?"

I shook my head, stood up on wobbly legs, sat back down again.

"Um, I think I should. You don't look good."

"Stop talking," I said, rocking slowly back and forth. I breathed in deep, tried to block out the noise, tried to get my heart to return to its normal pace.

"Who are you?" I whispered.

"Alex Chester. Peggy's son."

I opened one eye, took in the slim build, the darker skin tone, not one feature resembling Finn. I heard Hope's voice from the other night talking about Peggy, and Jess, and some kid I didn't know. I remember she'd said, *Are you awake? It's* important.

"Chester? Finn's not your father?"

"Stepfather. Well, for now." He glanced up at the house. "He's not living here anymore," he said.

"Where is he?"

"I don't know. He came by earlier, but he left. He's probably on his boat. He keeps it on the waterfront. Not far from your boat."

"You've been on my boat?"

"No . . . I've seen it, that's all." His face went red again.

"You're sure about that?"

"I'm positive. We sat at the slip when you were gone, and I've seen you motor in and out, but we never went on the boat. You can ask Jess."

"Right," I said, "Jessica."

"Mr. Kelly," he said, "I'm not sure what you want me to say."

"I came here for Finn. I don't have a clue what you're talking about with Jessica. When you apologized, I assumed it was for stealing from my traps."

He let out a long breath. Then he bent and put his hands on his knees, breathed out.

"Jesus," he said. "I thought you thought . . . you know, that something happened with me and Jessica. I mean, something more than what happened."

"Tell me what he said when he was here. Finn. Where was he going?"

"He was looking for my mother. He left her some flowers and said he had to take care of some things."

I turned and looked through the screen door into the house. On the table was a vase full of roses. "That's it?" I asked.

His forehead creased. He paused, thinking, it seemed. "No. He was rambling. Sort of manic. He said he wanted me to know that things would be different from now on."

"Different how?"

"I don't know. I didn't ask. His face was a mess. Black eyes, crooked nose. But he was sober. I figured that's what he meant. He said to tell my mother he'd be out on the water for the next couple of hours. That he had traps to bait. Then he left."

I heard his voice, but it seemed far away, and the world was suddenly spinning. I heard him call my name. But I was walking away, already in the truck, heading back to the water.

Things would be different.

Finn would have banked some money selling my catch. The roses, the new outlook. I'm sure everything looked brighter now that he'd moved in on my territory. Now that he had a way to make money.

Traps to bait.

My cell phone buzzed on the passenger seat next to me. I must have left it in the truck while I was out on the boat. I picked it up, and saw Boon's name on the screen. I let it ring, not wanting to go another round with him. I saw that he'd called a dozen times. I tossed it on the seat. He never knew when to leave it alone.

I drove as fast as the truck would allow, slowing only when I reached the dock, the truck skidding sideways and lurching into the parking lot. I didn't bother parking, just drove straight to the loading dock and jumped out, leaving the keys in the ignition. I heard Boon calling my name from above when I reached the boat. I ignored him, untied the lines, climbed aboard, and started the engine, reversing out of the slip.

In less than five minutes, I passed the No Wake Buoy, pressing my palm against the throttle, the engine screaming, the hull slamming against the swells, the buzzing in my head deafening.

Ten minutes later, I swung the boat around Turner Point, my

territory in front on me. A boat with twin engines idling, surrounded by my traps. My empty traps.

I headed for the stern of the boat, steaming for it, my head screaming, a fury inside that had slipped away from me, uncontrollable now.

When had he pulled them? Saturday maybe.

But most likely Sunday, when it was illegal to haul. When no one would have seen him. And then he'd had the girl sell the catch.

The *Hope Ann* was less than twenty yards off Finn's port side when he looked up, his face registering that a forty-foot lobster boat was bearing down on him. He was at the rail, my buoy on his deck, a trap at his feet. He put his hand up, words coming out of his mouth that were lost in the air.

I headed straight for his twin engines. Finn waved at me to stop, the bow of the *Hope Ann* barreling at him, the engine needle pushing into the red on the tachometer on the dash. Finn put both hands up now, screaming *STOP* over and over.

He scrambled to the middle of the boat and crouched in a squat, clutching the seats to steady himself against the collision, against the blow of my boat plowing into his stern.

But I threw the engine into reverse at the last second, spun the wheel, slamming her into neutral. The *Hope Ann* rocked violently with the motion, throwing me to the deck but barely scraping against the side of Finn's boat. I'd planned to be on his boat before he even had time to think. But suddenly I couldn't breathe, couldn't move hardly, the pain in my back making me gasp for air. I was flat on the deck, gulping, a fish out of water.

I closed my eyes and made myself get up, my knee underneath me, pushing up onto one leg, then the other. When I stood, Finn was lifting his head up from his hands, his eyes wild.

I ignored the pain, letting the rage inside of me do all the work.

The knife was next to me in the sheath at the rail, but I knew if I took it on his boat, I'd use it. My fists would have to do the work, and the black bruises on his face told me I'd done some damage the other night.

I grabbed hold of the pot hauler, put a leg up and pulled myself up on the narrow rail. The boat pitched in the waves, and I grabbed the metal bar of the hauler with two hands, clinging to it to steady myself.

Finn saw me and screamed something I couldn't hear, motioning for me to get down.

The rail was slick, my boots sliding, my legs screaming under the strain of trying to balance on the thin strip of wood. The wind had kicked up, the swells crashing into the side of the boat, and suddenly I knew I wouldn't make the jump over to Finn's boat, that whatever sickness I'd been fighting had won.

My legs were rubber underneath me. The water and wind swirling around my head. My hand was clinging to the metal bar of the pot hauler, stopping me from falling to the deck or into the ocean below.

Finn's boat was drifting away from me, the water dark and swollen between us. I squeezed my eyes shut, trying to stop the spin in my head, the numbness that was spreading through me.

My foot slid off the rail. My head smashed off the metal bar, and for a moment, I was balancing on one leg, my arms around the hauler, straining to hold my weight.

The heel of my boot slammed against the rail, and I was on two feet again. A voice in my head screamed at me to *get down,* or maybe it was Finn, standing across from me, pointing to something behind me.

I turned, but it was too late, a wave already cresting over the bow of the boat, slamming into the hull of *Hope Ann.*

My legs collapsed. There wasn't anything left in me to hold on. The hauler slipped through my arms. My body pitched forward, the black water below me rising with a swell, coming, it seemed, to swallow me.

There was no sound when I hit the water. Just the enveloping cold. And the tug downward. The pull of the water against my drained body.

My head was above the water, my face tilted to the sky, but there was no air left to breathe. Black stains edged in from the corners of my eyes.

And then there was nothing but darkness and a paralyzing cold and Hope's voice, begging me over and over and over to go to the doctor.

22

Jess

I could've slept in on Monday. Boon said not to come in until noon. But my eyes opened and it wasn't even eight o'clock and I was wide awake.

I gave it another half hour before I finally gave up and got out of bed. There was a note on the kitchen table from my mother that she was out to breakfast with my grandmother and Kat. I poured a glass of orange juice and sat down at the kitchen table when my cell phone buzzed. I looked at the screen and saw Alex's name. I felt my heart speed up.

I reached over and answered it and heard a rustling noise on the other end.

"Jess," Alex shouted. "You're there."

"What's wrong?" I asked, my heart jumping at the sound of his voice.

"I'm not sure. Maybe nothing. It's your dad. He came to my house."

"Did you say my dad?" I asked, confused. I felt the room spin. He was at Alex's house? My *father?*

"Yeah. He was upset. Something about someone stealing from his traps."

He was talking fast, his voice dropping in and out. Through the phone, I heard a car horn wail.

"Where are you?" I asked.

"Driving to the dock. I just wanted to tell Ryland. See if I could catch him before he went out. I don't know what happened, but your dad seemed kind of crazy. Like he wanted to kill me kind of crazy."

"Kill you?" I yelled.

"Well, me at first. But then Ryland. Or somebody. Whoever messed with his traps, I guess."

"Did he say where he was going?"

"No. But he left here in a hurry. I'm thinking he went looking for Ryland."

"Pick me up," I said. "I'm going with you."

There was a pause on the other end. Then, "Jess. Let me check it out and I'll call you—"

"Alex. Pick me up, or I'll ride my bike down. Either way, I'm going."

I heard him sigh. "Fine. Be ready in five minutes," he said. "I'm not far from your house."

I tossed the phone on the counter, ran to my room, and changed into the first shorts I could find, holding the waistband with one hand while I dialed my father's cell phone with the other. It rang for what seemed like an eternity until it went to voice mail. I hung up and called again, tripping over my feet as the shorts stuck around my ankles. I hit the speaker button on the phone and pressed redial two more times in the time it took me to get dressed.

When I got his voice mail the fifth time, I gave up, threw the phone on the bed, and ran down to the front porch just as Alex pulled up to the curb.

He leaned over and opened the door and I got in, shutting the door in a hurry.

"I'm sorry," he said, glancing over at me as he pulled away from the curb. "I don't want to scare you if it's nothing."

I looked over at him. "Did it seem like nothing?" I asked, and he shook his head.

He was driving fast, and we both concentrated on the road ahead. A minute later, we were in the center of town when I heard a siren. I looked out the back window to see an ambulance on the road. A fire truck behind it.

Alex pulled over to let them pass, and we watched as they turned into the fish shop parking lot in front of us.

Alex stepped on the gas, maneuvering through traffic, following the ambulance. I was out of the car before he shut the engine, sprinting down the dock. I turned the corner and saw Boon at the end of the dock, near the water.

Two policemen stood next to him, all of them watching a boat tearing through the water, full throttle, straight at them, the No Wake buoy launching in the air from the large swells behind the speeding boat.

My feet hit the gangplank at the same time as Alex's, a loud clang ringing out over the sirens. Boon turned and saw me, a panic-stricken look on his face. He said something to the policeman, and then Boon was running at me, turning me around, pushing me back in the direction of the shop.

"Get in the shop," he shouted, then pointed at Alex. "Get her in the shop now, and don't come out until I get you." He stood in front of me, blocking my view of the water.

Behind him, the boat roared into the dock, slamming into the slip so hard that the wood shifted under our feet.

We stumbled, caught our footing. Boon looked over his shoulder at the boat, then looked back at Alex.

"Make her go. Now," he growled, grabbing my hand and motioning for Alex to take it. I felt Alex's arm around my shoulders, turning me. Two paramedics ran past us, a stretcher rolling between them.

I looked over my shoulder and saw a man on the boat. He was screaming at the paramedics, pointing at something on the deck of the boat. It took me a minute to realize it was Ryland Finn, his face bruised, black circles under each eye.

I yanked away from Alex, running toward the boat. Boon caught me and swung me around, trying to shield my view with his body, but it was too late. I saw Finn bend over and lift something up, throwing it over his shoulder. A rag doll, the limbs flopping lifelessly. Then Finn stepped off the boat onto the dock, turning to the stretcher, and the lifeless rag doll's head was in front of me, my father's face resting against Finn's back, blood in streaks down his face.

My legs gave out, and then Boon was half carrying, half walking me up the dock, lifting me in the air, pushing me forward. Tears were blinding me. I tried to turn around again, but Boon tightened his grip. "Walk, goddammit," he shouted.

He pushed me through the back door of the shop, Alex following behind us, and slammed the door once we were all in.

"Is he dead?" I cried, and Boon grabbed me by the shoulders. Alex was next to me, his face white.

"Stop it," Boon yelled. "I need you to calm down. Understand?" He glared at me. "Calm." He spread his hands out at me, gesturing for me to slow down. I gulped, my breath coming out in ragged hiccups.

"Now, listen to me. I'm going to call your mother, and then we're going to get in my truck and go to the hospital." He blew out a breath, rolled his eyes. "What a fucking shit show," he muttered.

The front door of the shop opened, and we heard footsteps, heavy and quick, and then Finn was in front of us, blood covering the front of his shirt.

"He's on his way," he said, motioning to the ambulance pulling out of the parking lot. "He's breathing, but I don't know how long he was under. It took me a couple of minutes—"

"Got it," Boon cut him off, and Finn glanced at me.

"Didn't you tell him I gave it back?" Finn asked, and Boon's face grew sharp, his eyes flaring at Finn.

"You think I have fucking time to unravel this mess right now?" Boon barked, and Finn put his hands up, nodding again.

"Where's his boat?" Boon asked.

"Still out there," Finn said. "Drifting. After I pulled him, I didn't want to waste time with the anchor. I didn't know, you know, if he was breath . . ." He glanced at me. "I just wanted to get him some help. Anyway. I'll go find the boat. Tow her in if I have to."

"I'll go with you," Alex offered. "I can drive her in." He looked at Boon, who held out his hand for Alex to shake.

"Thanks, man," Boon said to Alex. He walked to the front door, and I followed him.

"Jess. Wait," I heard Alex say from behind me. I turned and he was in front of me, his arms pulling me in, my face pressing against his T-shirt. He let me go, bending until his face was even with mine. "He's going to be fine," he whispered, and pressed his lips to my cheek, held them there for a moment before he pulled away. "I'll come to the hospital as soon as I can," he said, and jogged after Finn, who'd disappeared out the back door.

I walked out the door, feeling numb. Boon was waiting in his truck, the passenger door open. I climbed in, and when my seat belt was fastened, he reached over and gave my shoulder a squeeze.

"He's a tough nut, you know, your dad."

We watched as the firefighters piled into the truck in front of us. It was blocking our way, and it seemed like forever until the fire truck moved and we pulled out of the lot.

Boon gunned the truck, heading to the highway. The hospital was fifteen minutes away, in the next town over. The way Boon was driving, we had a chance of making it in ten.

"Your mother is on her way," Boon told me. "She wanted you to call her, but I told her to concentrate on driving."

I imagined my mother having a meltdown in the car after talking to Boon and my grandmother tapping her arm and saying, "Drive now. Enough nonsense. Life is ninety-nine percent how you handle it."

I knew it drove my mother bananas, my grandmother's one-liners. The other day my mother was sitting at the table with her head in her hands, her laptop in front of her when Grandma walked in and asked her what was wrong.

"Writer's block," my mother grumbled.

"Where there is no struggle, there is no progress," Grandma quipped.

After she left, my mother had looked at me.

"At least it wasn't 'that which does not kill us,' " I told her.

My grandmother never even finished that one. She'd just nod her head and let her voice trail off.

I was relieved my mother had Grandma with her now. Maybe she'd say something aggravating and keep my mother's mind off my father.

Boon turned the truck sharply to the right, and we merged onto the highway, my shoulder pressing against the soft pad of leather on the door. I saw the needle pushing eighty as we eased into the fast lane.

"Tell me what you know," he said, looking over at me.

I told him what I knew, which was next to nothing. He crinkled his nose when I mentioned Alex.

"How is this Alex character involved?"

"He's my friend. The one that called about Dad at his house."

"His house?"

"Yeah. Alex said Dad showed up there and was angry. Something about someone stealing from his traps."

Boon hit the steering wheel with his hand, swore under his breath.

"What?" I asked, alarmed, twisting in the seat to face him.

He shook his head, hit the steering wheel again.

"Boon!"

He glanced over at me and sighed. "God forbid he pick up the goddamn phone or answer the radio."

"Boon. I have no idea what you're talking about."

Boon looked over at me, sighed. "I got a call from Finn this morning. Right after your father left on his boat. Apparently, Finn's been going several rounds with your father these last couple of months. Things got messy the other night. Physical. And Finn went on a drinking bender and pulled your father's traps. Managed to off-load it somewhere down the coast. He woke up this morning with a hangover and an envelope of cash. When he put two and two together, he came to me. Rock-bottom sort of moment, he said. Anyway, I took the money back, said we wouldn't press charges, and sent him out to bait your father's traps. Then I spent the next hour trying to hunt down your father, but he wouldn't pick up."

"He must have found his traps empty. That's why he was at Alex's."

He looked over at me, confused. "Why would he go to your

friend's house? Wait. Is this the kid you had lunch with that day? Brown hair, had a baseball hat on, kind of goofy?"

"He's not goofy." It came out defensive. My face went from pink to red.

"Ah, the lady doth protest. . . ." Boon winked, and I saw he was just being Boon.

"Finn's his stepfather," I said.

Boon turned and looked at me. Looked at me for so long that I gave him a look and pointed at the road, reminding him that he was *driving*. He shook his head, his eyes sliding to the highway in front of us. "This keeps getting better," he muttered under his breath.

"What?"

"Nothing."

He kept his eyes on the road, his thumb drumming the edge of the steering wheel. But I saw his leg tense and felt the truck pick up speed, as if this news had sent a jolt from his brain to his foot.

"Um. What's going on?"

"Let's change the subject. When's school start?"

"I don't want to change the subject. What's the deal with Ryland Finn?"

Boon sighed. "It's old stuff. Nothing to do with your friend."

"Well, what does it have to do with? Why were they fighting in the first place?"

"Let's just say your father and Finn have a history. And not a good one."

I looked at him to continue, and he held up his hands, letting the wheel go for an instant before he put them both back on the wheel.

"I'm not going to say any more, Jess. It's not my business. Wasn't then and isn't now. I will say I'm glad it was Alex he found

and not Finn. Your father left the dock like he was shot out of a
cannon. Your friend must be able to hold his own to deal with your
father when he's like that."

"Wait. You saw him leave the dock this morning?"

"Saw him? I yelled to him, damn near chased him down.
Thought about getting in my truck and following him, but he was
gone. I didn't know where to start looking."

He turned off the exit and pulled into the entrance of the hospital, a sign marked *Emergency* leading us to a semicircle in front of
a pair of glass doors.

"You found him," I said quietly, looking out the window.

The electronic doors opened, and my mother rushed out to the
car. I opened the door and jumped down.

"He's okay," she said, pulling me into her. I felt my body go
slack when I leaned against her. "He's in with the doctor, but he's
okay."

She tilted forward with me still in her embrace and squeezed
Boon's outstretched hand through the passenger window.

"I'll park and be in," Boon said.

"What's wrong with him?" I asked my mother as we walked
into the hospital.

"Double pneumonia to start. Maybe a lung infection because
he ignored it." She muttered *stubborn* under her breath, then kissed
the side of my head. "A gash on his head from something. The
doctor was surprised his temperature wasn't higher with the infection, but he thinks the time in the water cooled his body down. But
he swallowed a bunch too, so there's that. That's all I know for
now. Go sit with your grandmother. I want to check in with the
nurses."

My grandmother was in the waiting area, and I gave her a hug,
sat down next to her. I let my head rest on the back of the chair and

closed my eyes. The relief I'd felt when my mother said my father would be okay was so overwhelming, it was almost numbing.

Over the last few weeks, it had felt like there was one of those metal merry-go-round things you find on old playgrounds living inside of me. There'd been one on the beach playground down the street before the town tore it down. Mom hated it, called it a *dangerous contraption*. Kat and I would beg to go on until she'd give in. She'd stand next to it, yelling at us to be careful while Kat and I got that thing spinning like crazy. I'd feel dizzy for hours after. But the ride was worth it.

Now, sitting in the chair with my eyes closed, my father alive and breathing somewhere in the hospital, all I felt was tired, as if whatever had been going round and round and round inside of me had simply run out of the oomph it needed to keep going.

We sat there for what seemed like years. Boon was on the phone, pacing in the hallway. I'd just stood up to stretch my legs when Alex walked through the door. He walked over to us, his hand already on the brim of his hat, fiddling with it nervously.

I introduced him to my mother and grandmother. After a round of hellos, we stood awkwardly in silence. My grandmother looked from me to Alex. Then excused herself to get a cup of coffee. My mother gazed blankly at us until my grandmother said, "Hope. Keep me company."

"Oh," my mother said, reaching down to get her pocketbook. When she saw that it wasn't at her feet, she turned to the row of chairs.

"It's on your arm." Alex pointed to the patchwork bag looped over her shoulder.

My grandmother snickered, and my mother slapped herself on the forehead, both of them shuffling down the hallway. When I looked at Alex, he was smiling.

"They're funny," he said.

"A hoot," I replied.

I thought we might have a moment alone, but Boon hung up the phone and walked over. He shook Alex's hand again, and before I knew it, we were seated in the chairs while Boon and Alex talked about *Hope Ann,* how he'd put her back on the slip and she seemed intact except for a broken pot hauler.

Then there was a noise in the hallway, and my mother was rushing toward us, my grandmother trailing behind. I got up and met her in the hallway. Boon followed behind.

"What's wrong?" I asked.

"Oh, nothing. I mean, it's not your father. In all the confusion, I forgot your sister has a half day at camp. She needs to be picked up. I want to be here when your father wakes up. I tried Peggy, but she's not answering." She looked at her cell phone and grimaced at it.

"Apparently I'm an unsafe driver," my grandmother huffed from over my mother's shoulder.

"That's not what I said. What I said was that the last time you drove my car, you said you couldn't reach the brake pedal."

"I said it was *difficult* to reach. Obviously I reached it or I wouldn't be here." She waved away my mother, who sighed.

"Let me do it," Boon suggested. "I haven't seen the squirt in days."

"You can't," my mother said. "There's a pickup list, and you're not on it."

"I'm on the list," Alex said from behind us. He got up from the chair and joined us in the hallway.

"I get my brother sometimes. I can drive, and Jess can get Kat. You know some of the counselors, right?" He looked at me.

"Are you sure you don't mind?" my mother asked. "Your whole morning has already been taken up by us—which frankly is another thing I'm confused about."

"I can probably take a stab at that," Boon said, and she looked at him, surprised. He gave her a look that said this wasn't the time to talk about it.

"I don't mind," Alex said, and turned to me. "Ready?"

I nodded, even though I felt the opposite of ready. My feet felt rooted to the ground.

"Wait," I said to my mother. "What should I tell Kat?"

"Don't tell her anything. She'll worry herself silly—" my grandmother said before my mother put a hand on her arm, cutting her off.

My mother led me a few feet away until we were alone. When she faced me, a crease in her chin appeared. She pressed the back of her hand to her mouth and looked down. I knew it was how she looked before she cried. Tears suddenly filled my eyes. A lump in my throat made it hard to breathe.

"Oh, now," my mother said. She pulled me into her, pressed my head against her shoulder. She patted my back lightly while I snaked a hand up between us and wiped my eyes.

"I'm sorry," I said to her when we separated.

She tucked a piece of my hair behind my ear. "It's okay to cry. He'll be okay. But it's scary."

"No. I mean I'm sorry about everything. Sorry for lying about Alex. And for what I said to you about Kat. I didn't mean it."

"I want you to hear it from me that I don't know if what I did was right. Everything just happened so fast." Her lip quivered. A tear slipped down her face.

I started to say that I understood. That she didn't need to explain, but she held up her hand.

"I don't have all the answers. Your father either. It's just, you have children and you want to protect them."

She paused and dug in her pocketbook for a tissue. When she

had wiped under her eyes, she took a deep breath, took both of my hands in hers, and stood in front of me so close, our foreheads almost touched.

"You tell Kat whatever you feel is best. The doctor said as long as Dad responds well to the antibiotics, he can be home as soon as tomorrow."

"Grandma said Kat will worry, and she's right. I could just say he's working on the boat."

My mother pressed her lips to the side of my head. "Go," she said. "Do what feels right."

Alex walked behind me through the parking lot, one step behind. Neither of us spoke. When we reached the truck, I got in the passenger seat and buckled my seat belt. We were on the highway, ten minutes into the ride before Alex looked at me.

"When your dad first showed up, I thought it was because of us, I mean, you—you know what I mean. But then it was obvious he had no clue who I was."

He looked over at me when he said this. When I didn't say anything, he looked at the road, then back at me.

"I thought you were going to tell him about us?" he asked after a minute.

In all the frenzy, I hadn't said anything about Alex's disappearance.

I hadn't mentioned that he'd fallen off the face of the earth after we'd kissed. And now he was acting surprised that my father didn't know about *us*? What *us*?

"Tell him what?" I asked. "That you're a guy who fixed my boat. That we had lunch a couple of times?"

He looked over at me, a wounded expression on his face. For some reason, it made me even angrier.

I saw how he'd looked at me that night. I felt the way he kissed me. And then he'd said he couldn't kiss me anymore. And then he disappeared.

He didn't have the right to look wounded.

"Besides, you didn't tell your mom about me. You told me that night at the Salt House that she didn't know about me."

"That's different."

"How is it different?"

"I'm eighteen, Jess. It's different."

"Not this again," I scowled. "That's a stupid thing to say," I said, feeling my face flame with anger.

He looked over at me, raised his eyebrows. "Why are you so mad?"

"Because you're sitting over there acting like you didn't keep me a secret. I have my own reasons for not telling my parents about you. But at least I didn't lie."

"Lie? What did I lie about?"

"About Amy," I snapped before I could stop myself.

If he was surprised I knew her name, he didn't show it. He put his blinker on and followed the curve into the parking lot. We were quiet as he pulled into a space at the back of the lot.

We were early for pickup, and I opened the door and got out of the truck, finding the small space claustrophobic.

I leaned against the bumper and watched the campers run around on the field in front of us. I tried to find Kat, but my eyes were tired from crying, and their small bodies all looked the same from where I stood.

I felt the truck dip when Alex got out. I watched as he hoisted himself up on the hood and slid his legs over until he was sitting next to where I was standing.

"I'm sorry," he said quietly.

I turned my eyes back to the field. All the emotion of the day had worn me out.

"Look, Jess. I'm not defending myself, but my mother didn't know Amy and I had broken up before we even moved. I guess that's why I didn't tell her about you. I didn't want to have to explain what happened with Amy."

"So she was your girlfriend?"

"For four years. Since we were freshmen in high school. We were in over our heads. Both of us. She was . . . is important to me, but . . ."

I caught the tense change. "Is that why you went home? For her?"

"When I decided to go to college up here, we agreed to see other people. She's going to college in Florida, and we didn't want to start lying to each other. But now that I look back on it, it was me pushing the idea."

"How come?"

"Amy was great, but the only thing we ever did together was go to parties or . . . stuff . . ." He leaned over and tied his sneaker, even though it wasn't untied. Then he untied and retied the other sneaker. When he straightened, his cheeks were red, and he didn't meet my eyes. I got the message of what stuff he was talking about.

"I sort of wanted to just be alone. To figure things out. And then I met you, and, well . . ."

I snorted. "Don't sound so enthused."

He nudged me with his elbow. "Cut it out. What I mean is that getting in another relationship was the last thing I was looking to do. And then you came along, limping up my street. And then that night on the couch with you, I realized I was really into you. And it freaked me out."

I felt my heart race; the palms of my hands grew wet.

"Anyway. I went home to tell Amy that it wasn't just a break for me."

I looked at him, waited for him to continue.

"Being here, meeting you. It's different. It's like a fresh start, you know? Just . . . I don't know how to explain it . . . sort of like there are things I didn't even know existed."

"Things in Maine?" I asked.

"No," he said, surprised, as if it had just dawned on him. "Things in me." He made a small self-conscious noise, fiddled with his hat. "Anyway. I'm sorry I didn't tell you about Amy. I was sort of lying to myself that I thought of you as just a friend until I kissed you. And then . . ."

". . . And then you fell off the face of the earth," I finished for him.

"Well, that I can explain. Look."

I squinted at him, blocking the sun with my hand. He dug in his pocket, held the tab of the key ring up to me.

"You got the apprenticeship." I smiled.

"That's where I was all last week. They wanted to meet me, show me around. I didn't want to tell you in the shop when I came to say good-bye. I just wanted to put all that other stuff behind me first."

"It's like another country up there," I warned.

"I heard. Some girl told me that." He looked at me. "Too far for a girl to come visit?"

"I don't think friends visit. I mean, that seems serious."

"How about friends that do this?" he asked, pulling me into him, his legs on either side of me. I felt his lips on mine, gently, his eyes open, looking right at me. After a minute, I pulled away, turned, and leaned between his legs, my back against him. His fingertips rested on my hips. His knee was next to me, and I reached out and traced the scar with my fingertip, the skin even softer than I imagined.

On the field, a whistle blew, and we looked over to see groups of kids lining up behind their counselors, ready to go home for the day. Alex nudged me forward and slid off the car, and we walked toward them, his hand brushing against mine.

I caught Kat out of the corner of my eye and watched her skip over to us. Her counselor was waiting with a clipboard, and I walked over and signed my initials next to Kat's name on the sign-out sheet. When I turned, Kat was giving Alex a high five.

"You've met," I said.

"She scored the winning goal in the soccer game." He held out his hand again, and Kat slapped it even harder this time. He winced and shook it playfully.

"Where's Mom?" Kat asked me. I opened my mouth to answer, but nothing came out. She studied my face. She stopped walking and looked from me to Alex and back at me. I thought I saw her hold her breath.

A year passed in my mind. The flashing lights of the ambulance outside my house; my mother asleep in Kat's bed; my father walking into the kitchen behind me whispering, *Jess, that's not your mess.*

I thought of my mother, crying in the hospital, giving me permission to tell Kat the truth this time. But now Kat was looking at me, waiting for me to say something. The corners of her mouth began to droop, her smile fading, creases of worry beginning to form on her forehead.

I looked into her eyes and thought of what she'd been through. How they were the eyes of a girl who got off the bus one summer day and found out her baby sister was never coming home. How they were the eyes of loss. And they were looking at me, waiting.

I thought of my mother, crying in the hospital, talking about protecting us.

Suddenly I knew what to tell Kat. I took her hand and swung it as we walked to the car.

I told her the truth. That our mother was with our father. And soon, they were coming home together.

23

Hope

An hour after Jess and Alex left, Dr. Schmidt came to get me. I left Boon and my mother sitting in the waiting room and followed the doctor to a small room, where he shut the door and delivered Jack's prognosis. The pneumonia had been so advanced that he had a lung abscess. They'd drained it, but if he didn't respond to the antibiotics, part of his lung would have to be removed. But that wasn't the worst of it. His blood pressure had been sky-high when he'd been brought in, and now it was only moderately better. Jack was on medication for both issues, but Dr. Schmidt stressed that the most important thing Jack needed now was rest, and not just for a week or so. Prolonged rest was how he put it.

"You know Jack, right?" I sighed. "What are the odds that he listens?"

Dr. Schmidt looked at me from over the top of his glasses. "Given the first thing he said when he woke up was 'Hope is going to kill me,' I think they're pretty good." He winked and squeezed my hand. "I'll let you know when you can see him."

In the waiting room, Peggy was sitting between my mother and Boon. She stood up quickly when she saw me and gave me a hug when I reached her.

"I just got the message," she said. "How is he?"

"He's doing okay. He's got some work to do to get better."

"I'm so sorry I missed your call. Who ended up getting Kat?" Peggy asked.

I frowned at her. "I take it you haven't talked to Alex?"

"Alex? No. He was sleeping when I left the house this morning."

"Damn. I was hoping you'd have some insight as to why Jack was there."

Peggy gave me a confused look. "Jack was where?"

I turned to Boon. "You said earlier that you knew something about it."

"Wait. Jack was at my house?" Peggy asked. "Is that where this *happened*?"

Boon held up his hands. "I said I can take a guess. Given Finn and Jack's history, it doesn't surprise me that they're tangling with one another again."

"What exactly is their history?" I asked.

"Yes," Peggy added. "You took the words right out of my mouth."

There was a long pause while Boon looked at me and then at Peggy and then back at me.

"Christ," he muttered.

"Can someone please tell me what happened and how Alex is involved before I have a heart attack," Peggy pleaded.

"I'm sorry, Peg," I said, pressing my fingers against my eyebrow. "Jack showed up at your house and Alex was there and Jack was angry and Alex thought it was about Jess but then it came out that it had to do with some stolen traps. Jack left in a hurry, and Boon got a call from Ryland that he'd pulled Jack out of the water and to call an ambulance and here we are."

I said this all in one breath, and my mother stuck her bottom lip out and said, "Whew."

"Alex and Jess left to get Kat and now they're all at my house. And what history?" I demanded, turning to Boon.

Boon didn't speak, but he didn't need to. His expression told me it was something I wasn't going to like.

"I'm going to check on the kids," Peggy said quietly.

"I'm going with you," my mother blurted out, gathering her purse with the quickness one usually reserves for emergency-type exits. Peggy squeezed my hand and mouthed, *Call me*. My mother gave Boon a hug and turned to me, pressed her face against my cheek.

"Now, you tell Jack that tomorrow is a new day," she told me in a chirpy voice.

"Mom," I said wearily. Out of the corner of my eye, I saw Boon smile. But when I looked over at him after they left, the smile was gone.

I crossed my arms. "He didn't cut his hand on the engine, did he?"

He motioned for us to move to the chairs in the far corner of the room. When we were seated, he looked at me.

"I'm guessing not."

"Guessing?"

"Yes. Guessing. I heard there was some shit going down on his boat the other night. I asked him about it this morning, and he told me to mind my own business. Then he went out on the boat and the next thing I know, Finn's in my office, handing me a wad of cash, telling me he stole out of Jack's traps, his face smashed in. I'm not a detective, but I'm guessing the cut on Jack's hand was probably a right hook to Finn's face, not the engine."

"Wait. Back up. Finn stole his catch? When? How?" I thought of Peggy. I'd talked to her on Sunday. She'd said she hadn't heard from Ryland in days.

"We didn't get into details. I took the money, and he said he was

going to buy some bait, head out to Jack's traps, and make it right.
I got on the phone and called Jack. No answer. Tried the radio and
got the same. Then Finn's calling me from his boat, screaming at
me to call an ambulance, that he's got Jack on the deck, barely
breathing."

My mind raced, trying to process it all, to piece it all together.

"Why would Ryland steal from Jack's traps? Was that his territory? Is that the history you're talking about?"

Boon studied me, a somber expression on his face. "This is
where I'm out of this, Hope," he said quietly. "I don't know what
you know. You need to talk to Jack about it."

"Well, given that the first time I heard Ryland Finn's name was
when he was standing in my living room, I'm assuming I don't
know anything."

Boon's jaw dropped. "He was at your house?"

"Yes. Earlier this summer. I invited them over. Jack was angry,
said he never wanted Finn in our house again. I brought his name
up a couple of weeks later, asked Jack why he didn't like him, and
he wouldn't answer. Said it had nothing to do with me."

Boon shook his head, studied his hands. I sighed and sat back
in the chair, frustrated.

"Just tell me what it is, Boon."

"He's such a pain in the ass," he muttered. Then, "I don't want
to get in the middle of this."

"It's a little late for that."

"Hope. This isn't my information to give."

"Well, apparently Jack can't give it either," I said. "And look
where it landed him." I waved to where Jack was, somewhere in
the hospital, hooked up to tubes and lines and monitors.

Boon swore under his breath, shifted in his seat.

"Boon, please. As his friend. And mine."

He was silent, staring at the floor.

"Whatever it was, it was a long time ago. This is ridiculous." I was angry now, and it came out in my voice. "Was it about fishing? About a girl? What?"

Boon groaned and threw up his hands, faced me. "I don't see how this is going to help, but what do I know? It was a girl. Hannah something. I don't remember her last name. She moved here our senior year, got serious with Finn right away. They were *that* couple, you know? Pretty cheerleader meets the football guy, the golden couple. Only problem was he had a drinking and steroid problem, and she had a temper. They'd have these colossal fights in the middle of the school parking lot. Didn't matter who was around. Anyway, the summer after we graduated, she got a job working at the Wharf Rat as a waitress."

"Enter Jack," I said.

"Yes and no. He wasn't interested. And that made her more interested. I swear whenever we pulled in on the boat after hauling traps, she'd be on the patio, watching for him, waiting to take her break just at the right time. He didn't stand a chance."

"She was pretty?"

"Not pretty," he said. "Beautiful." But his voice was hard.

"You didn't like her?"

"No."

"Why?"

"Finn was a jealous guy. Add the alcohol, the steroids, and he's a gasket waiting to blow. I think he cheated on her, pissed her off one too many times, and she used Jack to get back at him."

"Used him how?" I asked.

He looked at me, waited. "For his stunning conversation skills," he said after a minute.

Boon had his eyebrows up, and when he saw that I understood

what he meant, he rolled his eyes. I took a deep breath and motioned for him to continue.

"You sure?" he asked, and I nodded.

"Jack got pretty lit after work one night, drinking beers with
me and Eddy on the dock. She showed up after her shift, and that
was that. Game over."

"Meaning they started seeing each other?"

"If that's what you want to call it. It didn't last long. Maybe
a couple of weeks. Long enough for her to get what she needed
to make Finn jealous. She found him at a bar one night and told
him about Jack. Threw it in his face from what I heard. Publicly.
Eddy was there, and he said she came right over to Finn and lit into
him." He paused. "Finn left the bar with a bunch of his buddies
and they went looking for Jack." His voice grew quiet. "Beat the
shit out of him. He couldn't see out of his eye for weeks."

He touched the place over his eye where Jack's scar was. My
eyes went wide.

"He told me he was on the boat when that happened."

Boon bit his lip, let it go. "He was. That's where they jumped
him. Four of them. The defensive line, basically. When I found
him, there was so much blood on the deck, I thought he was
dead."

I looked over to see if he was exaggerating, but his face was
drawn, serious.

"Turns out the blood wasn't all his. Four on one, and he managed to break Finn's nose." There was a hint of pride in his voice,
but I saw from his face that he was bothered by the memory of it.

We sat in silence while I tried to wipe the image of Jack lying
in a pool of blood from my mind. Jack hated to talk about his past,
said the day his life really began was the day he met me. It used
to drive me insane, the way he'd dodge my questions, kiss me to

make me stop grilling him. But then we were married, and the years passed, and suddenly we had a history of our own.

I thought back to the night of the party. I heard Jack shouting, *They're not allowed to come over here again.*

What he'd meant was you're not allowed to bring my past back like this. You're not allowed to do that.

"Why wouldn't he have told me this?" I asked out loud, more to myself than to Boon. "It was so long ago. He couldn't think I'd be upset over something as stupid as two guys fighting over a girl."

Boon looked at me. Stared at me. Stared at me the way someone stares at you when they're about to change your reality, your perception of things.

And suddenly I knew what it was. I don't know how. Maybe it was Boon's face, full of regret. I held up my hand so he wouldn't say it out loud, and we sat in silence.

I blinked several times. I concentrated on breathing. I wondered how to ask Boon if there was a child out there that belonged to Jack that I didn't know existed.

Instead I asked him if he'd fallen in love with her. This Hannah I'd never heard of before now.

"God, no. I think he just thought they'd fool around for a while. Then after Finn jumped him, Jack tried to break it off with her and she told him she was pregnant."

"It was his?"

Boon turned to me. "Sort of a moot point."

He paused, cleared his throat. "A couple of days later, she swallowed a bottle of her mother's meds and chased them back with a fifth of vodka. Never woke up."

There was a flipping sensation in my belly. I swallowed the hard lump that had formed in my throat. Swallowed again. I felt the tears well up behind my eyes.

"He kept all of this a secret from me," I said, dumbfounded.

"That doesn't surprise me."

I shook my head. "Why?"

Boon sighed. "It really messed him up. Jack was always the straight-and-narrow guy. Only child, never knew his father, and his mother was always in one crisis or another with some guy. His grandfather was the only thing stable in his life. And he was always working on the boat. So that's where Jack went. He was the same then as he is now. And you know how that is. He doesn't talk about anything that bothers him. Took him over a year, drunk one night, to tell me he felt responsible. That it was his fault. That if he'd stayed away from her, none of it would have happened."

"That's a burden to carry all these years."

Boon shrugged. "If you want my two cents, I think the reason he didn't tell you has to do with forgiving."

"I would have forgiven him. I didn't even know him when this happened."

"I wasn't talking about you. I was talking about him," Boon said. "I don't think he's forgiven himself. I'm not sure he knows how to."

There was a long stretch of time we sat without talking. Then the nurse came to say Jack was out of recovery. She looked at me and said, you can see your husband now, and the first thing that came to mind was yes. Yes, I can. But was my husband ready to be seen?

~ 24 ~

Kat

It turns out Smelliot isn't so bad after all. I almost fell over when Mom said he was staying with us for a week. She was putting sheets covered with soccer balls on the bed in Maddie's old room when she told me this, and I had to sit down on the edge of the bed and ask her what this meant. She couldn't mean sleep at our house. As in use the toilet, eat at our table, wake up in our house. I told her this and made my eyes wide to show how awful that would be.

She waved her hand at me to stand up so she could tuck the sheet under the mattress and told me that, yes, staying with us did mean sleeping here, and eating here, and using the bathroom. And I was to be a perfect hostess. I shook my head at her and left the room. The only hostess I knew was the girl with the big fake smile who carried menus and brought us to the table whenever we went to the Wharf Rat, and if Mom thought I was going to smile like that the whole time Smelliot was here, then I had an even bigger problem.

My first thought was to go upstairs and stay with Grandma. Then I remembered Grandma was back in Florida. I'd tried to convince her to stay longer, even made her an ice-cream sundae with caramel sauce mixed with coconut flakes. But she reminded me that she'd already stayed extra long so she could help spread the rest of Maddie's ashes. She said it was time she went home so Mom could get back to regular business. I asked her what regular business Mom had to get back to, and she looked over at me and said *her life* in a serious way, and since I wasn't feeling all that serious, I shrugged and went back to eating my ice cream.

Jess had come up with the idea to put the rest of Maddie's ashes in the sunflower garden at the Salt House. Or maybe it was all of us. We'd been sitting at the table after dinner one night, and Dad was in the best mood. Maybe it was because he was taking a long vacation. Or maybe it was because we were moving when the construction was done. Or maybe it was because Mom had made brownies and cut them up in wedges and put the whole pan on the table and we were eating out of it with our fingers. Piece by piece. Like a cake. And Mom wasn't even telling us to stop. She was just watching us, and then she left the kitchen and came back carrying the wooden box with Maddie's ashes.

I still felt bad for stealing them and making such a scene that day. But Mom had promised she'd tell Dad and he wouldn't be mad at all, and she was right because even though the box had water rings all over from when it fell in the ocean, Dad reached over and pulled me onto his lap when Mom sat down and asked everyone to think about a good place to spread them.

Dad said, "She liked dirt," and I nodded, because she did. She'd crawl as fast as she could to dig her hands into it before anyone could grab her. And then it seemed like everyone thought of the same thing at once. Jess said, "Sunflower," and Dad said, "Garden," and Mom said, "Perfect," and I just smiled and took a bite of my brownie. Because it was perfect.

And then the day had come, and the sun had been so bright and the sunflowers so tall and yellow, bent over and looking down at us like a family of happy faces, that I wasn't even sad like I was that day at the ocean. I told Mom this before I went to bed that night. She said she felt the same way, and wasn't life funny like that? Sometimes, she said, what you think is going to happen is nothing like what actually does.

I had to agree because not in a million years would I think we'd be moving to the Salt House. Like to *live*.

Which was why Smelliot was staying with us. Peggy was taking Alex to some boat-building school way up in the part of Maine that always made Grandma do a fake shiver. And when Peggy got back after dropping Alex off, she and Smelliot were renting our house. Mom thought it was a good idea that Smelliot spend some time here. Plus, Mom kept telling Peggy to take her time coming back, that she should take a mini-vacation after all her hard work.

Peggy had spent the last two weeks decorating Mom's new office. Mom had loved it so much she got her editor to do a story on it. A bunch of people came over to the Salt House with big lights and cameras with these long lenses. After the magazine came out, Peggy said her phone started ringing off the hook. Mom and Peggy couldn't stop talking about it. They'd say, *Can you believe how good it looks?* And then they'd start hugging and talking over each other, saying no, I didn't do anything, you did it all, and blah, blah, blah.

Now Mom was telling me to cheer up—that it wouldn't be so bad. I scowled at her and went to my room. I made a sign for my door that said *No Boys Allowed* and taped it right up so Smelliot would know that my part of the house was off-limits to him. But then Dad walked by and stuck his head in and said he's a boy and how would he lie with me in my bed at night and read me my book if he couldn't come in? So I crossed out *boys* and wrote—*No Smelliots Allowed*—and then Mom walked by and gave me her look so I took it down and decided when Smelliot got here, I'd ignore him.

That was still my plan when they pulled up in Alex's truck, but when Smelliot got out, he walked right over to me. He was holding a plastic bag, and he stuck it out to me. It swung back and forth in front of my nose.

"It's for you," he said.

"Me?"

"Yeah. Take it."

I folded my arms in front of me and asked him if he thought I didn't know better. There was probably dog poop in it. Or worms. Maybe even a lit firecracker waiting to blow up in my face. But he put the bag on the step.

"Suit yourself," he said.

Everyone was down on the sidewalk, saying good-bye to Alex. Dad shook Alex's hand and told him if he wanted a job in the summer, all he had to do was ask. Then there was a pause when nobody said anything until Dad said maybe we could all go inside and have a cup of coffee and give Alex and Jess a minute alone. I told him I didn't drink coffee, and he picked me up and put me on his shoulders, so high up, my head was as tall as the stop sign, and Mom said, "Jack, please, the doctor," and Dad let out a sigh. But he put me down. Then he leaned over and kissed Mom on the cheek.

Smelliot was still standing next to me. I waited until my parents and Peggy went upstairs to say, "See. They're not getting a divorce."

I put the emphasis on the *v*. It had taken me an hour to find it in the dictionary after *deforest* only said something about trees. Believe me, Jess had heard about *that*.

I thought he'd have something stupid to say, maybe even another lie. But he just shrugged. Like that was that.

I folded my arms and stuck my face out at him. "And I heard

you're moving in here and your Dad's not. So who's the one getting the divorce now?"

I expected to feel good after I said this. He had it coming, after
all. But the way his head tilted back, as if what I'd said was a punch
he never saw coming, made my stomach hurt, like the words had
turned right around and socked me too. Grandma would say
it served me right. If I didn't have something nice to say, then I
shouldn't have said anything at all. Too late now, I thought to myself.

I pressed my tongue into the roof of my mouth, tried to think
of what to say. I could lie and say I hadn't heard that his dad wasn't
moving in, even though I had heard it. Mom had said that Mr. Finn
was going away for a bit to try to get better and to not ask Smelliot
about it. When I asked what he needed to get better at, Mom had
just sighed and said, "Better choices, Kat. Learning how to make
better choices." I hadn't asked anything more because I had no
idea there was a place you could go for that. I'd gone outside, out
of sight, before she got any bright ideas about sending me to the
better-choices-place.

"Don't tell my mother I said that about your father," I blurted out.

He kept his face blank, as if none of it mattered. "He's not my
real father. He's my stepfather."

I considered this. It was a twist, all right. "Where's your real
father?" I asked suspiciously. He was a known liar, after all.

"In heaven. He died a long time ago. I don't remember him."

I thought about telling him I knew someone in heaven too.
Usually people made a sad face when I told them this news. And
then I'd have to make a sad face too. It was tiring. So I stopped telling people about Maddie.

But he didn't look sad when he told me about his dad. So I gave
it a shot.

"My sister's in heaven too," I said.

Smelliot's face didn't change at all. If anything, he perked up, like he was happy we found something we had in common.

"What'd she die of?"

"She stopped breathing. She went to sleep and didn't wake up."

"It's not a bad way to die," he offered. "Better than getting ripped to pieces by a man-eating sloth." He bent over and pretended to rip into something with imaginary claws. I didn't ask, but I hoped that wasn't how his father died. I watched him until it seemed like he was never going to stop.

"So what's in the bag?" I said loudly, and pointed behind him.

He stopped what he was doing and looked at me. Then he reached in the bag and pulled out something shiny and silver. The sun caught it and sent a light in my eyes.

"It's yours," he said, holding it out to me.

When my eyes were back, I saw that it was the trophy from the last day at camp. The one he took home after he tripped me and I fell.

"So you did trip me," I said accusingly.

"Not on purpose. If your legs didn't fling every direction, it wouldn't have happened."

That was the stupidest thing I'd ever heard. "That's what your eyes are for. You see someone in front of you, you go around. You don't go through them," I told him.

"Do you want it or not?" he asked in a tired sort of way, as if he'd rather be anywhere else in the world.

I held my hand out, and he gave it to me. It was heavier than I thought it would be. Not like the cheap plastic trophies they gave out at the swim meet last summer. Even the girls that held their noses when they jumped in the water got one. Not dove. Jumped. Like they were at a backyard cookout instead of a *race*. I remember

I'd been so mad in the car on the way home that Mom had pulled over and told me she was not going to drive one more inch until I calmed down.

"But why bother giving out trophies if everyone gets one," I'd shouted.

She'd started to speak, then looked at the road. Finally, she looked back at me. "They wanted to make everyone feel special. That's a nice thing, isn't it?"

I hadn't answered because what I wanted to say would've only got me in trouble for using bad words. I'd tossed the trophy in the trash when we got home. Who wanted a trophy for first place when Mary Ellen Arnold took the same one home and she came in dead last after she doggy paddled over to the side because the water was getting too deep. Too deep in the *shallow* end.

Smelliot was still waiting for me to answer. As if I had to think about it. Of course I wanted to keep it. But the whole thing seemed kind of fishy.

"Why fess up to it now?" I narrowed my eyes at him, turned the trophy this way and that. Maybe he'd rigged it to blow up.

"I don't know," he said, but he looked over at his brother, who was leaning against the truck next to Jess. Alex gave him a thumbs-up, and Jess mouthed to me: *Say thank you.*

Thank him for stealing my trophy? Was she nuts?

"My brother said you told him I won."

"I told him you won the trophy. I didn't say anything about the race," I pointed out. I was no tattletale.

"You're hard to give something back to," he said, turning away, toward the house.

"Hey," I called after him.

He turned when he reached the steps, and I said, "This doesn't mean we're friends. I still think you're a jerk for what you said."

He kept walking up the steps, slowly though, as if he didn't want to reach the top and have to go inside. Jess and Alex were sitting in the truck now, and the street was empty. I was still holding the trophy in one hand and the bag in the other. My face burned with anger. Who did he think he was, acting nice? Didn't he remember calling me Kat Poop? Pinching my arm? Suddenly I wanted to throw the trophy at him. Make him take back his stupid words.

I caught up to him, ran up to the top step, and stood in front of him.

"Here." I thrust the trophy out to him. "I don't want it. And you can't sleep here. It's my house, and I say so."

He stared at me for a second. Then he looked down at his feet. When he looked back up, I lowered my hands. I know what people look like when they're about to cry. And he looked like that. Mom was going to kill me if she came out here and he was crying.

"I'm sorry," I said. "Don't cry."

"Who said I was crying? I don't want to move into your house anyway," he shot back. But he didn't look up again. His ears were dark red.

I was still holding the trophy out. I looked at it. Maybe he'd brought it as a peace offering. Sort of like the tomahawks that Indian chiefs gave to one another to make friends. We'd studied it in school last year, and Mrs. Whitley read us a book about it out loud, and even with her squeaky voice that made my ears ache, I still paid attention. And that says a lot.

Grandma would say one good deed deserves another. And that people sometimes forget what you said and did, but they usually remember how you made them feel.

"I didn't mean that about you moving in. I take that back."

He shrugged. But his ears went back to skin color, and he didn't look like he was going to cry anymore.

"And I take back that I don't want the trophy." I moved it so it was partly behind my leg, so it wasn't fully in sight, and cursed my big mouth for saying I didn't want it.

"And I'm sorry for bringing up your da— I mean your stepfather . . . you know, what I said."

"Okay! Jeez. Can you just take it and be quiet?" He looked at me out of the corner of his eyes, like I was a lunatic. I stood up as straight as I could. Who was he to say anything? A few minutes ago, he'd been pretending to be a man-eating sloth.

"Do you want to come in?" I asked, sweeping my arm toward the door like the hostess did when she showed us to our table.

He shook his head, opened the door, and went in. I stood on the porch. Mom's laugh trickled out, and the smell of coffee filled the doorway. I held the trophy in front of me, traced the edges of it with my finger.

I thought of Smelliot walking into my kitchen, into his new house that he didn't want to live in. How his brother was leaving and his dad was in heaven and now his stepfather was gone too.

I went inside and ran into the kitchen. Everyone at the table stopped talking and looked up, except Smelliot. He had his chin in his hand, staring at the tablecloth, a piece of date nut bread untouched in front of him. I wrinkled my nose. I hated that bread too.

"Do you want to see my room?" I asked.

He looked up at me, his face blank while our mothers nodded furiously.

"I have a huge bullfrog," I added, and Mom frowned. But Smelliot got up and walked over to me. Behind him, Dad winked at me.

He didn't find out until we got to my room that the bullfrog was a stuffed animal with a missing glass eye.

But by that time I was telling him how cool his new house was. How the tree outside his bedroom window lost its leaves in the winter and you could see the dock in the backyard. And in the summer when the tide was out, there was always a little puddle of water at the bottom of the ladder that was as warm as bathwater.

And there were these tiny little fish that you could catch in a jar, and at night, under a flashlight, they looked like streaks of silver under your blanket. Like a jar full of fireworks right in your hands. I told him not to mention that part to his mother. Taking fish from the ocean into your bed wasn't one of those better choices Mom talked about.

I thought he might look at me like I was strange again. But he looked out the window at the dock. When he looked back at me, he was smiling, as if he already knew how bright those fish would look under that black quilt covered in soccer balls.

It'll be our secret, he told me, and I knew from the way he looked back at the water, his eyes wide, that he was telling the truth. And just like that, me and Elliot were friends.

Jack

Late-August mornings on the water are the pearl in the oyster shell. The air is still cool from the night and it gives you that first taste of September. Wait an hour or two, and the sun is high, and you're stripping down to a T-shirt, the water so flat and clear, it's like hauling traps in a bathtub. The wind nothing more than a whistle past your ear.

This was what I was telling the girls over breakfast when Hope reminded me that I wasn't cleared to be hauling until the doctor said so. As if I needed reminding. As if the horse pills I downed three times a day to fight whatever nonsense had taken residence in my lungs weren't reminder enough.

I didn't say that to her, though.

Boon had told me in the hospital room that it was Finn who'd fished me out of the water. Finn who'd slammed on my chest until water stopped spurting out of my mouth, until I was alive and breathing.

Boon didn't let me speak, told me shut up and listen. When he was done, he said that every man gets a limited number of free passes on being an asshole, and he was pretty sure mine were used up. He crossed the room and closed the door before he said it. Like he knew if someone heard him harassing a patient, he'd get thrown out.

"Exhaustion play tricks with your mind," I told him, repeating what the doctor said.

But Boon had grunted, grimaced. "So can stupidity," he said.

Then he told me that a string of traps had washed ashore off Turner Point not thirty yards from my territory. Hank Bitts's string, the dark blue buoy in pieces on the rocks. I thought of the traps I'd cut, the ones marked with a purple-striped buoy that I thought were Finn's.

Boon didn't accuse me of cutting them. He didn't need to. He just put the envelope full of cash on my chest and folded his arms, his way of telling me that he knew I'd played my part in this thing. That it was over, this back-and-forth with Finn, whether I wanted it to be or not. I nodded, not saying a word, thinking that I'd have to remember to give Bitty some cash, tell him I'd run over the string by accident.

Not that it mattered. Any of it. What mattered to me was sitting across from me in the chair next to my hospital bed when I woke up, looking at me like I was someone she didn't know.

I had to work my way back into Hope's good graces.

Finishing the Salt House helped. That kid Alex turned out to have a knack for carpentry. And he worked cheap too, said he'd give me a week's work for free if he could have the skiff behind the warehouse. I told him the skiff was junk, a crack in her hull the size of the Grand Canyon. That's why I want her, he told me. It seemed like a fair deal to me until he gave me a day's work. He got more windows framed in two hours than Boon did all day.

When I pointed this out to Boon, he put down his nail gun, went to the cooler, and cracked open a beer. "If you like that speed, you're going to love this one," he said.

Boon had told me in the hospital room that Hope knew about Hannah. He'd been pissed about that too, being put in that position. But he was more worried about what Hope was going to do to me.

"If I were you," he said, "I'd go back into surgery. It'd be less painful."

Hope waited until I was home from the hospital, in my own bed, my head propped up on the pillow, and my eyes just about shut before she closed the door and sat on the edge of the bed.

"Tell me about Hannah," she said. "And don't make me ask again."

I saw from the look on her face that we'd go around and around until she got what she wanted.

"What do you want to know?" I asked, too tired to argue.

"I want to know all of it," she said.

I didn't sugarcoat it, pretend it was something it wasn't. I told her the truth, said I was sorry for not telling her before, but I hated thinking about it.

"That's not enough," she told me. "I deserve to know what happened."

"I told you what happened."

"You told me the events."

"Isn't that what you asked for?"

"I want to know how you felt about it. I want to know what it meant to you." She was angry, shouting at me.

"Stop yelling," I said. "Calm down."

"Tell me what happened."

"I told you what happened."

"No. There are other things I want to know."

"Like what?"

"Just things!"

"Like what, Hope? For God's sake."

"Like did you love her?" she shouted at me.

I felt something inside of me let go. "I didn't even like her," I said, and Hope flinched. "Is this what you want, Hope? Is this the stuff you want to know?"

She nodded, but her face told me she wasn't so sure. But she'd pushed and pushed, and now I couldn't reel it back in. I'd have been shouting if I had the voice for it.

"You want to know I slept with a girl I didn't like? That I knew it was wrong, and I still did it?"

Hope stared at me. I waited for her to look away, but she didn't. She sat next to me on the bed, looked me straight in the face.

"You want to know that when she told me she was pregnant, I told her it wasn't mine, even though it could've been. I left her crying. Did you know that? This wonderful husband of yours left a girl just one year older than Jess crying in her house all alone."

Hope reached for me, and I pushed her hand away. I felt empty inside.

"I left her standing there. Then two days later, she walked up-stairs, swallowed a bunch of pills, and killed herself."

"And you're blaming yourself for all of it? Jack. You were eigh-teen. And what about Finn?"

I scowled at her. "None of that matters. Doesn't make what I did any better. I knew she was trying to mess with Finn's head. I pretended it had nothing to do with me. That I was getting what I wanted. And Finn was getting what he deserved. I was too stupid to realize she needed me to walk away. She needed me to be one of the good guys. And I wasn't."

"How could you not tell me this? I can almost understand you didn't tell me because you don't like to think about it and it was a long time ago, but I've been asking you about what hap-pened between you and Ryland, and you said it was nothing to do with me."

"It doesn't have anything to do with you. This was my fault. My mistake. The last thing you needed this year was this. The last thing you needed was me making it even harder for you."

She started to speak, and I put up my hand, shook my head.

"There's nothing more to say, Hope. I wasn't one of the good guys. And I'm sorry that I wasn't. That's all I can say. I'm sorry that I wasn't."

"But you're a good guy now, Jack. You're a good husband. A good father."

"Am I? I'm lying here useless. Instead of fixing everything, I'm out there making it worse, screwing it all up."

"What are you talking about?"

"Fixing it, Hope! Making it better. For you. For the girls."

"You can't fix what happened, Jack. You can't make it better for everyone."

"So I just do nothing? Well, I can't do that, Hope. I won't do that."

"Well, what? You'll do this? Working a hundred hours a week so you end up in the hospital. After all that happened with Hannah, you went to work. Boon told me. You refused to talk about it, refused to deal with it. And here we are, twenty years later."

"One has nothing to do with the other, Hope. That was a million years ago."

"It's grief, Jack!" Her voice was loud now, full of emotion. "Grief!" She leaned into me, her face inches from my own, finding my eyes, making me look at her.

"It's called grief," she said again, her hand on my cheek, stopping me from turning my head away from her crumpled face, the anguish in her eyes, the tears streaming down her face.

The knot in my throat unraveled and a noise slipped out, guttural and raw.

Hope stood up, went to the door and locked it, pulled the shade, even though it was the middle of the day. She walked to my side of the bed, took off her clothes, and climbed into bed next to me. We didn't speak. It hurt to move, but I wanted the pain. As if everything that hurt inside of me needed a way to get out. We stayed in bed for hours, not saying a word.

And later, when Kat knocked on the door, and Hope opened it and told her, go tell Daddy how good he is, how much we love him, I pressed into the pillow to hide my face.

Maybe it was the medicine clearing my lungs, or the sleep clearing my mind, but things seemed different after that day. There wasn't that heavy feeling inside of me anymore, and the dread that had hung in the air was gone.

Hope was different too. I'd waited for her to close back up again, but she went the other direction. I told her after the third night in a row that we'd made love that I wasn't sure this was what the doctor meant when he'd said to rest. She slipped out of her clothes and said, *Then let me do all the work*. How can you argue with that?

We'd put the last window in at the Salt House this morning, the last day of summer vacation before the kids went back to school. Hope was writing her column in her office and it was already a day late, and all the hammering wasn't helping. She yelled out to everyone that we should go look at paint colors for the house, but what she really meant was take the kids and go look at paint colors so I can get some work done. Anything but red or green or yellow would work she told us, and Kat shouted "Purple!" and Hope had looked up from her computer and told us that anything actually meant white or tan.

What she didn't mention was the number of different shades of white and tan.

So Jess and I had been standing in front of the paint samples for almost an hour now, while Kat played with a stack of them on the floor next to us, arranging the square cards in a pyramid, the puff of air that came in when the front door opened threatening to demolish the delicate structure.

We'd picked out a dozen colors and placed them on the flat edge of the display in front of us when Jess reached out, picked one up, and handed it to me. It was a light, clean color, but not what I had in mind. I shrugged and held it back out to her.

She didn't move to take it. "Mom picked it out," she said. "Last year. When she was thinking of doing Maddie's room over."

I looked down at it. It wasn't a color I thought Hope would've wanted for a little girl's room.

"Really?" I asked. "It's so . . . white."

"Read," Jess said, pointing to the small letters on the bottom right.

I pushed the paint sample away, squinted, and brought it closer. "I don't have my cheaters, Jess. What is it?"

She leaned in, pointing to the word as she said it. "Salt," she said. "The name of the color is salt."

I looked down at it, then up at Jess.

"I was with her when she found it. She got all weird. I didn't get it then," Jess said. "I mean, I got that it was the name of the summerhouse, but I didn't get why she was so excited. Why it had anything to do with Maddie."

"It was where we . . . It's um . . ."

"Where Mom got pregnant," Jess said, rolling her eyes. "I know how it works."

"Right," I said, looking back at the color, remembering that weekend with Hope.

It had been the second weekend in September, and we'd gone

to the Salt House one last time before closing it up for the season. The weather had been unseasonably hot for that time of year, and the girls had gone to sleep in our room, the only one with an air conditioner.

After they'd gone to sleep, Hope had grabbed a cold bottle of white wine from the fridge, and we'd sat outside on the Adirondack chairs, a breeze finally stirring off the water. At some point I opened another bottle.

Later, we'd pulled a mattress down from upstairs, put it on the floor of the screen porch off the kitchen, and made love. I remember Hope scrambling to find her tank top and shorts the next morning, throwing my boxers at me when she heard our bedroom door open, the girls' feet slapping against the linoleum floor.

It's like camping, Kat had said when she saw the mattress where we'd slept, and Hope had caught my eye and pressed her hand against her mouth to hide the smile. It was a joke between us now. *Let's camp tonight,* wink, wink. Or it's been forever since we went camping. A month later, Hope missed her period.

I looked over at Jess now, thinking of how it didn't seem that long ago that Hope was pregnant with Jess. And just the other day she'd turned seventeen. I cleared my throat. Thought of where to start.

"That Alex kid. You like him?"

She glanced at me and nodded.

"Your mother said I should apologize to you." I cleared my throat again. "And she's right, as usual." Jess's cheeks colored, and I saw that Hope had talked to her. Had told her that I wanted to speak to her. Not that I wanted to talk about this. But I knew I needed to.

"It wasn't about me not trusting you. Not wanting you to date," I said. "I just . . . I made some bad decisions when I was younger.

And um, well, it was my stuff, Jess. I mean, heck, you've got so many more smarts up here than your old man does." I tapped my knuckles on her head, and she flushed and laughed.

"Okay?" I asked, and she leaned her head against my shoulder.

"Do you think your mother will like it?" I asked, holding the sample out in front of us.

"I think it's not purple," Jess said, and snorted, a sound that made Kat look up from the floor and grin, even though she hadn't heard a word we'd said, the paint samples arranged in front of her, a house of cards two stories high.

We bought the paint and were heading for the door when Kat turned and tugged on my sleeve.

"Look, Dad," she said. "My house is still standing."

She pointed to the structure she'd built, the paint samples bright against the dull concrete floor.

Behind us, the door opened and a rush of air came in. I heard Kat gasp, but her house stayed intact. The colors balancing against each other, leaning on one another.

So as not to collapse.

~ *Epilogue* ~

Hope

I'm in my new office and the blue water sparkles outside my window. There is a leather-bound journal in front of me, my pencil poised over the cream-colored paper.

I started seeing a grief counselor this past week. She suggested keeping a journal as a way to write about my feelings. When I told her I was struggling with where to begin, she gave me an exercise.

"Get in the habit of writing three words at the start of every journal entry," the counselor had said. "Whatever comes to mind. Three words to describe how you're feeling."

It sounded easy enough.

But an hour has passed, and the blank page is staring back at me.

Jack is outside my office sanding a banister. Now and again, he comes in and I feel his lips against the top of my head or the side of my neck. When he leaves my office, I hear him whistling a catchy, upbeat tune and I find my foot tapping along to it.

Jess and Kat are on the lawn below, doing cartwheels through the sprinkler, wet pieces of grass clinging to their ankles. From time to time, their laughter drifts in through the window. Like wind chimes tinkling in a breeze. It's like hearing my very own symphony, so I am content to listen and wait. It strikes me that this is why I haven't been writing this past year. So much of writing is listening. Waiting to hear what will arrive in the silence.

I think about this house. How there is a memory behind every door: the story of our family between these walls.

Outside my window, the ocean sits. Limitless and teeming with life. My daughter now a part of the eternal ebb and flow. Her eyes reflected in the blue expanse in front of me.

I put my pencil to the paper and write the first three words that come to mind.

The Salt House.

Acknowledgments

I t's old news that writing is a solitary act, yet bringing *The Salt House* into the world required the effort, generosity, inspiration, and patience of many people. I'm indebted to the following for their contributions to this book.

First and foremost, my agent, Danielle Burby, who took a chance on a slush-pile manuscript by an unknown author, and forged ahead with unrelenting enthusiasm and unwavering faith. She does her job in the most elegant and admirable way possible, and I couldn't ask for a better guide and advocate.

Thank you to my editors, Etinosa Agbonlahor and Tara Parsons, and the entire team at Touchstone, who championed this book from the beginning and embraced it with more heart than I had any right to hope.

I am grateful to the University of Massachusetts Boston, the MFA program, and alumni who offered wise critiques on early drafts. Particularly Calvin Hennick, who encouraged me to write it to the end, and Kathleen McKenna, who said exactly the right things to keep me going.

This book would not exist without extraordinary teachers and mentors, Joe Torra, who told me I could write, and Askold Melnyczuk, who encouraged me to go farther than I thought I could.

A heartfelt thanks to Pam Loring and the Salty Quill Writers Retreat for Women for the gift of time and support while I completed the novel.

Special appreciation to K. Stephens, author of *The Ghost Trap*, for her insights on the Maine fishing community.

There were many cheerleaders behind this book. My deepest gratitude to friends and family who offered countless contributions along the way.

Special thanks to Jennifer Russo Roopenian, Nancy Schofield, Jen Tuzik, Leah Collum, Lisa Roe, Kimmery Martin, Kristin Contino, and all of the wonderful writers in the Curtis Brown Creative Spring 2015 group, specifically Dolores Gedge, Kathleen Kern, Susan Paul, Sophie Whitley Flavell, and Derek Routledge.

To Chris and Tina Hamilton, for their love and support.

My late father, Ken Hamilton, left this world while I was writing this book, but his belief in me and my writing never faltered, and the marks of his love are in these pages.

My heartfelt thanks to my mother, Peg Hamilton, for her friendship and strength and guidance and good humor, and for talking me off the ledge at regular intervals.

And last but not least, to my tribe at 25,

Lauren, Heidi, and Alyssa, daughters extraordinaire,

Samantha, Matt, and Mia, loves of my life,

and Tommy, my greatest champion,

this book belongs to you.

About the Author

Lisa Duffy received her MFA in creative writing from the University of Massachusetts Boston. Her short fiction was nominated for a Pushcart Prize and can be found in *The Drum Literary Magazine*, *So to Speak*, *Breakwater Review*, *Let the Bucket Down*, and elsewhere. Lisa is the founding editor of *ROAR*, a literary magazine supporting women in the arts. She lives in the Boston area with her husband and three children.